CW00456373

Acknowledgements

A huge thank you to my Beta readers and friends/family, for their contributions at different stages of the creative process.

Our 'team' has been going for a number of years now and I'm enormously appreciative of the time you give to help me make my stories the best they can be. Thank you all.

NONE SO BLIND

CAROLYN MAHONY

PROLOGUE

'I'm sorry we killed your husband.'

The words dropped into the air, bald and ugly. Barbara Harding sat in the visitor's office in her local community centre trying to hide her distaste at being there. She wasn't sure she believed the person who'd spoken. Was he genuinely sorry? It was difficult judging such things when you were blind. It was also difficult hiding her anger. This man was responsible for everything that had gone wrong in her life, but she tried to keep her voice unemotional.

'Really? Could have fooled me. That wasn't the message I got when I heard you all whooping for joy at the pathetic sentences you were given. Are you the one that shouted out, "Serves you right, you bitch"?'

The youth was sitting directly opposite her, and she could hear the nervous tapping of his fingers on the table between them. She knew he was mixed race and twenty-one years old but other than that, she knew little about him. Her choice, and her way of distancing herself from what had happened.

'No. I felt bad about what we did. We killed a man and that ain't right.'

'So, who was it? Your best buddy? I heard he's an important man on the estate where you live. Isn't he your gang-leader?'

'He ain't no friend of mine and I ain't in no gang. There's no way you'd get him here saying he was sorry for what we done to your husband.'

And what about me? she wanted to scream. *My life was taken, too.*

It was stupid to have come here. What did she think she could achieve? When her victim support worker had suggested this so-called restorative justice meeting, her instinct had been to reject it. Why on earth would she want to meet the man who'd been responsible for Roy's death and her blindness? By all accounts, the youth in front of her was from a rough estate and probably spent most of his days pilfering and living on the wrong side of the law. She should never have agreed to this.

Melanie, the victim support liaison officer, stepped into the awkward silence.

'This is difficult for you both, I know, but I hope you can both gain something from the meeting.'

'You can't begin to imagine how your recklessness changed my life,' Barbara finally said. 'My husband and I had been married over thirty-five years – no children, and I have no siblings. He was all I had. And as if losing him wasn't bad enough, look at me now – I've been blind since you ploughed into us. Can you even begin to imagine what that's like?'

It was a relief giving vent to feelings that had been suppressed for so long. She hated the pity she sensed as she moved around with her stick, diligently counting out her steps, feeling her way with her hands; not a day went by when she didn't feel a burning rage. Her husband had lost his life. The man who'd killed him – this young man sitting opposite her now – had been given a pathetic seven years and was now out, after less than five. Where was the justice in that?

'I didn't mean to hurt no one,' the young man said. His name was burned onto Barbara's memory. Offin Abara, although evidently he preferred to be called Finn.

'What did you think was going to happen? How old were you? Sixteen? Not even old enough to have a licence. And yet there you were, behind the wheel of a car, going too fast and on the wrong side of the road. What chance did we have?'

'It weren't my fault.'

'Whose fault was it ... ours?' Barbara snapped back.

'Why don't I pop into the kitchen and make us all a cup of tea?' Melanie said. 'I think you might find it easier if I'm not here. I'll just be in the kitchen through the hatch here if you need me.'

Barbara heard her footsteps receding. They were alone. Another uncomfortable silence ensued.

'It weren't me driving the car,' Finn said in a quiet voice. 'You won't believe that but it's the truth. My mum used to say that if you knew you'd done nothing wrong it don't matter what other people think.'

Barbara ground her teeth so hard her jaw hurt. So, he was going to try to deny it? Is that the way this was going to go? No way was she going to let him off the hook that lightly.

'So how come you said it was you, then?'

'Had my reasons – don't want to talk about it.'

Oh, for heaven's sake. What was the point of all this?

'Why did you come here today?' Barbara asked abruptly. 'What did you hope to gain by seeing me?'

'Dunno. Mel knew I felt bad about stuff and thought it might help both of us. Couldn't see it myself – didn't think you'd want to meet me. When you agreed ...' She could sense his shrug even if she couldn't see it. 'My foster mum said I should do it.'

'Your foster mum?'

'Yeah. I'm not like you. My life's nothing like yours.'

'And what do you know about my life? My husband and I had nothing when we started out. But he worked hard and so did I. If you're determined to succeed and work, you can have a good life without nicking people's cars or breaking the law. Your background is no excuse.'

'You don't get it, do you? I live on an estate that someone like you would never even drive past, let alone walk through or live on. I'd work hard if I could, but have you got any idea how hard it is getting a job, for someone like me?'

He sounded so passionate she could almost believe him. But what difference did it make really? It didn't change anything. Roy was still dead, and she was still blind. Even so, she found herself daring to hope that perhaps he might have learnt something from what had happened. A small positive outcome. She sat back in her seat and drew a breath. 'Listen, you can sit there feeling sorry for yourself and do nothing about it, or you can try and change things for the better. I can't believe there aren't any youth programmes out there to help you. How long have you been out of prison now?'

'Three months.'

'And what have you been doing in that time?'

'Nothing you'll think worthwhile. I've been looking for jobs but there ain't much around and especially not when you've got a record.'

'So just lounging around, then?'

'No – if you really want to know, I've been writing songs.' He sounded defensive, as if expecting ridicule, and when she didn't respond immediately, he added, 'It helps me, right? Otherwise, I'd go mad doing nothing all day.'

'What sort of songs?' She was interested, despite herself. Roy had worked in the music industry all his life.

'Rap, mostly.'

'You know my husband was a music producer? Is that what you want to be – a songwriter?'

The change in his tone was instant. 'It'd be my dream. When I'm spitting rhymes and putting them to a backing track, I feel like ... like me. The person I really am, not the one living my shit reality.'

The passion was there in his voice again, along with the wistfulness and hope that couldn't quite be extinguished despite the fact it was so unlikely to happen. All the things she remembered Roy feeling when they were young. Maybe they weren't so different after all ... but it was their circumstances – the things they couldn't change – that led to their different chances in life.

Silence. Then he said in a quiet voice, 'I really am sorry for what we done. I wished it were me that died. Especially when I heard about all the good stuff he done in the music world and charities and all that. Why should someone like him die and a no-hoper like me live? There ain't no sense to it.'

She agreed but didn't voice the thought. Something in her had shifted. Roy was dead but this young man was still alive. He had a future. Could she play a part in making that future more positive than it otherwise might have been?

'Do you believe in God?' she asked.

He laughed scornfully. 'Are you kidding me?'

'Fate then? Maybe there's a reason why you were spared.' She paused. 'I'd like to believe that. It might help me make some sense out of losing my husband.'

'Tea?' Melanie's bright voice cut into their conversation. 'How have you been doing?'

Barbara wasn't sure she had an answer to that question yet. Incredibly, the ghost of an idea was beginning to form in her mind that was ludicrous ... one she wouldn't even have contemplated before this meeting. Was this what madness was like, or was she going soft?

Whatever it was, she needed time to think things through, maybe have a couple more meetings before coming to a decision. She was so vulnerable in this invisible world she inhabited. She didn't want to make a choice that might jeopardise her security even more, and she could already imagine everyone else's reaction to where her thoughts were taking her.

'We're doing okay,' was all she said. 'One sugar, thanks.'

CHAPTER ONE

Nine months later:

She may have lost her sight but at least she was still alive.

It was a consolation that Barbara often forced herself to fall back on when she found life overwhelming. Today she felt angry with Roy for leaving her at the mercy of people who meant well, but who drove her nuts with their smothering care of her, treating her as if she was incapable now that she was blind. She'd had to fight hard to have the house to herself at weekends. If they knew what she got up to while their backs were turned, they would have been doubly horrified. Finn would be here soon and would be spending the next few hours pottering in Roy's studio, using his equipment and mixing his raps. It wasn't her kind of music but, against all the odds, they'd formed a bond of sorts. Occasionally, doubt crept into her mind that maybe he played on her sympathy, but he seemed genuinely appreciative of what she'd been doing for him.

She crossed the hallway and felt her way cautiously up the stairs. The smoothness of the banister beneath her fingertips soothed her. She didn't need her eyes to remember the beautiful gleaming wood that she'd painstakingly polished over the years.

At the top of the stairs, she turned right, tapping with her stick and walking six steps before turning right again; another five steps and then left into her bedroom. A cold breeze was coming from the window, and she walked over to close it. For a moment she stood there, letting the crisp air brush her cheeks. Below her, on the front lawn, she could hear a robin's tweet. She breathed in deeply, picturing it, recalling how the trees and shrubs in her garden looked in the spring and summer. It was only a few weeks to Christmas and the trees would be completely stripped of their leaves; the bark laid bare to the chill of winter. But even that was a sight, especially when the snow fell, covering the branches with a thick coating of white. It saddened her that she'd never again see the wondrous sights of nature, but she could still touch them with her fingers, breathe in their scent.

A creak out on the landing distracted her. She turned towards the bedroom door, frowning.

'Is that you, Finn?'

No answer.

'Elena?'

It shouldn't be Elena because her housekeeper was off at the weekend and had left earlier that morning. Had she come back for something?

'Elena?' she repeated louder, her sightless eyes staring vacantly in the direction of the doorway. Her skin prickled, when still there was no response. Someone was there, she knew it. Why weren't they answering her?

'Come on, who's there? Tell me.'

She edged cautiously forward with her stick, feeling suddenly vulnerable here on her own. Her heart was skittering all over the place, but she squashed her rising panic, focusing instead on counting her steps as she headed for the bedside table where the panic button was. If she could reach that...

She sensed the closeness of the intruder as soon as she drew level with him, *or her,* the composition of the air around her changing, closing in, smothering her. They were so close, she knew if she reached out a hand it would touch another body.

She stopped. 'Who is it?' she said again. 'What do you want? Just tell me.'

Her voice was querulous, a single thought now racing around in her head. *Was this how she was going to die? Alone, at the hands of some anonymous person?*

A lifeline, as she remembered the pendant alarm around her neck. Her fingers moved quickly up to grab it. But not quickly enough, as a hand came from nowhere and knocked it from her grasp, yanking it roughly over her head. She screamed, making a lunge for the panic button by her bed, but those same hands now swung her viciously to the floor, knocking the wind from her body.

'You coward,' she cried, scrambling to get up. 'Why won't you identify yourself?'

Arms grabbed her, hooking under her armpits to drag her across the floor and out onto the landing. She clawed at the wrists as she was hauled to her feet and had barely got her balance before another violent push in the small of her back sent her hurtling forwards. She cried out, clutching at air as she fell, tumbling down the stairs over and over, until she came to a crashing halt on the hard marble floor at the bottom.

She was badly injured, she knew that. It wasn't just the blood she could feel flowing from her head onto the cold floor beneath her. She couldn't move her body, couldn't speak, or open her eyes. A small moan escaped her.

Footsteps coming down the stairs. Padding into the lounge.

What was happening?

They returned to her side. A cushion was placed over her face, pressing, suffocating. A moment of panic ... a twitching of her fingers ... and then there was nothing.

***

He bent over the body, putting his ear to her chest to listen for a heartbeat. Nothing. Then he drew back on his haunches and focused on the blank, lifeless eyes staring up at him. They were as dead as she was, and he couldn't drag his gaze away. The horror of those last few moments was etched on her face, and it was as if he could see right into her soul. He tore his eyes away, picking up a wrist to feel for a pulse. Nothing. Up to now, he'd kept calm, clinical even, but as he released her hand, panic swept through him. He had to get out of here.

He looked at his hands. Blood. *Wash them*. He moved swiftly into the cloakroom, keeping an ear out for any noises outside.

Then he was out through the door, slipping as unobtrusively as he could to where his scooter was parked on the drive. A quick glance around – one more look at the house – and he was gone.

CHAPTER TWO

Detective Inspector Harry Briscombe stood back from the small group of mourners and observed them from his secluded position beneath the large oak tree. What was he doing here? It was crazy. He didn't even know the woman. But the obituary notice and details of the crematorium service from an anonymous source had sat on his mantelpiece for the last couple of weeks, relentlessly drawing his curiosity. Why had someone sent them to him? It had tugged at him all weekend, and in the end curiosity had got the better of him.

He scanned the group of people at the entrance to the crematorium, but it was as he suspected. No one he knew – not a familiar face amongst the forty or so people gathered there. His hand moved to his pocket, his fingers curling around the funeral notification. Should he move over to the group and introduce himself – try to find out who sent it to him? What would he say?

He hesitated, but... he'd come this far. *Just do it*, he told himself.

About to take those steps that would close the gap between them, his phone sounded off in his pocket. Damn.

He looked at the screen. Beth, back at the station. He fumbled with the buttons to silence it, aware that people were looking at him. Straightening up, he turned away from them and headed back towards his car.

'Hey, Beth.'

His colleague's rich Northumberland accent trickled down the line. 'Harry, where are you? We've just been notified of a woman's body found in a house. I'm on my way over there now. Do you want to meet me there?'

He picked up pace. 'Sure. Message me the address.'

As he reached his car, he turned for one last look at the gathered mourners. Most of them had lost interest in him but his eyes met those of a young woman. She was fair-haired, about his age, and clearly upset. There was something familiar about her, but he couldn't place it. Then she turned away, slipping her hand through the arm of a middle-aged man, as together, they walked into the crematorium. Was she the one who'd sent the details? Did he know her? He was sure as hell he didn't. Yet there was something about her...

He sighed as he pulled his keys from his pocket and hit the remote. It had been stupid to come, and there was no point him hanging around if he didn't have the courage to wade in and ask questions. Why all the secrecy, anyway? The moment had passed, and he'd missed his chance. Now he had a body to deal with. He tried to ignore the niggling disappointment that he'd never get to the bottom of it.

His phone pinged and he looked at the address Beth had forwarded. Hadley Wood – and one of the most expensive roads.

Twenty minutes later he parked the car in the driveway and looked around him as he climbed out. Number 103 was a large mock-Tudor house, set on its own plot with a circular in-out driveway. Both house and front garden were meticulously presented. No shortage of money here.

In the hall, Beth was waiting for him with protective clothing and covering for his shoes. He did a double take, noting her sleek auburn bob in surprise.

'Wow, what happened to the spiky bits?'

She rolled her eyes. 'I got fed up with the comments, alright?'

'It looks great.'

And it did, somehow enhancing the unusual green of her eyes. He wondered what their boss would make of it. DCI Murray was old school and Harry knew it had been a personal challenge to him not to comment on Beth's hair, which as well as being spiky had frequently changed colour. He hoped Murray would have the sense not to make some fatuous remark that would put her back up.

'Yeah, well thanks, but ... end of subject, please?' Beth said.

She was embarrassed and that surprised him, but he said no more as he pulled on the clothing and put the paper coverings over his shoes.

He didn't need her to tell him where the body was because he could see the woman lying in a heap at the bottom of the stairs.

'Do we know who she is?'

'Barbara Harding. She was married to the music producer, Roy Harding.'

'Never heard of him.'

'He was big in the music industry. You remember ... died about five years ago in a car crash – big news at the time.'

Harry shrugged. 'It'll probably come back to me when I look it up.'

He walked to where the pathologist was examining the body. Simon Winters was tall and lanky, with dark brown hair that flopped over one eye.

'Morning, Simon. A suspicious death, Beth says – she didn't just fall down the stairs then?'

The pathologist sat back on his haunches and looked up. 'Barbara Harding, white female, mid to late fifties, and no, I suspect she didn't just fall down the stairs.' He lifted the woman's hands, which had been covered with transparent plastic bags, and showed them to Harry.

'There's blood and what looks like skin particles beneath her nails which suggest a struggle.'

'How long has she been lying here?'

'Not conclusive, but a while, I'd say – certainly a day or two.'

'Who found her?' Harry asked, turning to Beth.

'The housekeeper. She's through there, in the lounge, if you want to speak to her. She's in a bit of a state.'

'Anything else you can tell me?'

'Only that the victim was blind. The housekeeper lives in during the week, but apparently Mrs Harding insisted on maintaining her independence and having the weekends to herself. Not a wise choice by the looks of it.'

Harry surveyed the scene. Nothing seemed out of place and from what he could see, the house looked spotless. Almost too tidy. It looked more like a hotel than a home. He followed Beth to the lounge.

'Housekeeper's Elena Mancini, and she's Italian,' Beth said in a low voice. 'Her English is good.'

They walked into a large, airy room looking out on a beautifully maintained rear garden. Elena Mancini was hunched on a cream leather chair. She was a tiny, bird-like woman in her fifties, and she looked up, dabbing at her eyes with a crumpled tissue as Harry approached.

'Mrs Mancini? I'm Detective Inspector Harry Briscombe and I'll be trying to find out exactly what happened to your employer.'

'We kept saying she should have someone with her over the weekends when I wasn't here.' Her voice was subdued, her accent heavy.

'What time did you find her?'

'About half past ten. Normally I'm in by nine, but I had a dentist appointment today.'

Harry settled himself on a chair opposite her. 'You work every weekday?'

She nodded. 'I have weekends off – she insisted on that. I have worked for her for twenty years, but I have only lived-in since the accident. I leave on Saturday mornings and come back each Monday.'

'It was a car accident, I understand. Could you tell me about it?'

'Oh, it was terrible. Her husband died and she was blinded. I told her that it was not safe being here on her own, but she would not listen.'

'So, you left here on Saturday morning. What time would that have been?'

'Around nine? We have breakfast between half past seven and eight, then I clear everything away and go.'

'And where do you stay over the weekend?'

'At my house in Finchley.'

'Did she have any enemies? Anyone who might want to harm her?'

She looked at him, shocked. 'Why are you asking that? Do you think it was not an accident?'

'We have to cover all possibilities,' Harry said.

'No one I can think of who might have wanted to hurt her. But no one very close either.'

'Family? Friends?'

'It was very sad. She had no children and no sisters or brothers – just a cousin and her daughter, pah...' She shrugged, making it obvious what she thought of them. 'They came to her doorstep after her husband died and then they tried to take over her life. But she isn't stupid. She used to say to me, "Elena, they are just here to see what they can get out of me – to see what I have left them in my will."'

'What about friends?'

'A few, but after the accident most of them disappeared. She led a lonely life. We both did.'

'You're not married?'

She sighed, her fingers worrying at the balled-up tissue in her hands. 'Yes, I'm married – over thirty years. Our son has left home, and the house is too quiet without him, so it is good for me to be here during the week.'

'Could you give me a list of names of Mrs Harding's friends and the cousin you mentioned?'

'Of course.' She got up from her chair, looking relieved at having something to do.

'Who should we contact about her death?'

'I have already done that. As soon as I found her, I ran next door to our neighbour, Yvonne, and we phoned Mia – she's the daughter of Barbara's cousin, Sylvia, but Barbara and Sylvia don't get on. Mia lives here most of her time, but even she was forced to go elsewhere over the weekends.' There was no missing the glint of satisfaction in the housekeeper's eye. No love lost there.

The housekeeper shuffled off to find pen and paper and Harry turned to Beth. 'Anything you've found?'

'Not a lot. I took a quick look at her bedroom upstairs – a couple of wardrobes and drawers tipped out, but nothing much. One of the windows was open – could have been a point of access, but it's quite high and no sign of a ladder. And her white stick was lying on the floor.'

'Her white stick?' The housekeeper stopped in her tracks and turned back to face them. 'No, no. She never went anywhere without that. She wouldn't have come down the stairs without it.'

Harry and Beth exchanged glances.

Beth stood up. 'I was about to give uniform a hand questioning the neighbours.'

Harry nodded. 'Good. I'll check a couple more things here, then head back to set up the incident room.'

A quick check of the bedroom didn't reveal anything that hadn't already been noted. Some clothes and trinkets were tipped over the floor. Forensics were already checking them out. A white stick lay in a random position that might indicate a struggle had taken place and it had been dropped. Harry conducted a careful walk through of the rest of the house and couldn't help thinking that it was extremely large for a couple with no family. There were five bedrooms in all, one of which was converted to an office and a second appeared to double up as a spare room and some sort of music room, with various instruments and equipment on display. Drawers and cupboards in all rooms had clearly been gone through, but otherwise the place was tidy, with no obvious point of entry for a break-in. SOCO would conduct a thorough sweep, so not much more he could do here.

Harry was just taking the list of names and contact details from the housekeeper when the front door opened. A young woman with shoulder-length light brown hair was trying to push past the policemen on duty.

'This is Mia Carroll, sir,' the police constable said. 'Mrs Harding's niece. I've been trying to explain to her that she can't enter the house.'

'What's happened?' the girl asked, peering past Harry.

Her eyes fell on the body lying at the bottom of the stairs and she gasped, her hand flying to her mouth. 'Oh my god! Elena said there'd been an accident.' Her eyes turned to Harry in horror. 'Is she alright?'

'I'm sorry, Miss Carroll. You can't come inside, I'm afraid, until my team has finished checking things out. But I do need to talk to you.'

'Yvonne will let you talk next door,' Elena Mancini suggested.

'That would be good if we could go somewhere else, and if you could come with us? I'm afraid no one will be allowed back into the house now until we've finished our examination of it. One of our officers can accompany you upstairs to pack a few things if you need them and we'll wait for you outside.'

A few minutes later, they were welcomed into the lounge of number 101. Yvonne and Elena went to the kitchen to make tea while Mia Carroll sank shakily into one of the chairs and buried her face in her hands. Then she looked up at Harry. 'She's dead, isn't she? Elena didn't tell me that. What happened?'

'We're not sure yet. We're still trying to establish the facts. But it looks like she fell down the stairs.'

Mia moaned as she rubbed her palms over her cheeks. 'I told her it wasn't safe to stay on her own, but she wouldn't listen to me — she insisted on having the house to herself at weekends. And now look. This was an accident waiting to happen.'

She was clearly upset but Harry knew that these early stages of any investigation were crucial in moving it forward. He pulled out his notebook. 'Was she expecting visitors over the weekend, do you know?'

Mia shook her head, tears glistening in her eyes. 'Not that I'm aware of, and I doubt it. She hasn't entertained much since Uncle Roy died. I offered to cook for her if she wanted friends over, but she always said no.'

'I understand she doesn't have much family?'

'There's just me and my mother. Mum and Auntie Barbara are first cousins. Their mothers were sisters.'

'Where do you spend the weekend, when you're not here?'

'At my boyfriend's usually. He lives in Mill Hill.'

Harry scribbled a note in his book and looked back up again. 'Do you work?'

'Yes. I'm a freelance window dresser. I'm working for a shop called Cocoa at Brent Cross, designing their window display for Christmas.'

'When did you last see Mrs Harding?'

'Saturday morning, before I headed off.'

'And she seemed alright? She didn't appear to be anxious or worried about anything?'

'No ... why are you asking these questions? She was fine, same as she always is.'

'Was there a particular reason why she liked the weekends to herself?'

He couldn't help thinking that it was a strange thing to want for someone who was blind.

Mia slumped back in the chair. She pulled a tissue out of her jeans pocket and blew her nose. 'I don't know. She's very independent. I never really thought about it. She just said she wanted some time to herself, and we respected that even if we did think it was stupid.'

Harry flicked to a new page in his book. 'What time did you leave on Saturday morning?'

'A little after nine. I start work at ten on Saturdays.'

'And your work can verify that? I'm sorry to have to ask, but we need to establish everybody's whereabouts on Saturday.'

'Oh.' She frowned. 'I'm sure someone will remember. I finished at four and went straight over to Paul's, stayed at his for the weekend and went into work from there, this morning. I usually do that because he's closer to Brent Cross than here.'

She broke off and shook her head in disbelief. 'God, if I'd come back last night ... it would have been me that found her. Poor Elena.'

Harry looked up at her, his antennae twitching. 'How do you know she was dead yesterday? It could have happened this morning, no?'

Mia's eyes widened in panic. 'Oh! I thought ...' She broke off and sat on the edge of her seat, rigid with tension.

Harry raised an eyebrow. 'We're awaiting the official report, but we believe she's been dead a bit longer than that.' He shut his notebook. 'I'll probably need to ask you some more questions later. Will you still be here?'

'You're welcome to wait here if it makes things easier,' Yvonne Carter said, walking into the room with a tea tray, and Mia nodded. 'Thanks. That would be great. Mum's already on her way over and it'll save me having to call her to change her plans. But ...' She looked at Harry. 'I don't understand why you're asking these questions. Her fall was an accident, wasn't it? You're not suspecting anything else?'

'We won't know for certain until we've established the facts. Until then, we need to keep an open mind. I'll hopefully be back within the next two to three hours. I'll want to speak to your mother as well.'

Harry left the house and went back next door to his car. He stood in the drive and took another, more detailed, look around him. The houses were all quite large, all detached on reasonable-sized plots. Most of them had shrubs edging their perimeters which meant it wasn't as easy as it might have been to see what went on in the next-door gardens. His gaze was drawn to the upstairs windows, and he tried to imagine what had gone on up there. Had it been a random attack, a burglary that had gone wrong? Or had there been a more personal motive as to why someone had wanted Barbara Harding dead? At this point they didn't know, but if he had anything to do with it, they'd find out.

CHAPTER THREE

'Is everyone here?' Harry asked, looking at the team of seven or eight people in the incident room. 'Where's Geoff?'

'He's just following up on a couple of things and then he'll be with us,' Beth said.

'Right. We're investigating the death of Barbara Harding, a fifty-five-year-old blind woman found dead at the bottom of the stairs at her home in Hadley Wood this morning. On first impressions, it could appear that she'd simply fallen, but according to forensics there are signs that she'd been involved in a struggle, so criminal activity is a definite possibility.'

Everyone turned as the door opened and DS Geoff Peterson entered the room. He pulled an apologetic face, 'Sorry. I was just checking out a few facts on our victim.'

'Good, you can share them then. We need to know who we're dealing with.'

Geoff stepped forward, his broad, six-foot frame dominating the room. He pinned a photograph of a man and woman to the board. 'Roy and Barbara Harding,' he said. 'Roy Harding was a well-known music producer with some big successes to his name. He was killed in a car crash five years ago and his wife was blinded in the same accident. The lads who caused the accident were caught and were well known to the police. They showed no remorse. Offin Abara, the driver and youngest lad in the group, was driving illegally, aged sixteen. He got seven years and came out six months ago having served less than five.'

'What price a life, eh? Harry said.

'Yep. One of the others in the car was Connor Stephens. The local police know all about him. He was an up-and-coming thug back then, but in recent years he's risen to dizzy heights.'

'Okay,' Harry said. 'Anything else?'

'Not yet. I've still got some digging to do.'

'What about you, Beth? Anything interesting from the neighbours?'

Beth flicked through her notebook. 'Most of them said she kept herself to herself pretty much. The people at 101 are Yvonne and Alan Carter. Mr Carter was at work, but Yvonne's the one that the housekeeper ran to when she found the body this morning. She confirmed what Elena Mancini said – no close relatives apart from Mia and Sylvia . Mia's been living there for part of the week for the last year or so and Barbara apparently wasn't too happy about that, but the girl said she didn't want to live with her mother and didn't have anywhere else to go unless she moved in with her boyfriend, which she didn't feel ready to do yet. Yvonne Carter said that neither she nor her husband heard or saw anything suspicious on Saturday, but they were out most of the day visiting their daughter and grandchildren. She said she hadn't seen Barbara at all over the weekend but that was nothing unusual because there's a high hedge between their gardens.'

She looked up and Harry took over. 'Mia didn't have much to contribute either, as she was apparently at work on Saturday. We'll need to speak to her and her boyfriend in more detail. Can someone check her movements with work for Saturday? Did you check the neighbour on the other side, Beth?'

'Yeah. She was out when I knocked, so I pushed a card through her letterbox asking her to call when she got back, which she did a few minutes ago. I told her someone would be round to talk to her later today.'

'Good. I'll do that when I go back. The housekeeper gave me a list of friends and we can divvy that up between us. Geoff, you can carry on with research here.'

Geoff nodded. 'I thought I'd do some more probing into the lads involved in the accident. They all live on the Hathaway estate in Hatfield so it's a good bet they've got form.'

The room cleared, and Harry glanced at his watch. One o'clock. 'Fancy grabbing a bite to eat before we go?' he asked Beth.

'Yeah, sure.'

They made their way to the canteen and grabbed a couple of sandwiches and coffees.

'Sorry for interrupting your morning off,' Beth said when they were seated. 'But you did say to call if anything urgent came up.'

'No worries. I'm glad you did.'

'Hope I didn't spoil your fun. How's Claire?'

'She's good, but I wasn't with her this morning if that's what you're angling after.' He hesitated. 'As it happens, I was at a cremation.'

'Oh, God. Sorry, I had no idea. Was it someone close?'

Harry frowned as he peeled the plastic wrapper off his ham sandwich. 'No. In fact it wasn't even anyone I knew as far as I'm aware.'

Beth raised her eyebrows. 'Sounds like there's a story in there somewhere,' she prompted, when he didn't elaborate.

He shook his head. 'It's a weird one. Someone posted a Telegraph obituary notice to me about three weeks ago, for a woman I'd never heard of. A week later, I get the cremation details. No letter or indication who it was from, but in the end I decided to go on the off-chance I might recognise someone there.'

'And?'

'Nada. Your call came through just in time to stop me making a complete prat of myself, I reckon. I guess that's the end of it, but it's frustrating.'

'Maybe they'll get in touch again?'

'Maybe … if it's important. I doubt it, somehow.' Harry shrugged and took a swig of his coffee, wincing. How did they manage to make it taste so vile?

Beth hesitated. 'While we're on the subject of funerals… my dad died ten days ago and his funeral's this Friday. I'm under pressure from my family to go.'

Harry looked at her, shocked. She never talked about her family, but from bits and pieces she'd let drop, he'd gathered they didn't particularly get on.

'God, I'm sorry to hear that. Why didn't you say? Of course, you must go. I know you weren't close, but–'

She sighed. 'That's an understatement. We've not talked in years. I'd feel a hypocrite going, but my brother who lives in Scotland can't – or won't – go, and my sister's begging me to go and support her. My mam and my older brother, Mitch, will be there and I can only see it ending badly.'

'Tough call.'

'Yeah.' She avoided Harry's eyes as she screwed her sandwich wrapping into a ball.

'Do you want to book Friday off, just in case? You're entitled to compassionate leave.'

'I don't know.'

'Do it,' Harry said. 'You can always change your mind. And I'm here if you want to talk anything through.'

'Thanks, Boss.' She smiled, then pulled a piece of paper from her pocket. 'So ...' she said, changing the subject. 'This is the list of names Elena Mancini gave us, of people we could speak to about Barbara Harding. Not many people on here, are there? A few friends and her cousin, Sylvia Carroll, who lives in Stanmore.'

'That's Mia Carroll's mother. She was on her way to the house when I left, according to her daughter, so hopefully she'll be there when we get back. How about I take the neighbour and the cousin, while you look into the friends?'

CHAPTER FOUR

105 Beechwood Way was a different design to Barbara Harding's house, but equally impressive in size and decor. There was a car parked on the drive which hopefully indicated that the owner was in. As he looked around at the leafy road and expensive cars parked in the drives, he couldn't help comparing it to where he lived in Enfield. Not that he wasn't bloody lucky to own his house there, courtesy of his grandmother – but these houses were worth a mint.

The door was opened by a well-groomed woman in her mid-fifties.

'Mrs West? I'm Detective Inspector Briscombe from Hertfordshire police.'

She peered at his ID and opened the door wider. 'Come in. What a terrible business. I couldn't believe it when Elena told me what's happened.'

She led the way through to an open plan lounge and dining room and indicated to a settee. 'Can I get you a drink of something?'

'No, I'm good thanks.'

Mrs West sat down in the chair opposite him and folded her hands in her lap. 'Elena said that you suspected it might not be an accident, but ... who would want to hurt Barbara? Was it a burglary, do you think? There have been a number in the area over the last few months.'

'We don't know what happened yet. That's what we're trying to establish. When was the last time you saw Barbara?'

'Friday afternoon. She came over for a cup of tea.'

'Did you notice anything unusual? Did she seem worried or tense in any way?'

Mrs West shook her head, tears in her eyes. 'No, she was fine – looking forward to having time to herself, as she always did at the weekend.'

'I understand her family and friends weren't happy about that?'

She shrugged. 'Barbara was very independent. She wasn't easily talked out of something once her mind was made up. One of her friends persuaded her to have one of those personal safety alarms that you wear around your neck – she hated it but agreed to wear it just to shut everyone up."

'Did she always wear it?' Harry was thinking that he hadn't noticed it when he'd seen her.

'I think so. She always had it on when I saw her. She was wearing it on Friday.'

Harry opened his notebook and scribbled a note. 'How friendly were you with her?'

'We've got more friendly since her husband died. I'm divorced.'

'Anything else you can tell me about Saturday? Did she have any visitors that you noticed, or was she expecting anyone?'

'She didn't mention it if she was. But now I come to think of it, there was a car parked in her drive late morning. It wasn't there long but it looked quite smart and was white.'

Harry's head jerked up. 'Can you be a bit more specific with the time?'

'Around eleven thirty maybe?'

'I don't suppose you recall the make or registration?'

'Sorry, I'm not very good on cars.'

'Do you remember seeing it there on other occasions?'

She shook her head. 'But that doesn't mean it hasn't been there before. I don't spend my time looking in her driveway to see who's visiting.'

'And no one else that you recall seeing on Saturday?'

'Only the gardener on his moped. His usual day is Thursday, but he sometimes comes on a Saturday too. He was turning into her drive as I was nipping out to the shops, around two-ish. He'd gone by the time I got back an hour or so later.'

'His name?'

'Finn. I don't know his surname.'

'Can you give me a physical description?'

'Early twenties maybe? Mixed race, about five foot ten. I don't think he was that great a gardener to be honest, but Barbara used to love gardening before the accident, and I think she enjoyed trying to teach him.' She gave a small smile. 'She said it was like the blind leading the blind.'

'How long has he been coming?

'A few months. Elena, Barbara's housekeeper, would be able to tell you more.'

This was good. This was good. At least they had a starting line now.

'You've been very helpful, Mrs West. Is there anything else you can think of that might be relevant?'

She hesitated. 'Not unless you're interested in gossip.'

Harry smiled. 'In my job some of the best information comes from gossip, so please, fire away.'

'It's just that there's a chap who lives opposite us in number 110. His name is Elliot Frith and he had a bit of a thing for Barbara. People round here think he's odd. He's probably quite harmless but he lives with his mother and has a telescope up at the window. He says it's for looking at the stars and planets, but I'm sure it's sometimes pointing towards Barbara's bedroom.' She shrugged uncomfortably. 'I feel bad saying it really, because he's been quite helpful to both me and Barbara, being on our own, but he was definitely put out when Barbara took Finn on as her gardener. Up to then he'd been doing it for her. She told me she felt he was getting a bit overfamiliar. I didn't tell her about the telescope thing because I didn't want to worry her. And anyway, I couldn't be sure.'

Harry made a last note and closed his notebook. 'Okay, thanks for that. He's probably already been spoken to by one of my team, but I'll check him out.' He stood up, handing her a card. 'If you think of anything else, please don't hesitate to give us a call.'

She rose to escort him to the door. 'It's horrible to think—' She broke off and shook her head. 'My son's coming over later and he's going to stay a couple of nights. I'm not normally a jittery person, but...'

'There'll be a police presence here overnight, but it's always good to have company at times like this. I wouldn't worry too much – there's no reason to think you're in any danger.'

Nipping over the low wall between Mrs West's house and Barbara Harding's, Harry nodded at the policeman standing guard outside the door.

'Everything okay?'

'Yes, sir. They've removed the body, but CSI are still here. The other occupants of the house are still next door waiting for you to talk to them there.'

Harry nodded. 'I'll just have a quick word with the forensics guys first.'

It was Charlie Fraser heading up CSI, and Harry found him on his knees poking at carpet fibres in Barbara Harding's bedroom.

'How's it going?' he asked from the doorway.

'Oh, hi, Harry. Getting there.'

'Anything interesting?'

The man looked up. 'Couple of things. A cushion on the settee downstairs had some blood on it and we've taken it away for analysis. The pathologist seemed to think it might have been used to smother the victim. Hopefully, he'll come up with evidence to support that at the PM. We've dusted for fingerprints on the wooden arm of the settee it was taken from.'

'What was the other thing?'

The officer stood up. 'I think the incident could have kicked off here in the bedroom. The way her stick was lying indicated it had been dropped, not placed. Too much danger of her tripping over it where it was, and the housekeeper is adamant that she wouldn't have gone downstairs without it. And we found one of those personal alarm pendants on the floor that could have been forcibly removed from around her neck.'

Harry nodded. 'I was wondering about that. The neighbour mentioned she had one. It would make sense if her attacker was trying to stop her from calling for help. Okay, so they start up here ... did she let him in, do you think, and then he followed her up?'

'No signs of forced entry but the backdoor to the garden was unlocked. Difficult to know if that happened before or after the attack.'

'Any sign of sexual activity did they say?'

'Nothing obvious apparently, but you'll have to speak to Simon about that.'

'Right.' Harry took a quick look around the bedroom scene, logging it to memory, then turned to leave. 'I'm off next door now to speak to the family and housekeeper.'

'Perhaps you can make sure they know this place is off limits to them until we've finished?'

'Will do.'

CHAPTER FIVE

H arry was shown into the next-door neighbour's house by the owner, Yvonne Carter.

'Mia and Sylvia are in the kitchen,' she said, leading the way.

Mia was talking to an older woman with blonde hair when Harry walked in, and next to her a man was sitting close, holding her hand.

'Who are you?' The older woman queried officiously.

Her manner put Harry's back up straight away, and he felt like responding that he was the one asking the questions. But he was used to dealing with all sorts and had long since learned that people reacted to grief in different ways.

He showed her his card. 'DI Briscombe. And you are?'

'Sylvia Carroll, Barbara's cousin. This is a terrible business. Do you know yet exactly what happened? Mia said you're suspicious it might not have been an accident. I can't believe that can be the case.'

'We're still looking into it. I can't confirm one way or the other yet. But I'm glad you're here, it saves me a visit. Is Mrs Mancini here?'

'She's in my lounge watching the television,' Yvonne Carter said. 'Shall I get her?'

'Not yet, thanks. Would you mind if I had a private word with Mia and her mother?'

'Of course. I'll be with Elena if you need me.'

He shifted his gaze to the man, who he judged to be in his late twenties.

'Paul Cunningham,' he introduced himself, rising to go. 'Mia's partner. I'll take myself off too.'

'No, it's okay, you can stay, please.'

'Have you got any news?' Mia asked, as Paul sat down again.

'No, but I do have a few more questions. I've just been speaking to Mrs West next door. She mentioned that your aunt had a visitor on Saturday. Someone in a white car. Can any of you think who that might have been?'

They all shook their heads.

'She didn't have many visitors, but none of her friends have white cars that I can think of,' Mia said.

'I understand she also had a gardener; Finn is it? Can you tell me anything about him?'

Again, it was Mia who answered, her expression disapproving. 'Only that he was my aunt's protégé, and none of us approved of him,'

'Do you know his other name? Where he lives?'

'No. Hatfield somewhere. Elena might know.'

'What do you mean when you say he was her protégé?'

'Aunt Barbara was involved in a car crash several years ago that killed her husband. It was a gang of yobs in the other car, driving dangerously, that caused the accident and Finn was the driver. He went to prison for it but not for long. When he came out, he did one of those restorative justice meetings where the person who commits the crime meets the victim?'

Sylvia Carroll gave a derisive snort at that, and Mia glanced at her briefly before continuing, 'Whatever he said, he clearly convinced Aunt Barbara that he was sorry because she ended up giving him a job as a gardener and doing general DIY stuff. We all told her it was a terrible idea, but she wouldn't listen. He was into music like her husband had been and as far as she was concerned, that was a good enough reason to give him a second chance. And now this happens. I hadn't thought of it before but...' She shrugged. 'He's definitely someone you should check out.'

Her eyes filled with tears, and she grabbed a tissue from the box on the table. 'It's all so horrible, are you sure it wasn't just an accident?'

'We're not sure about anything yet,' Harry said carefully. 'But at this point, forensic evidence does seem to suggest the presence of another person and the possibility that that person may have contributed towards your aunt's death.'

He turned to Sylvia Carroll. 'When did you last see Barbara?'

'I don't remember exactly. A couple of weeks back?'

'And nothing untoward that you noticed? She wasn't stressed or anxious about anything?'

'No more than usual. She wasn't particularly happy with her lot as you might imagine. But no, she seemed fine.'

'Does she have no other family?'

'Not that I know of.'

'Do you mind telling me where you were on Saturday from mid-morning onwards?'

She stiffened. 'At home doing my housework until lunch time. We can't all afford to have staff. After that, I went shopping, and in the evening I went to friends for supper.'

'And can anyone verify your whereabouts during the day?'

'Not really. Do they need to?'

'It's just helpful if we can eliminate people from our enquiries. But no matter for the time being.'

He looked enquiringly at Paul.

'I was at home most of the day doing general stuff in my flat, until Mia got back from work late afternoon. Then we went to the cinema with friends in the evening, to see that new film, Direct Hit.'

'And you last saw Mrs Harding, when?'

'The Friday before last. Mia and I went away for a Spa weekend, and I came to pick her up.'

'Did you see much of her?'

'Barbara? Not really. Sometimes I'd stay for a cup of tea if Mia and I were heading off somewhere – or the occasional supper. But she wasn't particularly sociable, as I'm sure people will tell you.'

'Okay, thank you all. Has someone taken formal statements from you?'

They all nodded.

'That's fine for now then, although I'd be grateful if you could drop into the station in the next day or two, to have your fingerprints taken.'

'Is that really necessary?' Paul asked.

'We need them for elimination purposes as you've all been in the house recently, and the sooner the better, please.'

At the door, Harry turned. 'I don't know if anyone's said, but Barbara's house is being treated as a crime scene and as such, I'd ask you to return to your own homes for the time being, until our forensic people have finished. Leave your number with them, and they'll call you when it's okay for you to return.'

'What about her ... body?' Sylvia asked. 'When will she be released? We'll need to get on and arrange the funeral I suppose.'

'I can't say yet. It could be a while, so I wouldn't rush to make too many firm arrangements. If you'll excuse me, I'm going to speak to Mrs Mancini now.'

CHAPTER SIX

Elena Mancini and Yvonne Carter were talking in quiet voices as Harry entered the room.

'Mrs Mancini. Can I have a few words with you, please?'

'Of course, and please, my name is Elena.'

'I'll take myself off,' Yvonne said. 'Can I make you a drink, Inspector?'

'I'm fine thanks.'

He walked further into the room and took a seat in the chair opposite the housekeeper. 'It must have been very upsetting for you, finding your employer?'

'I will never get over the shock of it,' Elena said, her hand going to her heart. 'I have worked for her for twenty years; it was awful to come in and find her like that.'

'I know this is difficult, but can you think of anyone who might have wanted to harm Barbara?'

'Of course not. She hardly ever went out, so who could even know to hurt her? Although...'

'Yes?'

The woman shrugged. 'I was not happy about her hiring that man, Finn, to do the gardening and odd-jobs.'

'Because?'

'I could not trust him, you know? Not after what he did. But Barbara, she would not hear anything against him. She said he was very talented at his song writing, and we all need a second chance in life. Perhaps she is right about that. When I moved to England with my husband thirty-three years ago, it was a second chance for us, and I do not regret it.'

'Were you aware the gardener sometimes came on a Saturday?'

'No. I was not. Who told you that?'

'Your neighbour, Mrs West. Do you have a full name and address for him?'

'We have his mobile number, but no address.'

'Could you give me that before I leave?'

'Of course.'

'Mrs West also mentioned there was a white car in the drive on Saturday. Do you have any idea who that might belong to?'

She shook her head.

'Has anything unusual happened recently? Anything at all?'

'No.'

'She didn't argue with anyone?'

The woman shrugged. 'She did not see many people.'

'And was anything taken, do you know? Did you get a chance to see if anything was missing?'

'Only after your people got here. They showed me some pictures of her room.'

'And?'

'I could see straight away that her jewellery box was gone from the wardrobe where she kept it, as well as some money that is usually in the top drawer. It was open and things had been thrown out. The envelope was apparently gone – it had over one thousand pounds in it. I told her it was too much, but she would never listen. I think because she could not get out, she liked to have money in the house so she could pay people in cash.'

'How did she get the cash out of the bank?

'Usually, I got it for her. She would give me her card and I know her pin. I got four hundred pounds out for her on Friday and added it to what was in the drawer.'

'Did she want it for a reason, do you think?'

'If she did, she did not say.'

'Do you handle all her finances?'

'Most of her bills are paid by direct debit and she has ... how you call it ... a financial person who deals with her investments? It is a company in Totteridge. But I have always helped her to pay for everyday bills, like the gardener, window cleaner, shopping. That is why she likes to keep cash in the house. Mia has also recently got involved with her finances. She convinced Barbara it would be a good idea to have a power of attorney appointed in case she got ill and was unable to manage things herself. Barbara was reluctant to do it, but when she spoke to her accountant, he agreed it was a good idea, so that's what they did, and she also added Mia's name onto her bank account.' She pursed her lips making it very plain what she thought of that idea.

'Anything else missing, that you noticed?'

'Her coin collection, which I know was very valuable. She kept that in the wardrobe near her jewellery – and some extremely valuable handbags, Hermes, Chanel and Louis Vuitton, that she had collected over the last thirty years or more. She was very proud of them and had about four or five. They are also gone from her wardrobe.'

'Can you name any of the jewellery items that are missing?'

'My mind is not working properly at the moment, but I can write you a list when I think about it. She had some very beautiful pieces that Roy bought her over the years. A Rolex watch, a diamond necklace that he gave her. A silver Tiffany heart necklace. I can find pictures of those for you probably – she had photos of everything for her insurance policy. Also, I noticed …' She took a breath. '… when I found her, she did not have her engagement ring on. She never took that off. It was a diamond surrounded by a circle of sapphires. Very beautiful.'

'Thanks, you've been very helpful. If you could draw up a list of her jewellery when you feel up to it, and tell my officers where the photos are, that would also be helpful. What about security? How good was she about that?'

'There's an alarm that we put on at night or if we go out, a panic button by her bed and good locks on the doors. But she didn't worry about security too much in the daytime – the back door is often unlocked, and neighbours and friends know they can come in that way rather than make her walk to the front door.'

'Spare keys? Who has keys to the house?'

Elena gave it some thought. 'I have one of course, Mia and Sylvia both have one, Yvonne, and there is a spare in the garden hidden in a brick. I can show you if you like?'

'Yes please. In fact, if we could do that now?'

They walked to Barbara Harding's back garden, where Harry caught the attention of one of the SOCO team busy at work. 'There's apparently a brick with a spare key to the back door hidden in it. Can you have a look?'

'It's just over there, behind the bird bath near the fence,' Elena said. 'It is the only brick with a slit in the top.'

They waited while the man went over to the brick and slipped his gloved hand inside. He looked up. 'Nothing here, it's empty.'

'Has anyone used it recently, that you know of?' Harry asked Elena. She shook her head.

'Who else knows it's here?'

'Mia, Sylvia, Yvonne. That is all I think.'

'What about the gardener?'

'Maybe. He sometimes did odd jobs in the house for her.'

'One last question, when did you last see Barbara, and can you tell me where you were on Saturday?'

She looked affronted and said frostily. 'I saw her on Saturday morning. I cooked supper for that night and prepared easy meals for Sunday, and then I left for my own house at about ten o'clock, as I always do. For the rest of Saturday, I was at my home, clearing up the mess my husband had made all week.'

'Can anyone confirm that?'

'My husband was there for part of the time, until he went out to the pub. Otherwise...' she shrugged. 'I spoke to my son for perhaps half an hour when I first arrived home. That is all.'

'Thank you. This is my card if you remember anything else. If you can just tell me where they can find the phone number for the gardener now, I'll ask one of the investigating team to get it for me?'

'Of course. It is in the bedroom at the top of the stairs, the first one on the left. It is used as an office and Barbara's address book is in the top right-hand drawer. The number will be under F, for Finn. He was mixed race you know, and he had a strange name, but his mother was English and he told us she always called him Finn.'

While they were waiting, Harry wrote a couple of things in his notebook. Then he turned back to Elena. 'What was Barbara and Mia's relationship like?'

She shrugged. 'They got on okay, but Barbara did not get on with Sylvia, Mia's mother. She said she married her first husband for his money, and she was not surprised the second marriage hadn't lasted because she was an impossible person to live with and no man would be able to put up with her for long.'

She smiled. 'You will find out that Barbara was like that – not slow to say what she thought – although I am not aware that she ever said that to Sylvia's face. Even she was not usually that tactless.'

CHAPTER SEVEN

A s Harry was walking back to his car, he rang Geoff. 'How's the research into Offin Abara and his mates in the car, going?'

'Put it this way, they're not the sort of people you'd want house sitting for you while you were away. They all live on the Hathaway estate, and we were right, Connor Stephens is their ringleader, or Conn as he's more commonly known. I was about to head off to see if I could catch any of them at home.'

'Well, I've just discovered that Offin Abara was Barbara Harding's gardener.'

'What? How did that come about?'

'I'll fill you in when I get back, but meantime why don't I take him, and you try the others. We can compare notes later. Can you text me his address?'

'I'll do it now. I'll also email you some background stuff on him.'

'Send the address to Beth as well. I'll see if she wants to meet me there.'

Harry ended the call and searched for Beth's number. She picked up straight away.

'How are you getting on?' Harry asked.

'I've finished here. Luckily for me, two of the friends were together, consoling each other, so that saved me a trip to Hertford. I'll fill you in at the briefing. Anything you want me to do now, or shall I head back to the station?'

'You can meet me at Finn Abara's house – the one who was driving the car that killed Barbara Harding's husband? Turns out he did a restorative justice visit – after which Barbara took him on as her gardener.'

'No!'

'Yup. Geoff's texting you the address now. If you get there before me just wait until I arrive.'

Twenty-five minutes later Harry was pulling up outside 16 Elder Avenue. Beth wasn't there yet so he parked the car and opened his emails to skim read Geoff's information on Abara. There was surprisingly little on him by way of police cautions and the only conviction he had was the one relating to the accident that they already knew about. It wasn't unusual though for people to skirt the law and manage to avoid being caught. He'd known examples where it had taken years before finally managing to nail people for crimes they'd committed, only to have them then turn around and ask for dozens more, going back years, to also be taken into account.

So, Offin Abara was twenty-one years old, clean record apart from a couple of minor public order offences and possession of class B drugs. After his release he'd moved back to this address, where the woman who'd fostered him lived, although clearly she would no longer officially be classed as his foster mother.

He looked up as Beth's car drove past and parked a few spaces further down. A minute later she was standing outside his car. He was still struggling to come to terms with the new look. There was no doubt, in his opinion, that it suited her. Her hair was back to its natural, and quite striking, auburn colour and her slim though curvy figure would attract any man's eye. Yet she seemed totally unaware of her attractiveness. He closed his emails and joined her. They both surveyed the road, which was long and winding, with identical cream-coloured houses on both sides, in varying states of maintenance. It was an estate they knew well, and this was one of the better maintained houses of what was a pretty eclectic mix.

'The house is in good nick,' Beth said, a note of surprise in her voice.

'Yeah, it is,' Harry said, consulting Geoff's email. 'The woman who lives here's a Mrs Marigold Lamb – goes by the nickname of Goldie. Widowed, and she's fostered Abara and his younger sister, Alyssa, since Abara was eight. Let's see what they've got to say for themselves.'

They walked up the path and Beth rang the doorbell.

Fin looked out of his window and saw them walking up the path. He knew who they were straight away, and his heart started an erratic beat.

Keep calm. They had nothing to pin on him. He'd gone over and over it in his head. He was as sure as he could be that he hadn't left any evidence to show he'd been there. The most they might have would be that one of the neighbours had seen him, and he had a good enough excuse for that. He mustn't panic or let his fear show – the bastards would jump on that straightaway and have him back in the nick in no time.

The doorbell rang and he heard Goldie walking to the front door to answer it. He resisted the temptation to tell her not to but stood in his open doorway so he could hear what was being said.

'Mrs Lamb?' It was the man who spoke.

'Yeah?'

'My name's Detective Inspector Harry Briscombe and this is my colleague, DC Bethany Macaskill.'

'Oh?'

Finn knew that tone of Goldie's. She'd give nothing away at this point, but he'd seen the looks she'd been throwing him all weekend, and she'd know this call was about him.

'I understand that Offin Abara lives here?'

'So?'

'Is he in? Can we speak to him?'

'What's it about?'

'We need to speak to him about that. Can we come in and can you get him please?'

'Have you got a warrant?'

'No, but I can get one if you'd rather. We just want to ask him a few questions.'

Silence for a few seconds, then...

'Finn?' Goldie called up the stairs. 'Come down. The police are here and want to talk to you.'

Finn banked down his fear as he walked to the top of the staircase. 'What about? I got nothing to say to them.'

'Just come down, lad, and find out.'

He sauntered down the stairs, trying to look unconcerned.

'Offin Abara?'

'Yeah.'

Harry looked at the woman. 'Is there somewhere private we could talk?'

She jerked her head sideways. 'Through there in the front room, but I'm coming in too, 'cos I want to listen to this – make sure it's not harassment.'

The front room was set up with a large rectangular table and six chairs. Goldie pulled one of the chairs out and sat down. She was a tall, well-dressed woman in her mid-fifties, curly dark hair and mixed race like Finn, with a look in her eye that warned she was no pushover. Her hair was short, and her nails manicured. The house too, was clean and well maintained. There was no offer of a drink and as soon as they sat, Harry got down to business.

'Right, Offin –'

'The name's Finn – no one calls me Offin, it's a shit name no-one's ever even heard of.'

'Oi, don't knock it. If it was good enough for your grandfather, it's good enough for you.'

Goldie's voice was severe, and Finn shrugged, but he didn't bite back.

'Okay ... Finn. We're investigating a serious offence that happened over the weekend – the death of Barbara Harding, who I believe you know?'

'She's dead?'

He didn't look as shocked as he might have and Harry mentally noted that. 'That's what I said, and I'm afraid, unless we get information to the contrary, we're treating her death as suspicious.'

Harry didn't miss Goldie's gasp, but Finn Abara's face was an expressionless mask.

'You don't seem very surprised at the news?'

Finn shrugged. 'Not much surprises me, especially the fact that you lot are already here, banging on my door and trying to pin it on me.'

His tone was belligerent, and Harry sought to defuse the situation. 'We're not trying to pin it on anyone, we just want to establish the facts. When did you last see Mrs Harding? I understand you did some gardening work for her?'

'I saw her Thursday, my usual day for going there.'

'Did she seem different at all? Anxious or distracted?'

'No.'

'So, you're saying you didn't see her on Saturday?'

'That's right.'

'That's odd, because one of her neighbours reckoned she saw your scooter in the drive and apparently you do sometimes go over on a Saturday?'

'Yeah, sometimes I do, and I did go over but when I rang the doorbell she didn't answer, so I thought someone must have taken her out. They sometimes do that.'

'Did you leave straight away?'

'No. I went round the back to water some plants we put in a couple of weeks back. Then I left and came home.'

'How long were you there?'

'Ten minutes?'

'And you didn't notice anything strange or out of the ordinary?'

'No.'

Harry broke off to jot something down in his notepad, then he looked up again. Finn's expression was clearly defensive, and he decided to change tack.

'Talk me through how you got to be given that job as her gardener.'

'What are you thinking? How come a rich white woman like her takes a punt on mixed race trash like me?'

'No, but I know that you were driving the car that killed her husband. It seems unusual that she'd end up offering you a job.'

'Yeah, well you don't know nothing then, 'cos it weren't me driving that car. But I don't expect you to believe that any more than the Judge did.'

'Okay, I'll rephrase that if it'll make you happier. Let's just say that you did time for the offence. Why would she then give you a job?'

'They told me she was messed in the head about her husband being killed, and that maybe if we met up it might be good for both of us.

I didn't want to do it, but my probation officer talked me into it.' He shrugged. 'We found we had some things in common – and I know you're standing there wondering what someone like her would have in common with someone like me, but I'm into music — and her husband was the same when he was younger. We had a second meeting and got on alright. I told her that it was hard getting a job when I had a criminal record and that was when she offered to take me on as her gardener. I've been going a while now. She was all right – why would I want to hurt her?'

'A considerable amount of money was stolen from the house, plus some valuables. Whoever did it, got away with some rich pickings.'

'Well, it weren't me. That's all I can say. I don't know nothing about it.'

'Nor of anyone else who might have had a reason to harm her?'

'No.' He turned to Goldie. 'Do I have to sit here listening to this?'

She shook her head and looked at Harry enquiringly. 'Was there anything else you wanted to ask, because if not, I think we're finished here. Finn's been in prison, but he's done his time and you lot need to get off his back.'

'Do you mind telling me where you were on Saturday afternoon, Mrs Lamb? Finn says he came back here. Can you confirm that and around what time it was that he got back?'

The woman hesitated. 'I wasn't here because I run the youth session at the community centre on a Saturday. Helps keep the youngsters off the street. We give 'em lunch too. I usually get home about three, and Finn was definitely here then.'

Harry inclined his head. 'Okay, we'll leave it for now, but don't disappear off anywhere, Finn. We might want to question you again.'

After they'd left, Finn made to go back upstairs but Goldie stopped him.

'Finn?'

'What?'

'I think you know what. We need to talk.'

'What about?'

'I'm not stupid. I've reared you since you was eight years old and I've been giving you space, biding my time because I could see you was upset on Saturday, but now I need to know why – especially if you're in trouble.'

Finn felt angry colour creep into his cheeks. 'You think I done it?'

'I'm not saying that, but you got some explaining to do. You know I'm on your side if you want to talk.'

When he made no response, she probed further. 'Were you telling the truth when you told them you knew nothing about it?'

'Of course I was, you're the same as them. Waiting for me to get into trouble again so you can all say I told you so.'

Goldie looked at him, disappointment in her eyes. 'Is that what you really believe after all these years?'

Finn wouldn't meet her gaze. He was being unfair, and he knew it. Theirs had been an open house for anyone in trouble, throughout his childhood, and all his mates had envied him living with her and Ted. She'd always been there for him – but now ... she just didn't get how hard it was trying to stay clean around here – the pressure he was under every day. It was exhausting. He just wanted to get enough money to escape from it all. But that wasn't easily come by. Not legally anyway.

'Look, just leave it out, will you,' he said, heading back up the stairs, two at a time. 'I'm gonna change and go for a jog. I need some air.'

'I'm here if you want to talk when you get back–'

But Goldie was already talking to thin air as his bedroom door shut with a resounding bang.

CHAPTER EIGHT

'What was your impression?' Harry asked Beth as they walked back down the path.

'He's lying,' she said uncompromisingly. 'Or put it this way, he wasn't being open and honest with us.'

'I agree. I should have asked to take a look at his bedroom.'

'He wouldn't have let you without a warrant. And anyway, whatever he is, he's not stupid. If there was any incriminating evidence he'd have dumped it by now.'

'Nonetheless, it might have been useful. And you never know – where else is he going to stash a thousand pounds if he nicked it?'

His phone pinged and he pulled it out of his pocket.

'Geoff says he's been delayed. He was going to interview Connor Stephens and the other guy involved in the accident. Stephens is only a few roads away in Hinchfield Road, we might as well wander over while we're here.'

'Did he also do the restorative justice thing?'

'No mention of it, and there's nothing linking him or the third guy to Barbara Harding, but they both live on this estate, so for the sake of completeness...'

'Are we walking it?'

Harry checked Google maps. 'Shouldn't tire us out too much and I could do with the exercise.'

Hinchfield Road may only have been a short distance away, but it was nothing like where Finn Abara lived.

'What a dump.' Beth said, her eyes taking in the peeling paintwork of most of the houses, the car body-parts piled up in different gardens and taped up windows that had been smashed and not repaired. 'Some people are just plain slobs, aren't they?'

'The do-gooders in this world would say you're being judgemental and maybe it's not their fault. Unemployment, lack of education...'

Beth threw him a disdainful look. 'I grew up on an estate like this in Newcastle, and yeah, those things are factors, but people can still make their own choices, have standards and a sense of pride. I'm not getting any sense of that here, are you?'

Harry agreed, but it was one of those weird situations where he didn't feel comfortable speaking out. The fact that she'd grown up somewhere like this gave her a rite of passage that he didn't have. He was one of the luckier ones; good education, parents and grandparents who'd cared about him – and the more he saw the random cards dealt out in life, the more he realised how fortunate he was.

'No, I'm not,' he conceded. 'But come on, the sooner we get it done, the sooner we can get on with other stuff.'

But when they rang on the doorbell, there was no reply. Harry stepped back to look up at the windows but could see no signs of movement. He pulled out a card and wrote on it for Connor Stephens to call him, posting it through the letterbox.

'That's all we can do,' he said to Beth. 'Maybe Geoff will have more luck. If he doesn't call back by tomorrow, we'll try again.'

He looked at his watch. 'I'm going to head back, but I meant to ask. Did you speak to a guy who lived opposite Barbara Harding?' He rummaged in his pocket and pulled out his notebook. 'Elliot Frith, at 110?'

'I tried. He lives with his mother, and she said he was out shopping. Any particular reason? I could try again now?'

'Yeah, do it. Barbara Harding's next-door neighbour told me that he's a bit of an oddball. Has a telescope apparently, that she reckoned was sometimes trained on Barbara's bedroom.' He smiled when he saw Beth's raised eyebrow. 'Might be an idea to check out exactly what sort of bird watching he's into?'

Finn's feet pounded the pavement as he headed for the local park. His brain was teeming, and his stress levels were at busting point. He needed a good run to bring him down again. He wasn't stupid, he'd known the police would call, but it had still thrown him. And the taste of fear at the thought of being banged up inside again was a constant bile rising in his mouth. He'd had a tough life living on the estate but even that hadn't prepared him for life inside. He'd walked out of those gates without a backward glance and sworn to himself, never again.

He kept his head down, not looking around him. Shutting the world out. He wasn't in the mood for talking. He needed to get rid of his anger.

'Hey, Finn...'

Shit. He picked up pace, pretending not to have heard.

'Oi, Finn!'

This time the voice was so loud, there could be no pretending, but still Finn kept running even though he knew it was pointless. It didn't take Conn and his mates long to head him off further up the path.

He came to an abrupt halt in front of them, bending over, hands on thighs, getting his breath back.

'You looked like you'd got half the cops in London after you,' Conn said. 'Didn't know you could move that fast, mate. What you been up to? Haven't seen you around lately.'

'This and that.'

'How's the gardening job in Hadley going?'

Finn looked at him suspiciously. Did he know? But he was reluctant to fill him in on the latest development if he didn't. Conn had been hounding him ever since his release, trying to get him back on board. He'd have no excuse to say no, once the news leaked out.

'It's going alright. Quite enjoy it.'

'Landed on your feet there, mate. She didn't want anything to do with me when I pulled the sorry card.'

'You went to see her? How did you know where she lived?'

Conn tapped his nose. 'Just keeping an eye on old mates.'

'You followed me?'

'Yeah, it weren't difficult. But as I say, she weren't interested in the likes of me.'

Finn wasn't surprised. Barbara was no one's fool; she'd have seen through the likes of Conn, no trouble. 'Perhaps she twigged you didn't really mean it.'

'And you did?'

Finn shrugged.

'A good place to do over, don't you think. What's the security like?'

'No way. They'd think it was me straight away, and we done enough killing her husband.'

'Ah, listen to you. Got a soft spot for her have you?'

'I need the job.' He broke off, realising that his job had probably come to an end.

'Well, that's all very weird mate,'cos a little bird tells me you might not have a job any longer, that in fact, she ain't around anymore and that the place is crawling with cops. What's that all about then?'

'How do you know that?'

Conn just stared at him, and he sighed, knowing it was going to come out anyway. 'Yeah, well, she died over the weekend. The police were round at mine earlier, asking questions.'

'Why?' Conn's eyes were sharp. 'What she die of?'

Finn shook his head. 'Dunno. They didn't say, but they was asking questions as if there was something not right. And they said she'd been burgled.'

He looked at Conn suspiciously. 'How did you know the place was crawling with cops? What little bird told you?'

Conn winked. 'Can't reveal my sources. So, what did they say to you, the cops?'

'Not a lot, but I'm on their radar. I need to keep my head down, that's for sure.'

'Pity. I got a little job for you.'

Finn eyed him warily. 'What sort of job?'

'Nothing much. A little delivery.'

'Not a good idea mate. Not at the moment.'

'I don't seem to have had any good ideas since you came out the nick. You've been avoiding me. What you doing? Running your own side-line? Cos you know I wouldn't like that.'

'I ain't doing nothing. Just trying to keep out of trouble.'

'I wanna believe you, Finn, but ... you know as well as I do mate, that round here you're either with me or Zach. Which is it?'

'Look. Conn, we known each other a long time, right? Truth is, I don't want to be in with anyone. I'm trying to go straight – do something with my music.'

Conn burst out laughing. 'You hear that, guys? This is Finn we're hearing ... wanting to go straight. Do we believe him?'

The other youths sniggered and shook their heads.

'See ... we know you too well. I gave your family protection while you was inside, cos I was grateful you taking the rap and all that. But that Goldie ... she's a rare one ain't she? And that lovely little sister of yours, Alyssa ... how old's she now? Thirteen, fourteen? You wouldn't want to see anything happening to them, would you? And it won't, while I'm looking out for'em. But get on the wrong side of me, mate ...'

Finn could feel his stress level soaring. 'I'm not on the wrong side of you. No way would I go with Zach, you know that. But I'm telling you, I need to lay low until this thing with the dead woman blows over. They'll be watching me. And maybe they'll call on you too. They knew about the car accident.'

'Just let'em try.' But Finn could see it was bluff, as an uneasy expression entered Conn's eye.

They were distracted by the arrival of a couple of young lads on bikes. 'Hey, Conn, we just saw some people at your door. Looked serious like, and they pushed something through your letterbox.'

'What did they look like?' Finn asked sharply.

'Man and a woman.'

'Did the woman have red hair?'

'Yeah.'

'It's them,' Finn said, turning back to Conn. 'They must have called on you after me.'

'What did you tell'em?'

'Nothing. Just that I'd been there Saturday but she was out.'

'What do they want to talk to me for, then?'

'How would I know? I told you, they knew about the accident. It's probably routine. It's not like you had anything to do with her, is it?'

'No.' Conn's tone was abrupt as he turned away. 'See you around. We'll catch up another time, but you have a think'bout what I said. I don't like my boys straying too far from my path. Come on,' he said to the others. 'Let's see what they wanted.'

Finn watched them go, before turning round himself and continuing his run. He felt more trapped with every day that went by. He'd avoided being sucked in again so far, but Conn wouldn't give up. He wanted Finn back, safe in his clutches where he could control him, and he'd find a way of achieving it.

By the time he re-entered the house half an hour later, he'd calmed down, but he couldn't shake off the despair that was beginning to overwhelm him. He'd thought for a short time there, with the help Barbara had been giving him, that maybe, just maybe, he could turn his back on his life here and all the crap that went with it – make something of himself with his beloved music. That had been his dream, the goal that had driven him – to get Goldie and Alyssa right away from this place – a new start in a new neighbourhood. But who was he kidding? Fate always seemed to butt in – forcing him to do things he didn't want to do. And then, the more he did them, the more trapped he became.

'Finn ... that you?'

Goldie appeared in the hall just as he was about to head up the stairs. 'Come in here,' she said, walking into the dining room.

He hesitated, but her voice brooked no argument, and he knew he had to face her at some point.

'What?' he asked belligerently, following her in.

'I've given you enough space now. But after that visit from the cops, we need to talk about the blood I saw on your hoody when I washed it.'

CHAPTER NINE

B ack at the station, as Harry headed for his desk in the large open-plan office, his phone rang. He looked at the ID and saw Claire's laughing face beaming up at him. No doubt ringing to see how he'd got on that morning at the crematorium. They'd been back together a couple of months now and it felt good having her sharing his life, but it still didn't come naturally to him letting someone in. That was a work in progress and wasn't going to change overnight.

'Hey,' he said into the mouthpiece, moving over to the window for a bit or privacy.

'Hi. Just wondering how the funeral went. I've been dying of curiosity – no pun intended.'

'Haha. But nothing to report, I'm afraid. I'm none the wiser.'

'What? You did go?'

Harry sighed. 'Yeah, I went, but it felt weird, turning up to some person's cremation service who I never knew. And just as I was deliberating whether to go in or not, Beth rang with a new case. I had to head over to Hadley and that was that. Guess I'll never know now.'

'Oh, Harry, how frustrating. Maybe they'll get in touch again.'

Harry hoped not. It all felt a bit of an anti-climax. He had enough mysteries going on in his life. Did he really need more?

'I don't know. It was all weird anyway, wasn't it? I'd never heard of that woman, I know that. So why would I be interested in going to her funeral?'

'I've been thinking about it. Maybe whoever it is knows you're a policeman and thinks you might be able to help in some way? It could have been a suspicious death or something and they're not happy with the coroner's report.'

'It's possible, but I'm not wasting any more time on it. I've got enough dealing with the case load I've got.'

'Are you coming over later?'

Claire had a small house of her own in Cuffley, and they tended to spend their time house-hopping between there and Enfield where he lived. 'That would be good, but I'm not sure what time I'll get away.'

'No worries. Just give me a call when you're leaving, I've got some ready-mades in the fridge. See you later.'

Harry switched off and looked about him. 'Anyone got anything new?' he called out. He homed in on Dave Freeman, the analyst. 'How about you, Dave? Where are you at?'

'I've been drawing up a network of associates of both the victim and potential suspects, and I'm looking at other crimes in the area to see if I can track any similar patterns. I've also been on to the prison governor where Offin Abara did his time. He was apparently a model inmate. Kept out of trouble and spent a lot of time in the library educating himself and learning about the music industry. He's a keen songwriter in the making, apparently. As for the other two – I've looked into them and it's a very different story. Thugs, the both of them, through and through. I've drawn up a couple of charts of timelines and significant events for both the victim and any suspects and pinned them to the board in the incident room. We can fill in and expand on those as we get more info.'

'Good work, thanks.'

Harry's mobile rang and he walked towards his desk as he answered it.

'DI Briscombe.'

'Oh ... hello, this is Elena Mancini, Barbara Harding's housekeeper?'

'Yes. Hello.'

'I thought I should call you because I forgot to tell you something that could be important. When you asked about anything unusual happening, I was agitated, you know? And I don't know how I forgot ... but a few weeks back – maybe three or four – two men turned up on the doorstep to speak to Barbara. They were the other two people in the car that killed her husband and they said they had come, like Finn, to say they were sorry. But afterwards ... Barbara, she said she did not believe that they were sorry at all. And they were not with a victim liaison officer like Finn had been. She felt very uncomfortable about the visit and was much stricter about using the burglar alarm at night after that.'

'Thank you, Mrs Mancini, that's very useful to know and we'll follow up on it. If you think of anything else, please don't hesitate to call again.'

'Thank you, Inspector. I will.'

Harry clicked off his phone, sat down at his desk to scribble some notes on his pad, then tore the page off and went back to Dave's desk.

'We need to check out everyone who's in the frame at the moment. I've got some info for you to flesh out here on the people I've interviewed today. First off, Sylvia Carroll, Barbara Harding's cousin. Find out what you can about her and her daughter, will you? And also, the housekeeper, Elena Mancini. But top priority is for you to check with the victim liaison services if they organised any sort of restorative justice meeting for the other two guys in the car to meet up with Barbara Harding. The housekeeper's just remembered that they turned up saying they wanted to apologise for what they'd done. But they were alone without a facilitator. I doubt it was a legitimate visit and if it wasn't, we need to speak to them about that soon as.'

'Reckon it's more likely pigs might fly than they'd apologise for anything, but sure, I'll look into it.'

'Thanks. I'm heading down to grab myself a sandwich. Want anything?'

'No, I'm good thanks.'

'As the others come back, tell them there'll be another briefing in an hour's time at five o'clock. We need to pool what we've got so we can hit it hard tomorrow.'

CHAPTER TEN

The elderly woman who opened the door eyed Beth suspiciously, even though she'd just shown her card.

'I don't know, police these days aren't what they used to be. Days gone by you could tell they were police by their uniforms.'

Beth grinned. 'You're right. But I'm CID, not uniform, and I'm sure you've heard of plain clothes detectives?'

The woman shrugged but opened her door wider. 'Well, you can come in. Elliot's back now. I'll give him a shout. Elliot...' she called up the stairs.

A pair of feet came into view, followed by legs and a body. He was what she'd describe as an innocuous looking man, slim build, early fifties, with a shock of untidy looking dark hair in need of a haircut, and horn-rimmed glasses; over which, he peered at her now.

'Mr Frith?' she enquired.

'Yes. What can I do for you?'

'I'm DC Bethany Macaskill. I wonder if I could ask you a couple of questions?'

'Of course. I'm guessing it's about what's going on over the road. My mother told me that Barbara's dead?'

'Yes, I'm afraid so. Did you know her well?'

'Quite well. I've been helping out where I can since her husband was killed. She was blind, as you probably know. What happened? Was it an accident?'

'We've yet to establish the facts, but we wondered if you might have seen anything unusual on Saturday?'

'Not that I recall. Mind you, I don't spend my whole day looking out of the window, and I was out a good part of the day, bird watching.'

'Wouldn't have thought there were many places around here to do that,' Beth commented, thinking that she didn't know of any.

'There are some if you know where to go. I went to the Tring Reservoirs. This is a good time of year for birds there.'

'Was that Saturday, dear, or Sunday?' his mother put in.

'Definitely Saturday, Mother.'

'What time would that have been from?' Beth asked. 'And can anyone corroborate that? Just so that we can eliminate you from our enquiry,' she added quickly, forestalling the usual indignant reaction to that question.

He shook his head. 'I doubt it. Not many people go there this time of year, but I like it for the walk as much as anything.' He shrugged. 'Someone might have seen me.'

'So, there's nothing you feel you can tell us that might be useful?'

He hesitated. 'Not about what happened to Barbara, but ... I've got a telescope in my room, and I've been keeping an eye on a couple of youths I've noticed a few times, parked further down the road. They seem to just park there and then take a walk along the road for ten or fifteen minutes and then get back in their car and drive off. It occurred to me they might be watching the houses. We've had a couple of burglaries in the road recently and I'm afraid your lot appear markedly unenthusiastic about catching the culprits.'

'Well, that would be uniform officers obviously but I'm sure they're doing their best. Did you report your suspicions to them?'

'No. I thought about it, but...' He shrugged.

'And there's part of your answer. People aren't always as quick as they could be to come forward with information. Something like that, that's noticeably unusual, would have meant that the police could park up and keep an eye out for them. Question them. What sort of car was it, do you remember?'

'A Ford I think. Fiesta maybe? Very dark colour, black probably. But it's always in the evenings, so I couldn't say that for sure. Could have been dark blue.'

'Can you show me from your window where it was?'

Beth had been wondering how she might casually ask to see his telescope and he'd just presented her with the perfect excuse.

'Sure. Come with me.'

Elliot Frith's bedroom was a tip, with clothes strewn everywhere, but if he felt embarrassed he didn't show it. Across the room pointing out of the window, stood a large telescope and Beth tiptoed her way over the mess on the floor to reach it.

'Mind if I take a look?' she asked.

He looked momentarily discomfited, but then, 'Help yourself.'

Without moving anything, she peered through the glass and yes, it was as the neighbour had said. It was focused directly on to Barbara Harding's bedroom window.

She pulled back to look at him. 'I see it's pointing at Mrs Harding's bedroom window. Is there any reason for that? Had you observed something unusual?'

'No.' His tone was abrupt as he moved over to join her, showing none of the reservations she had had about treading on his clothes. 'Let me see.'

He peered through it himself and then stood back, shrugging his shoulders. 'It must've dislodged when I was finishing up.' He shifted his gaze to look down the road. 'See the bend, there? That's where the car's been parked – several times over the last few weeks. Then the men got out and walked in this direction but on the other side of the road, past Barbara's and Yvonne's houses to the other bend up there. After that I didn't see where they went but they were back at the car within fifteen minutes or so.'

'Can you describe them?'

'I never got a proper look at them. You know what they're like these days. Dressed in jeans and dark hoodies that obscure everything, but both strong builds and quite tall.'

'When was the last time you reckon you saw them?'

'Well, that's the thing. I reckon they were there late Saturday afternoon when I got back from my day out. I didn't see anyone in it when I drove in, but next time I looked, they were getting back in, and they drove off up the road.'

'What time?'

'Sixish. Give or take?'

'You know Barbara's gardener? Could it have been him?'

'I couldn't say. It was quite dark by then.'

'Did you notice him at Barbara's house earlier on that day?'

'No. I told you; I was out.'

'What sort of stuff do you look at through this telescope then?' Beth asked.

'This and that. When the sky's clear I enjoy trying to spot the different planets and stars. It's quite a new hobby though, so I'm still learning.'

'Are you married, Mr Frith?'

He gave her a sly smile. 'No, why... you looking?'

If she was, he'd be one of the last people she'd call on, she thought. There was something distinctively unsavoury about him and it wasn't just the tip of a room and questionable use of the telescope that made her think that.

'Where are you from?' he asked. 'That's an unusual accent you've got there.'

'Northumberland – very different to around here.'

'I'll bet it is. Country lass then, eh? Maybe you'd like to come and birdwatch with me one day? Always room for a pretty girl in my car.'

'I don't think that's an appropriate remark, Mr Frith.'

'Maybe not, but sometimes it works, and you must be used to comments like that working with all those male coppers.'

'My colleagues have more respect for me than that. I'll head off now but if you remember anything else, I left a card with your mother this morning.'

This time, as she crossed the bedroom, she took great delight in treading on as many items of his clothing as she could.

CHAPTER ELEVEN

H arry's boss, DCI Murray, looked around the assembled room. 'Right. Can we cut the chatter? Where's everyone at? Harry, do you want to bring me up to speed?'

Harry had been standing behind him and now stepped forward. He cut an impressive figure, standing tall at over six feet, with chiselled good looks and air of assurance that commanded attention. All eyes were on him, as he opened his notebook and perused his notes. His voice when he spoke was authoritative and cultured, the latter of which was a natural by-product of the boarding school he'd attended due to his parents spending most of their working life abroad.

'Right, well, sorry if I'm repeating myself to some of you here, but I'll try and keep it brief. I spoke to the pathologist, Simon Winters, who was at the house doing his stuff before they moved the body, and he's confirmed it as a suspicious death. It wasn't a natural fall that killed her; there are signs of a struggle and there may be evidence to suggest that she was smothered with a cushion from the settee in the lounge. No sign of forced entry but a spare key she kept out in the garden is missing, so that could have been used. No obvious evidence of sexual assault and an alarm pendant that she wore around her neck could have been forcibly removed. Presumably to stop her from calling for help. So far, we have three chief suspects in the frame – the man, or men, who were responsible for the death of Barbara's husband several years back.'

He pinned a photo onto the board. 'This is Finn Abara. He was the driver of the car and did a restorative justice meeting with Barbara about nine months ago after his release from prison, following which, she seems to have taken him under her wing and he's been doing some gardening and odd jobs for her. According to her neighbour, Finn's moped was parked in her drive for a short while on Saturday afternoon. The housekeeper gave me his number and Beth and I called on him. At first, he denied being there but when challenged about his moped being seen, he admitted that he'd dropped round but he'd assumed she was out. Geoff, did you get to question the other two men involved in the accident? They were out when we called.'

'Yep. Connor Stephens and Daniel Redman. They arrived back just as I got there and said they were both at Stephens' house all day on Saturday and didn't go out. Flatly denied they knew anything about Barbara or where she lived.'

'Well, that's a lie for a start, because the housekeeper told me they called round a few weeks back, claiming to do a restorative justice visit – but without anyone from victim support. What do they look like? Have we got pictures?'

Geoff moved over to the board and tapped two more photos. 'This is them. Both white and heavily tattooed – hard as nails. You wouldn't want to argue with either of them.'

'We'll need to question them again urgently. Ask them how they knew where she lived and why they called on her. Any background on them so far, Dave?'

'Only that there are two rival gangs on that estate, one of which is headed up by Connor Stephens. He's got a list as long as your arm of suspected drug offences, burglaries, car theft etc., but nothing ever seems to stick.'

Harry turned back to his notes. 'The housekeeper also told me that jewellery, gold coins and over a thousand pounds cash, are missing from Barbara's bedroom drawer and wardrobe, as well as a valuable collection of handbags. She got some cash out for Barbara on Friday, so she knows the money was there. Who's checking bank accounts and finances?'

'I am, but still waiting,' Dave Freeman said. 'I've also taken a quick look at Sylvia Carroll, Barbara's cousin, like you asked. She lives alone in Stanmore after two marriages. Her first husband was thirty years older than her, quite wealthy and the marriage didn't last long. He died in a house fire not long after they separated. He was apparently a heavy smoker and drinker. He'd been drinking vodka that night and the blaze was thought to have been started by a cigarette that slipped down the cushions. She divorced her second husband, Mia's father, ten years ago. Acrimonious, because he went after her for spousal support and got it. Claimed back issues made him disabled and prevented him from working. She's still paying it.'

'Right,' Harry said, 'someone should speak to him for the sake of completeness. Make a note in the Holmes system to allocate that, can you?'

He turned to Beth. 'How did you get on with the friends and our bird-spotting neighbour?'

'It was interesting. Two of the friends were together. They told me that Barbara seemed to have grown quite fond of Finn and felt sorry for him. Apparently, she reckoned he was a talented song writer and I think she was helping him a bit with that. One of the friends also said she'd talked about changing her will and leaving most of her money to charities for the blind. She took her to see a solicitor but didn't know if she'd done anything about it. I've got the solicitor's name. The third friend lives in Cambridge. I called her and she said she hadn't seen Barbara for several weeks. They were meant to be meeting up next weekend.'

'And the neighbour across the road?'

'Lives with his mother. I'm not knocking that but he's a sleazy weirdo.'

'Just so we're all in no doubt.'

She grinned and a rumble of laughter went around the room. Beth never minced her words. 'Make your own minds up. The other neighbour was right about the telescope – it was directed straight at Barbara's bedroom window, though he said he must have nudged it that way by accident. He was quick to move me on to a car he reckoned he'd seen parked down the road. He said it was dark coloured and possibly a Fiesta and he seemed to think the occupants might have been casing houses in the road. He reckoned it was there when he got home on Saturday afternoon.'

'It's not impossible. We know there have been some burglaries in the area. I don't suppose he got a registration number?'

She shook her head.

'Did he have an alibi for Saturday afternoon?'

'Nope. Said he was at the Tring Reservoirs, bird watching, although his mother seemed to think that was Sunday, not Saturday. Either way, no one to vouch for him.'

'Connor Stephens drives a black Ford Fiesta,' Dave said.

'Does he now? Well, that can be our first priority for tomorrow morning – to bring him and his mate in for questioning. But we could do with checking the CCTV beforehand. How good would that be, if we could nail him parked up outside Barbara Harding's house the day she was killed? Which brings me to the other top priority issue to investigate. The neighbour also told me that she saw a white car parked in Barbara Harding's drive late Saturday morning. No-one could come up with ideas as to who that might have been, so we need to find out. Re-interview the neighbours to see if anyone else noticed and can come up with a make of car for us. Anyone else got anything to say?'

No one spoke and Harry turned to DCI Murray. 'Anything you want to add, Sir?'

'No, you seem to be getting off to a good start. Just bang on and if you need more feet on the ground, give me a shout.'

'Right,' Harry said. 'Does everyone know what they're doing, or anyone looking for work? If you are, check with Dave. He's been compiling a log on the Holmes system. Geoff, contact Connor Stephens and the third guy involved in the accident, and invite them to come in for interview first thing tomorrow morning. We'll push them about this so-called restorative justice visit and how they knew where Barbara lived.'

'Will do. But I'm not sure they're the type to respond to interview requests.'

'We can only try. Suggest they might prefer that to being arrested – it usually does the trick. I know I'm stating the obvious here, but we need to establish the last people to see Barbara Harding alive, and whether it was an opportunist burglary that went wrong, or someone out there had a motive to kill her.'

'Love, lust, loathing or loot, isn't it?' someone piped up from the back.

'I'm sure she was very nice, but she was blind and sixty,' Geoff pointed out. 'I think that probably takes out the first two.'

'Oi, no ageism,' Murray growled. 'I'm not that far off sixty myself, and there's life in the old dog yet.'

Everyone laughed and Geoff grinned. 'Sorry, Sir. You just look so young for your age.'

'Alright, alright, don't overdo it.'

'Shall I follow up on Mia's boyfriend and Sylvia Carroll's ex-husband, tomorrow?' Beth asked.

'Good idea – and the housekeeper's husband, while you're at it.' Harry said. 'Also, I questioned the boyfriend briefly, but you could perhaps get a bit more detail on his whereabouts on Saturday and we'll need to check we've got formal statements from everyone.'

As the group broke up and people drifted away, Murray turned to Harry.

'Well done. The most obvious suspects look to be Connor Stephens and his gang – a bit too much of a coincidence in my book that the one starts working there and then this happens. But sounds like they're slippery buggers, so we need solid evidence before we submit anything to CPS.'

'I agree. I'll update you tomorrow. I'll probably see Finn Abara again after the other two … apply a bit of pressure.'

Murray looked at his watch. 'Right. I don't know about you but I'm heading off home.'

'I want to do a bit more digging.'

'Well, take my advice, Harry, and don't stop all night. Set a timer and leave when it goes off. You don't want to let this place become more familiar to you than your own home. I learnt that one the hard way.'

CHAPTER TWELVE

Alyssa Abara looked at her watch. Six o'clock. Goldie would be wondering where she was. She'd better ring her. She looked at her friend, Hayley. 'If he doesn't show up soon, I'm gonna have to go. Goldie'll ground me if I'm back late again.'

'It's okay, here he is.'

A lad on a bike skidded to a halt in front of them. 'You got the stuff from Conn?'

It was Hayley who withdrew the small package from her pocket and handed it over, and without another word the boy swung round on his bike and sped off.

'Is that it? Can we head off now?' Alyssa asked.

'Yeah. Easy money ain't it?

Alyssa felt a twinge of guilt after her conversation with Finn. 'I don't like it. Finn'll kill me if he finds out what we've been doing. It felt all right while he was in prison, 'cos Conn looked out for us and I was grateful for that, but now Finn's out, he doesn't want me to have anything to do with Conn. Says we'll end up going to prison like he did if we get involved with him. I don't know what to do.'

'But Conn's been a good mate to us.'

'I know.'

And it was true. Conn had gone out of his way to befriend her after Finn had been sentenced, treating her to the odd kebab or pizza, reassuring her that she and Goldie would be fine whilst they were on his patch – he'd always look out for them. 'Cos Finn's a mate and he done me a favour,' he'd said. 'And Connor Stephens never forgets a favour.'

It had been a reassurance, even if she'd never actually had to ask him for anything.

'And it's such easy money,' her friend urged.

'I *know!* But I promised Finn I wouldn't get involved in stuff like this. What if we get caught? We'll get a record.'

'We ain't gonna get caught – the cops aren't looking for people like us. All we do is meet up somewhere quiet, where there's no one around and hand over a package. What's the harm in that? And we got Christmas coming up don't forget.'

Alyssa gave it some thought. Goldie did her best with her cleaning jobs, but money was tight, and really ... Hayley was right, it wasn't that risky what they were doing. Maybe she'd carry on up to Christmas, so she could buy something decent for Goldie and Finn – then she could stop after that if she wanted.

'I'll think about it,' she said. 'Look, that's our bus. Race you to the stop.'

***

Harry nipped home to pick up his overnight bag before heading to Claire's. He quickly sorted through his post and checked his emails, smiling to himself when he read the contents of one. He printed it out and slipped it into his jacket pocket before heading out to the car. Traffic was light and he got from Enfield to Cuffley in record time.

'How was your day?' Claire asked, sprinkling grated cheese on top of a lasagne and popping it into the oven. He watched her appreciatively, man enough to enjoy the willowy figure, yet shapely derriere, that she presented to him. As usual, her chestnut-coloured hair was tied back in the pony tail she wore for her work as a carer, but he didn't need to close his eyes to remember how it looked cascaded across her pillow. He resisted the temptation to get up and release it. He'd enjoy doing that later.

'Busy. Always is when a new case comes in,' he responded in answer to her question.

'Any clues as to what happened?'

'A couple, but early days. Hopefully we'll know more after we've interviewed a few people tomorrow. What about you? How was your day?'

'Good, but ...' She hesitated. 'You know, the more I think about it, the more I know I need a change. But I'm not sure the Doula course I'm doing is for me.'

'I thought you were keen on doing that.'

'I was, and I like the idea of helping prospective mothers out and being there for them, but looking into it, it's quite an erratic job, especially as people's delivery dates can vary so much. I'll be limited as to how many clients I can take on at any one given time because I'll have to keep times around their confinement free for just them, and what will I do with my spare time? I'm used to being busy and I'm not sure it'll be enough for me. You'll probably think I'm mad, but did I tell you I'd done a couple of counselling courses?'

'No.'

'Well, I have, and I really enjoyed them. I'm thinking I might carry it on to the next level and go all the way for a psychotherapist qualification.'

'Hmmm. Not sure what I think about that.'

Claire looked taken aback. 'Why? What do you mean?'

'I won't be able to get away with anything, will I?'

She grinned and threw the oven cloth at him. 'Cheeky sod. Seriously, do you think I'm mad? I feel bad changing direction again.'

'Well, don't. You've got to follow your instincts – and I think you'd make an excellent counsellor. You can sort me out any time.'

'Be serious!'

He laughed. 'I am. Really, go for it. I think you'd be great.'

'Thanks, Harry. I'm not sure what my mum will think of me changing tack again. But it's good to have your support. I'm sorry you didn't get any answers today at the crematorium. I know it's been playing on your mind.'

He shrugged. 'Don't worry about it, I'm not. I can't be bothered with it anymore, too much else on my mind – not the least of which is what I'm going to do with my parents when they fly in from Cairo on Thursday. They're here for a month and God knows what I'm going to do with them. They're going to want me to take time off I know, and it just isn't going to happen.'

'They're staying with you over Christmas, right?'

He nodded.

'Aren't they planning on seeing any other family members and friends?'

'They haven't said so, though I'm sure they will. They're just hopeless at organising stuff in advance.'

'Well, get them organised. Suggest they go off for a week or two doing that and come back in time for Christmas.'

'Yeah, that's not a bad shout, although … there's an added complication. Take a look at this.' He pulled out the email he'd printed earlier and handed it to her.

After she'd finished reading it, she looked at him in surprise. 'Who is this Mark guy?'

'Old school friend. We've known each other since we were eleven. He's been trying to get me out there for the last five years, since he took the hotel over. I've looked it up and it looks great, very picturesque on the bank of the river near the centre of Strasbourg.'

'Are you going to go?'

'I think I might. He's invited me over there several times and I've never taken him up on it, but Strasbourg's not difficult to get to, and I quite like the idea of doing the Christmas markets. My gran was always saying people should do at least one in their life.'

'Hmm … don't see you as a keen shopper, somehow.'

'I reckon I could be tempted, if I had the right companion with me.'

Claire stared at him. 'Are you saying what I think you are?'

He nodded. 'If you think you'd enjoy it? He's offering it at mates' rates, and Murray was saying only the other day that I was overdue some holiday. Substitute that for I haven't taken any in the four years I've been working with him and maybe you'll see why the idea is suddenly very tempting. You can see he's suggested the weekend of the 17th December. If I get this case sorted, we could go for a long weekend from the Friday to the Monday if you can get the time off work – and I can sort my parents out.'

'I'd have to clear it with my manager, and I'd insist on paying my own way, but, yeah, I'd love to go.'

'Great, that's settled then.' He got up from his chair and laughed as she threw her arms around him.

'Oh, that's the best Christmas present I could have had. Give me the dates, as soon as they're confirmed, and I'll be there. But you'd better solve this case quickly. I know you well enough to know you won't be going anywhere if you haven't.'

She looked at the clock. 'Come on, you can show me his website. We've just about got time to check it out before food's ready.'

CHAPTER THIRTEEN

H arry was in high spirits the following morning, and as he walked into the soulless open plan office and made his way to his desk, which was at least next to a window even if it did overlook the large car park, he forced himself to disengage his thoughts from Claire and their upcoming trip and concentrate instead on the case in hand.

'Right, Dave, anything new on Connor Stephens and his mate, Daniel Redman?' he called out.

'I spoke to them both last night,' Geoff chipped in, from behind him. 'Said we'd like to ask them a couple more questions and, cool as cucumbers, they said they'd come in first thing this morning. In fact...' He peered out of the window to the car park below. 'If I'm not mistaken, that's them there. Look at those swaggers, arrogant sods.'

'I've got something here you might find useful,' Dave said, walking over and handing Harry a sheet of paper. 'No CCTV in Beechwood Way, so we can't actually see Stephen Connors' car parked there last Saturday, but we see it approaching the road at 17.00 hrs and then nothing further up where the next camera is, which would suggest they turned into one of the side streets between the two cameras. One of which is Beechwood Way.'

'Good work,' Harry said. 'Let's see what they've got to say about that.'

Geoff's phone rang and he looked at Harry. 'That's probably downstairs telling us they've arrived.'

'Set them up in the interview rooms. I'll take Stephens, you take Redman.'

Harry grabbed a quick cup of water from the machine and checked his emails before heading up the stairs. In the interview room, Connor Stephens was lounging in the chair, looking as if he didn't have a care in the world.

Harry sat down opposite him.

'Thanks for coming in, Mr. Stephens,' he said facing the man across the table. 'My sergeant told you why we requested it?'

'Yeah, but I don't get it. I told him yesterday I never knew the woman. You're just picking on me like you always do.'

'Oh, don't worry, it's not just you. Even as we speak, my colleague's having a chat with your mate, Daniel Redman – and we've already spoken to Finn Abara, just to keep things fair. Now, would you mind going over your movements again for last Saturday?'

'I already told your mate, yesterday.'

'Just humour me. I want to make sure we've got it right.'

'I was hanging out with friends at mine, all day and night.'

'And you didn't leave your house at all?'

'Nope.' He leant back on the rear two legs of his chair and cupped the back of his head in his hands, a smirk playing around the corners of his mouth. 'I gave your mate some names yesterday if you want to check it out. They'll back me up if you ask them.'

'I'm sure they will. Until maybe, we point out that we have video footage of your car very close to Barbara Harding's road at five pm the day she was murdered. We've got a clear picture of your numberplate, and fortunately for us, although it's quite hard to see individuals in the car, the driver's wearing quite a distinctive hoody – in fact, pretty identical, I'd say, to that Gap one you're wearing today. The logo's certainly the same.'

Stephen Connors' chair bounced back to earth with a thud, as he scowled at Harry. 'That don't prove nothing. There must be thousands of these around.'

'We'll be running a check on that of course and, as part of our enquiries, I'll be requesting that you let us have that item of clothing for forensic testing. I'll send one of my men back with you so that you can remove it back home and hand it over. Don't want you freezing to death. So ... how about you tell me what you were really doing on Saturday?'

'No comment.'

'Okay. Perhaps you can explain why your car was seen in the vicinity of Barbara Harding's road then? Not only on Saturday, the day she was murdered, but also possibly on several other occasions over the past month or so – we have a witness who saw a car very similar to yours parked near their house. We'll be checking more CCTV to see if the dates tie in with any of the burglaries that have happened in that road.'

'Well, seeing as I didn't know this Barbara Harding, or what road she lived in, I can't answer that one, can I?'

'Beechwood Way, Hadley Wood.'

'Don't know it. I mean, sometimes I go walking out Hadley way, but don't know the names of the roads. As for Saturday, I'm remembering now ... I lent my car to a mate.'

'And that would be ...?'

'I'd have to think about it. All a bit hazy, you know? Had a few drinks and the like. Think it was Finn Abara.'

Harry raised an eyebrow but let it pass.

'You say you don't know Barbara Harding, but as I'm sure you're aware, she's the woman whose husband was killed in the car collision you were involved in. And we've been advised that you were one of two men who called on her a few weeks ago, supposedly to apologise – a bit like the meeting that Finn Abara did, except that his was an official visit set up by the victim support team and we suspect yours wasn't. What have you got to say about that?'

The man sniffed and eyed Harry insolently. 'Don't know what you're talking about, and I know my rights. I ain't saying nothing more without a solicitor. So, if you got more questions you'll have to wait 'til I call him.'

The two men stared each other out for a few moments before Harry terminated the interview.

'That won't be necessary for the moment, but I'd advise you that you're a person of interest in this investigation and, as such, I'd request that you don't leave the area without first notifying us of your plans. One of my colleagues will accompany you back to your house now so that you can change your hoodie and let us have the one you're wearing for forensics.'

He rose from his chair. 'Someone will be in to escort you soon.'

Out in the office, Dave pounced on him the minute he entered. 'Forensics have just been on and said can you call them?'

'Right, thanks.'

Harry moved over to his desk and picked up his phone. 'Simon? It's Harry Briscombe. Have you got something?'

'Yes. I thought you might like to know, that we got a match on fingerprints we found on the cloakroom door. A chap called Offin Abara. He's not been that long out of prison and the prints were tainted with blood – the victim's blood. My guess is he went in there to wash his hands. His prints aren't on the wooden arm of the settee, though, where the cushion was from, which is a disappointment. But there were a couple of other sets of prints there that we'll need to match up for elimination purposes.'

'We're getting those organised, but great stuff on Abara. That puts him in the house after her death, which he's denied.'

'Also, I can absolutely confirm now that Barbara Harding was smothered using that cushion. There are fibres around her mouth that match it, and more bruising discolouration is visible now. It's conclusive.'

'Thanks. Useful to know.' Harry put the phone down and looked up as Geoff came into the room. 'How did you get on with Redman?' he asked.

Geoff shook his head. 'Waste of time. He denied everything. Said it wasn't him in the car on CCTV and he hadn't called on Barbara Harding to apologise for the accident.'

'They're just playing for time, hoping we can't come up with the proof. We need to get on to that soon as and show the housekeeper their photos. Some better news – I've just heard back from Forensics. They've got a match for Finn Abara's fingerprints on the cloakroom door, mixed with her blood. It puts him firmly at the scene. I think send someone to pick him up. Stress it's a voluntary interview at this stage for a few more questions.'

'What if he says no?'

'Then explain to him that the alternative is to arrest him as a possible suspect. I don't think he'd like that.'

CHAPTER FOURTEEN

Goldie looked up as Finn walked into the kitchen.

'What you decided to do?' she asked. 'You need to form a plan.'

'I ain't doing nothing.'

'Finn, they'll know you were there. Listen to me–'

'No, you listen to me. I ain't going back inside again and that's all there is to it. I was careful. I just touched her to see if she was alive still, and if she had been, I'd have called an ambulance. But she wasn't and I panicked. I thought it was an accident, that she'd fallen down the stairs, but the police don't think that do they? If they know I was there, they'll try and pin it on me. You know that and I know it and I ain't taking the rap again for a crime I didn't commit. Not for anyone.'

'What do you mean?'

Silence.

'Finn…?'

'What's going on? Why are you fighting?'

They both spun round as Alyssa walked in, wearing jeans and a sweatshirt. She was turning into such a pretty little thing, Finn thought, and the realisation only added to his general level of anxiety.

'Nothing,' he said. 'We're not fighting.'

'Sounded like it to me.'

'Why aren't you at school today?'

'Inset. Can I go round to Hayley's after breakfast?' she asked, looking at Goldie.

'Got any schoolwork needs doing?'

'Only a bit.'

'Well, you know the rules ... get it done, then you can go.'

'I told her I'd go straight after breakfast and it's already late. I can do my homework when I get back.'

'You'll do it now, or you don't go. I don't want to be called in for any more meetings 'cos you're not keeping up with your work.'

'Oh, for God's sake.' Alyssa flounced over to the cupboard to get some cereal. 'You treat me like I'm a child. I'm fourteen.'

'Then act like it and take your schoolwork seriously. You're a clever girl, Alyssa, don't waste your education.'

The girl sighed dramatically but said no more on the subject as she sat down at the table with her bowl. She looked from one to the other. 'Why were you arguing, 'cos I know you were. Why won't you tell me what's going on? No one ever tells me anything in this house.'

'Hey, that's not true.' Finn moved over to ruffle his sister's hair. 'We've had some great talks since I've been home, haven't we? And as for Goldie, you know as well as I do, she never stops her jabbering.'

'You watch it boy, with your cheek.' But Goldie's smile was fond.

The sound of the doorbell interrupted them. 'I'll get it,' Finn said. 'Probably a delivery.'

But a few seconds later, he re-entered the kitchen, his expression wary. 'It's the police. They want me to go to the nick to answer some more questions.'

'No!' Alyssa cried out, grabbing Finn's arm and clinging onto him. 'Don't go. Don't let them take you away again.'

'Hey ... don't worry,' He disentangled her fingers gently. 'It's just a few questions, it won't take long. You do as Goldie says and get your homework done. I'll be back before you know it.'

⸻

Finn looked up as DI Briscombe walked into the room. He'd been waiting over an hour for this interview to start because once the detective had warned him he was being interviewed under caution, he knew what that meant, and he'd insisted on having a solicitor present. While he was waiting for that to happen, he'd received a WhatsApp message and he was still reeling from it. A picture of Conn with his arm around a smiling Alyssa. And she'd been wearing the clothes she'd got on that morning.

'If the police question you again, you better remember I lent you my car last Saturday. I forgot how sweet and innocent your little sister is...'

The inspector sat down and faced him and the solicitor across the table, while another officer switched on the recorder. Once it was set up and they'd gone through the procedures, he looked at Finn. 'You know why we've brought you in?'

'No.'

'You told us you didn't see Barbara Harding last Saturday.'

'So?'

'You were lying. We have evidence that puts you bang at the scene inside the house.'

Finn's insides froze. 'What evidence?'

'Your fingerprints on the cloakroom door handle, with traces of Barbara Harding's blood in them.'

Shit.

'You going to tell us what you were doing there?'

Finn glared at him. 'What's the point? You won't believe me.'

'Try me.'

Finn shifted in his seat. He didn't know what to do and looked to his solicitor for guidance. His advice had been to say nothing, but the cops had proof he'd been there. What was the point denying it? It only made him look more guilty. He felt a burst of anger against everyone and everything. He'd done nothing wrong and had nothing to hide. Maybe it was better to get things out into the open to help them catch whoever *had* done it.

He turned back to Harry, trying to ignore the sickening sensation that he was burning his boats. 'Okay. Yeah, I was there, but I didn't kill her.'

'So, what were you doing there?'

'I go round most Saturdays. One of the bedrooms is set up as a music room from when her husband was alive, and she let me use his equipment to mix my songs. She took an interest in my stuff and was helping me. Why would I want to kill her?'

'What happened that day?'

'I got there and let myself in through the back door. Sometimes she left that open for me and sometimes I used the spare key in the garden, to save her having to get up and answer the doorbell. On Saturday it was open. I called out but there was no answer, so I went into the hall. And she was lying there, at the bottom of the stairs. I ran over and felt for a pulse but there wasn't one. I could tell she was dead from the way she was lying – and her eyes were wide open and staring. She was gone,

man, and I panicked. I got no illusions. I knew if I called you lot, I'd
be taken in and you'd think I'd done something. Even the fact I was
in the house could have got me into trouble. No one else knew about
what we did them Saturdays. The neighbours just thought I was doing
gardening or odd jobs. They all disapprove of me. "Keep it between
us," she said. "No-one else's business."

'So, what? You just left her?'

'There was nothing I could do for her. I just wanted out. I went into
the cloakroom to wash my hands and then I left the way I'd come in.'

'And what about the cushion?'

'What cushion? I didn't see no cushion.'

Harry let that one go, not wanting to give too much away. 'When
you left the premises, did you go straight home?'

He nodded.

'What clothes were you wearing? We'll need to bring them in for
testing.'

'Jeans and a hoodie.'

'Did they have blood on them?'

He nodded, avoiding Harry's gaze. 'I washed 'em.'

The knot in his stomach twisted. They were going to arrest him, he
knew it.

'You realise none of this sounds good?'

'Course, I do. That's why I kept quiet. But I didn't do nothing to
Barbara. I wouldn't. She was helping me.'

'A considerable amount of money and valuables were stolen from
her house.'

'Don't know nothing about that.'

'I've just been interviewing your mate Connor Stephens this
morning.'

'He ain't a mate.'

'Oh? And yet he tells me he sometimes lends you his car and that in fact, he lent it to you that Saturday afternoon. We have footage of that car approaching Barbara's road on Saturday afternoon. Why did you borrow it? Were you going back to see if anyone had found her? Maybe to nick the stuff you hadn't taken first time around?'

'*No.*' Finn's knee seemed to develop a mind of its own as it started to jiggle up and down.

'But you did borrow Connor Stephens' car? Even though you don't have a driving licence?'

Finn leaned back, his mouth tightening. 'I ain't answering no more questions. I've told you the truth now about what happened. I know I should have said before, but I told you, I panicked – and you would have too, if you was me.'

Harry eyed him for a moment and then switched off the recording. 'Okay. You can go for now, but we'll keep you here until the warrant we've applied for to search your premises comes through. Whatever the truth, Finn, we'll get to the bottom of it. And if you're innocent the best way you can prove it is to tell us everything you know. A woman was murdered on Saturday. She was the wife of a man you killed, and we can place you at the scene of the crime. You're right, that does place you in top position as far as suspects go. But contrary to what you seem to believe, I'm not interested in pinning it on you for the sake of it. I want to get to the truth and the more facts I have, the easier that job becomes. Perhaps you can think about that. On the other hand, if you're guilty … we'll get to the bottom of that too. And you'll be put away for a very long time.'

The minute Harry walked back into the office, DCI Murray pounced on him. 'How did it go? Come into my office.'

Harry followed him in and closed the door.

'Sit,' the other man said, 'and fill me in.'

'Looks to me like you've got it fairly wrapped up,' he said when Harry had finished talking.

'I don't think we're there yet, Sir.'

'No, but it's looking promising. Think you've got enough grounds to hold him for further questioning?'

'There are a few angles I still want to flesh out.'

'Such as?'

'Connor Stephens' car being in the vicinity later that day, for one. They're blowing up a picture of the driver, and I'm not sure I buy the story about lending his car to Finn. I think it's significant that the hoodie the driver was wearing looks very similar to the one Stephens was wearing today.'

'He could have lent it to Abara, if his had blood on it?'

'True. But some of what Finn said rang true. Barbara Harding was helping him, almost mentoring him by the sound of it, why would he want to kill her?'

'Maybe that was his plan all along, to get on the right side of her? A thousand pounds combined with the coins and jewellery is a lot of money to someone like him. Or it could have been an argument that got out of hand?'

'I guess, and I accept that he's our main suspect, but I'm still happier letting him go for now while we check any other leads.'

'Well, you've got a free rein, you know that, but don't drag it out unnecessarily. The sooner we can shut this down, the better.'

Harry made his way back to the incident room, deep in thought. Was Murray right, was it all as simple as it looked? That Finn, for whatever reason, had murdered Barbara, and then gone back later in the day and stolen from her? His gut instinct for some reason, didn't sit happily with that. He'd been known to be wrong, of course, but for now he'd go with that instinct.

In the incident room, Beth and Geoff were comparing notes.

'How did you get on with Abara?' Geoff asked, turning as Harry walked in.

'He admitted he was there but says she was lying at the bottom of the stairs, already dead. He panicked because of his record and bolted. I've let him go for now.'

'Do you believe him?'

'I'm not sure. Murray thinks we've got our man, but I don't know; it all feels a bit too neat and tidy.'

'Nothing wrong with neat and tidy, for a change,' Geoff said. 'It all seems a bit of a coincidence that he had all that history with her and just happened to find her lying there. And we all know how you and the boss feel about coincidences. I mean, he's not going to say anything else is he, once it came out that we knew he was there?'

'I suppose not. How have you got on?' Harry asked, turning to Beth.

'I spoke to Barbara Harding's hairdresser – she went to the house every Friday. She said she went as usual on Friday and Barbara was on good form – nothing unusual in her behaviour. I also spoke to the local police and apparently there was another break in, further up the road the night she was killed, number 165. I called on the people there and they said they always play bridge with friends on a Saturday night. They leave at six and are usually home by 11. When they got back someone had broken in via the backdoor and nicked cash, jewellery, and a few personal effects.'

'So, it could have been an earlier burglary attempt gone wrong at Barbara Harding's – but they'd have to be pretty cool customers to come back and do another house the same night they'd killed her.'

'We'll extend the CCTV search to include the evening, see if anything sticks out.'

'What about the top end of the road? Where it joins the main road? They could have gone out that way.'

Beth nodded. 'I'll check that too.'

'Okay, moving on, let's go through our main suspects. Top of the list, Finn Abara, with or without the involvement of his mates, Connor Stephens and Daniel Redman, and apart from them, the only other obvious people in the running are Sylvia and Mia Carroll, the housekeeper and possibly Elliot Frith – motive unknown except that he's a bit of a weirdo and could have been spying on her from his bedroom window.'

Beth took the dig with good humour. 'Or the random burglary theory,' she added. 'If people have been watching the house, they probably would have known she was blind and on her own at weekends. She'd have seemed an easy target.'

'Yeah, that too. What are you doing now?'

'I'm calling on Sylvia Carroll's ex and Elena Mancini's husband this morning and Mia's boyfriend this evening after work, just so we have a full picture of everyone involved.'

'Good,' Harry replied. 'But keep your phone on. We're applying for a Warrant to search Finn Abara's house and I want you in on that when we do it.'

CHAPTER FIFTEEN

B eth exited the flat off the Cockfosters Road. What a wasted visit
that had been. Still, there were always a number of those in any
investigation and it was good to be able to tick them off. Derek Carroll
hadn't been a particularly inspiring character but neither had he come
over as being aggressive or having any axe to grind against Barbara
Harding. That there was no love lost between him and his ex-wife,
however, had been obvious and it was clear also that he had no contact
with his daughter, Mia.

'Haven't seen either of them in five years now,' he'd said with a
shrug. 'Their choice, not mine. You bring up your kids the best you
can and that's all the thanks you get for it. Mia's too influenced by her
mother, that's the problem. Still, I fared better than her first husband,
didn't I? She saw him into an early grave – and it wouldn't surprise me
if she'd had a hand in that either.'

'Have you got any facts to substantiate that?'

'Nope. Just that I wouldn't put it past her. She's got a one-track
mind when it comes to money, that one.'

'Do you work, Mr Carroll?'

'No, love. Bad back. I was forced to retire years ago.'

'Your ex-wife pays you an allowance, I believe?'

'Yeah, not much and she can afford it. She pays me because I've got back issues – I'm registered disabled and can't work. And that's how it should be, right? I mean, all these equality issues ... either it works both ways or it doesn't. I'd have had to support her if the boot was on the other foot.'

Beth stood up to go. 'Okay, well thanks for your help.'

'It's a shame about Barbara. We saw quite a bit of her when we were younger but there were always undercurrents between the two of them. I think Sylvia was jealous of her for having the kind of lifestyle she would have loved, and Barbara envied Sylvia having a child. They grew more and more apart as they got older.'

Outside the flat, Beth looked at her watch and noticed a coffee shop across the road. It was getting towards lunchtime, and she was hungry. No reason why she shouldn't stop off for a quick bite.

She'd just sat down with a toasted sandwich and coffee when her phone rang. She stared at the display, frowning as she picked up the call. Ryan, her brother.

'Hey,' she said, forcing a joviality she was far from feeling. 'Twice in one week – this has to be a first.'

'Beth, I just had another call from Isi. She said you're not going to Dad's funeral and she's in a right state about it.'

Beth took a breath. 'I can't help that, Ryan. You're choosing not to go, surely I have the same right? And if I might remind you, I got a lot more stick from him and Mum than you ever did.'

'I get that, sis, I do, but we're manic at work – you wouldn't believe the number of people that buy new cars for Christmas – and I don't want to let Ellie's dad down when he's gone out of his way to give me this chance. Isi said you're not picking up when she rings – at least speak to her.'

She sighed, but she knew she couldn't go on ignoring her sister's calls. 'Alright. I'll text her and tell her I'll call her when I can. But I'm in the middle of a case, so–'

'Yeah, yeah. I get the picture. But we decided to build fences with each other, didn't we? Let's not ruin that before it's even got off the ground.'

Beth finished the call and before she could change her mind, texted her sister. 'Sorry I missed your calls – things are hectic. I'll call you tonight/tomorrow. xx'

At least it bought her some time.

Her phone rang for a second time, and she picked up.

'Hi, Geoff.'

'Where are you?'

'Cockfosters. I've just finished interviewing Sylvia Carroll's ex.'

'Can you meet me over at Finn Abara's house? We've got the warrant through.'

'Sure. I'll see you there in about twenty minutes?'

She bolted her sandwich down, all thoughts about her father and his funeral pushed firmly to one side. The whole issue was a can of worms – she didn't want to go there.

When she pulled up at the Hathaway Estate, Geoff was already there, parked outside Finn Abara's house. He got out of the car, motioning to Finn to do the same, and they walked down the path in single file. They reached the front door and Geoff raised a hand to ring the bell, turning to look at Beth. 'You know the sort of thing you're looking for?'

She nodded, and his finger descended on the button.

'Hello, Mrs Lamb,' he said, holding up a card as the door opened. 'Detective Sergeant Peterson and DC Macaskill, who you've already met? We have a warrant to search these premises. Can we come in please?'

The woman looked from him to Beth and back again, hostility in her eyes. But she stood aside to let them in. 'You won't find nothing; Finn's been going straight since he left prison. Why can't you give him a break?'

'If he's done nothing, then he has nothing to worry about,' Geoff said, pulling on the forensic gloves Beth handed to him. 'Could you show my colleague to his room? I'll start down here.'

'I'll be watching from the doorway,' Goldie said, leading Beth up the stairs. 'And you keep an eye on the other one down here, Finn. We don't want any nasty surprises being planted anywhere.'

Finn's room was tidy, and it didn't take long to check his drawers and wardrobe to establish that there was nothing suspicious to take in. 'Have you got the clothes he was wearing on Saturday please? Jeans, tee-shirt and a hoody, that he says he's washed?'

'They're waiting to be ironed – I'll get them for you.'

'I'll collect them myself if you can show me where they are, to avoid further cross contamination.'

'Well, I've already handled 'em but suit yourself.'

Beth's eyes settled on a keyboard under the window. 'That's a nice piece of equipment. Is it Finn's?'

Goldie's expression was defensive. 'She gave it him—said he could borrow it to work on his music at home. He made sure he got a signed note from her saying it was alright.'

'Can I see that?'

The woman walked over to the shelf above the keyboard and picked up a piece of paper. 'This is it.'

Beth looked at it. It all seemed above board. 'Generous of her, but as she's dead, the relatives will want it returned to her house.'

'You're going to ruin that boy's chances forever, you know that? All he lives for is his music and she's been helping him with that. You should be asking yourselves why he'd want to kill her — it makes no sense. Just because someone lives on an estate like this, doesn't make them trash, or a criminal.'

'I know that. I lived on an estate like this myself,' Beth said. 'But Finn's got a record, and a woman's been murdered. We owe it to her and her family to get to the bottom of that.'

'Yeah, well just you remember you've got a young lad's life in your hands an' all. Finn and his sister have lived with me since he was eight and she was a baby. I know him inside out. While he ain't no saint, he's not a murderer. He's doing his best to go straight but it's not easy when you've got a record. You screw this up and you'll screw him for the rest of his life. And I can't bear to see that happen.'

Beth could see the genuine emotion in the other woman's eyes, and her attitude softened. If only she'd had someone like that looking out for her when she was younger. She looked at the keyboard, then back at the woman. She should probably return it to the house, the relatives may well want it back, but really, what harm would it do, leaving it here a little longer? As long as she made a note of it back at the station they could pick it up whenever they wanted. She understood what it was like battling the odds, being part of a community where everyone expected the worst of you even if you were trying to turn your back on that way of life. Innocent until proven guilty, that was meant to be the law of this land and yet too many times now, that was forgotten with social media and 24/7 news reporting. For now, she'd give Finn Abara the benefit of the doubt. If he was guilty, they'd find out soon enough, but if he was innocent he'd be feeling like shit and if his music helped him forget for a while...

'Okay, we'll leave it. But I'll have to mention it back at the station and someone might want to come and collect it at some point. I need to search the other rooms now.'

Goldie nodded. 'Thanks love. It's not going to be an easy time for him, I know that. And his music's the only thing that keeps him going.'

CHAPTER SIXTEEN

A s soon as the police had left, Finn turned to Goldie. 'Where's
Alyssa?'

'Round at Hayley's. Why?'

Finn shook his head and pulled out his phone, punching in a number. 'Alyssa? Get back here now. I need to talk to you … I don't care about any of that. You come back now. It's urgent.'

Goldie frowned at him. 'What's going on? You talk to her like that and you're gonna alienate her. And she's temperamental enough at the moment.'

'She's mixing with Conn and his mates. Did you know that?'

'*No*. She wouldn't do that.'

Finn brought up the photo on his phone and showed it to her. 'Conn sent me this while I was waiting to be questioned down at the nick.'

Goldie looked at the image and paled. 'Okay, we need to talk to her, but stay calm. She's at a difficult age. If you rile her it'll only make things worse. What does he mean about you borrowed his car? You haven't got a licence. Why did you do that?'

'I didn't. Don't you see what he's doing? He's setting me up – to cover his own arse. But I ain't going down for him a second time, that's for sure.'

'What do you mean?'

'Nothing.'

'Finn, it's about time you were honest with me. You've skirted around what really happened that night, but I never believed you would've driven away from an accident like that unless you were forced to. And now, if there's gonna be more trouble, we need to stick together, lad – and I can only do that if you tell me what's going on.'

'There's nothing going on. I'm just so tired of it all, Goldie – people like Conn manipulating my life. How do I ever break free of it?'

'You do what you've been doing. You keep your nose clean and get another job gardening. You said you enjoy it – working outside and all that.'

'And where am I going to get a reference from, now – when I'm about to be arrested for murder?'

'You listen to me. You done well since you came out of prison, you should be proud of yourself. Don't give up now. Something will come up. And in the meantime, while all this is going on, you keep your head down and bury yourself in your music like you always do.'

'I've got to go out.'

'Where to?'

He didn't answer.

'You're not going to cause trouble with Conn? Stay away from him.'

His look was hard. 'I can't do that, Goldie. Not when he's involved me and now he's involving my sister. They let me go today, but I don't know how long before they take me in and charge me – because they will, you wait and see. "None so blind as them that don't want to see."

That's what they say, and that's the cops for you – they've got me in their sights for Barbara's death and they ain't interested in finding anyone else. And I need to warn Conn off Alyssa before that happens. When she gets back, don't let her go out again until I've spoken to her.'

By the time Finn got round to Connor Stephen's house, his anger was at boiling point. He remembered how the man had groomed him as a young teenager, first paying him to run errands, notching it up a level to deliver a few packages, rewarding him with fags and booze, making him feel a valued member of the team, until finally, he was delivering drugs for him and doing anything he asked.

Oh yeah, he'd done a good job of luring him into it all and now he was doing the same with Alyssa and maybe even stitching Finn up for a murder he didn't commit. Well, he'd been stuffed by the man once and it wasn't going to happen again. He wasn't a kid anymore and Conn was about to find that out.

'We need to talk,' he said, as soon as Conn opened the door.

'Oh, yeah? What about? I've already had the cops breathing down my neck because of you. I don't want you involving me in any of your shit, man.'

'That's rich coming from you. What was that all about – texting me to say I'd borrowed your car? Was it you killed Barbara? Because if it was, I'm telling you now, I ain't going down for you a second time.'

'Don't know what you're talking about, mate. What interest would I have in killing the old biddy?'

'Why did you want me to say I'd borrowed your car?'

'Did you tell them that?'

'I said no comment.'

'Well, now, that wasn't what I told you to say, was it? She's a lovely kid, your sister, and pretty, too. There's some might take advantage of that when she's out with her friends and I'm sure you wouldn't want to see anything nasty happen to her.'

'Is that a threat?'

'Nah, just a fact of life. But I can protect her, make sure nothing happens to her if you play your cards right.'

'And that means saying I borrowed your car when I didn't?'

'Yep.'

'Only this time it's a lot more serious, isn't it? It puts me in the frame for murder.'

'Yeah, sorry about that but I reckoned yours was the best name to put forward seeing as you already had form for it.'

'Well, you reckoned wrong, because this time around I'm not some snotty nosed sixteen-year-old too frightened to say no.'

Without warning, Finn launched himself at Conn, catching him by surprise and pushing him hard against the wall, digging his elbow into the man's throat. He thrust his face into Conn's. 'Now it's my turn to threaten you, and you better listen hard. You harm one hair on my sister's head, and you won't live to see another day. And I ain't going down for you a second time, so you find some other mug to say they was driving your car, because I ain't gonna do it. You got that?'

When no response was forthcoming, he dug his elbow in harder. 'I said, have you got that?'

'Yeah.' Conn gasped the word out.

'Good.'

Grabbing the man by the scruff of his sweatshirt, he twisted the material in his hand and flung him sideways onto the staircase. 'I ain't the soft, scared teenager I was when I went to prison, Conn. It's survival of the fittest in there and I learned to look after myself the hard way. If you know what's good for you, you'll stay away from me and my family. As long as you've got that, things will be cool. But you step out of line…'

Conn glared back at him from the stairs, his eyes like flints of steel. 'You just made a big mistake, man. I ain't small fry now and no one threatens me and gets away with it. Looks like you'll have to learn that the hard way. '

'Did I threaten you? There's been no witnesses, and no one needs to know about it if you don't wanna lose face. Our little secret. But I swear to you, anything happens to my sister, and I won't even bother asking questions as to who done what. It'll be you I come for.'

Without another word, Finn swung on his heels and left.

Back at the house, he found a subdued Alyssa waiting for him. That Goldie had already given her a dressing down was clear and when he walked into the kitchen she looked up apprehensively. He was overwhelmed by the love he felt for her. He wanted to take her in his arms and hold her there. Keep her safe from the ugly world around them.

Instead, he said harshly. 'So, what was that all about, you and Conn in that photo this morning?'

'Nothing.'

'Don't give me that, Alyssa. You been running errands for him?'

'No.'

'Don't lie. I know what he's like and you're the age I was when he started taking me under his wing. He's bad news. You start mixing with him and his crowd and you'll end up in jail like I did.'

'No, I won't. I'm not *stupid*.'

'I thought that too. But he sucks you in without you knowing it and once he's got a hold over you, that's it. There ain't no way out. So, I'll ask you again, have you run any errands for him?'

'No.' She didn't look at him as she answered.

'You sure about that?'

He waited; his eyes fixed on her face.

'Only, taking a couple of presents to friends of his,' she said sulkily. 'That's all.'

'Yeah, little packages, right? 'Cos it's their birthday and he's kind like that. Except he ain't kind and they're not presents. They're drugs, Alyssa. You want to be involved in that sort of thing? Drug running?'

She stared at him wide-eyed.

'You can't trust him,' he said. 'He's bad news and you need to stay away from him.'

'He's not like that, he's nice to me. They all are. They treat me like I'm grown-up, not a child like you and Goldie do.'

Her voice was defiant, and Finn's sense of desperation grew. He knew exactly what she was saying because it was how Conn had made him feel when he'd been her age – valued, important, part of a team. He wished he could think of something to say that would really hit home but found himself falling back on the simple truth.

'But you are a child, that's why Goldie and I need to look out for you. You might not like it but that's the way it is, and people like Conn they exploit kids like you. They know you want to grow up before your time, so they make you feel good by telling you how cool you are, how pretty; they make you feel like you're one of them – but they're not nice people and they can turn nasty very quickly. They're too old for you to be mixing with. You should be hanging around with kids your own age.'

'I do.'

'I know and that's great. But keep it that way, and promise me that if Conn gets in touch with you again, you'll tell me?'

'You just don't like him because you went to prison, and he didn't. He told me you was angry about that.'

'And you know why?' Finn hesitated. He'd been warned not to reveal the true story of what had gone on all those years ago, but he knew now that the only way to convince Alyssa to stay away from Conn and his mates was to show her how dangerous that world was.

'Not even Goldie knows this because I never told anyone, but it weren't me driving that car. It was him. He made me take the rap for him and I was too scared to say no,'cos by then, I knew what he was capable of … and it wasn't only me he threatened.'

'What do you mean?'

It was Goldie who spoke. Finn couldn't bring himself to look at her; but he felt a sense of relief to be finally speaking out.

'You were an attractive woman,' he mumbled.

'Are you saying what I think you're saying?'

He looked her straight in the eye and nodded. 'And it wasn't just you they threatened.' He couldn't bring himself to put into words what Conn had spelt out to him could happen to Alyssa, who'd only been eight or nine at the time. And thank God, now, that part of it seemed to be going over his sister's head as she stared from one to the other in confusion. 'Did they threaten us? Would they have hurt us?' she asked.

Finn nodded. 'Yeah, and I wasn't going to allow that. Just like I'm not gonna let anything bad happen to you now. But you see why you must stay away from him? Promise me you'll do that, Alyssa. Look at me and promise.'

She looked at him, her expression subdued, but her eyes slid away as she nodded her head.

CHAPTER SEVENTEEN

G eoff Peterson was making coffee as Beth walked into the office, and she moved over to join him.

'Want a cup?'

'Thanks.'

'How did the house search go?'

She shook her head. 'Nothing. I dropped his clothes in, but we'll be lucky to find anything on them. I called in on Elena Mancini's husband after that. He lives in Whetstone.'

'And?'

She shrugged. 'Italian, late fifties. No fixed job but says he helps their son out in his restaurant in Cockfosters on an ad hoc basis. He confirmed that his wife was home most of the day on Saturday, although he was out at the pub for a couple of hours over lunchtime. I guess there's a slim chance she could have had time to nip back and do it, but why leave in the first place if she was planning that?'

'Only if something came to light after her return,' Geoff said. 'but I agree, it doesn't seem likely. It puts a question mark over his alibi as well, we'll need to check that out.'

'Already on it, I've got the name of the pub. I got the impression they're not that close as a couple – well, they can't be can they, if she's only at home two days a week? And he didn't have much time for those 'sponging Carrolls', as he called them. He reckons Mia had been worming her way into Barbara's life to see what she could get out of her and that the mother was behind all that. He didn't think for one minute that Barbara would have remembered Sylvia in her will, which is why Mia moved in – to remind Barbara that she was the only family that Barbara had.'

And where had he got those views from, Geoff wondered. It could only have been from his wife, which strengthened the view that she had no time for the Carrolls.

He shook his head. 'By the way, I forgot to mention earlier, that your brother rang. Ryan? Said it was urgent.'

'Oh, yeah, I've spoken to him, thanks.' She hesitated. Geoff already knew about her father dying. 'The pressure's growing to go to the funeral.'

'You thought it might. Want to talk about it? We could go for a pizza when we finish up here if you've got nothing better to do?'

'I haven't. But you probably have.'

'You're kidding me right? You know my life's as boring as yours. It'll be the highlight of my week.'

He grinned at her, and she smiled back as she said. 'We're a sad pair, aren't we? But yeah, okay. We could even go further and grab a pizza at mine? That way, we can have a drink and you can stay over if you want to, depending on how far we dip into the bottle.'

'Now there's an offer I can't refuse. Me and that sofa bed of yours are becoming quite pally. What time?'

'I'm seeing Mia's boyfriend at six. So, seven thirty?'

'Great. See you then.'

He sauntered back to his desk and Beth watched him go, noting how his easy stride matched the rest of him. They'd got closer these last few weeks and she appreciated the platonic friendship that had developed. She wasn't the easiest of people to get on with. She could be tetchy and was private, but Geoff seemed to get that and what little information he'd gleaned from her had been coaxed rather than forced, with her barely realising he'd been doing it. She'd even opened up to him about Andy, and how devastating that had been for her when he'd died. He'd been the first person to love her for who she was. The only person, other than Isi, that she'd loved unconditionally in return, and the sense of loss she'd felt had rocked her to the core. It was only since moving to CID and working with Harry and the team, that she'd finally found a sort of peace. It worked for her. People here were friends as well as colleagues. And Geoff in particular. There weren't many people she trusted but she reckoned he was one of them.

That evening, Harry parked up outside his house in Enfield and exited the car. In his hands, a McDonalds takeaway bag bore witness to a moment of madness on his way home. He hadn't had one in years and was sure now that he was going to live to regret it. What on earth had possessed him?

Approaching his gate, his attention was caught by a young woman who'd climbed out of a Volkswagen Polo ahead of him and was making a beeline straight for him. She looked familiar and he realised why. It was the woman at the crematorium yesterday morning.

His heart jerked in his chest, and he stopped in his tracks. Was he finally about to find out what all the mystery was about?

She came to a halt in front of him and it seemed as if she was suddenly lost for words, her manner awkward as she stared at him.

'Can I help you?' Harry was the first to speak.

'Hi ... my name's Angie ... Angela Kemp.' Her words seemed to tumble over themselves before drying up, and when she said no more, Harry prompted. 'Didn't I see you at the crematorium yesterday?'

'Yes ... my mother.'

'Oh, I'm sorry.' He paused to show respect, before adding. 'Was it you who sent me the obituary notice and cremation details?'

She nodded.

'Do you want to tell me why?'

She hesitated, clearly searching for the right words.

'You know I'm a policeman?'

'Yes.'

He gave her a bit longer, wondering if Claire was right that there was some ambiguity surrounding her mother's death that she wanted him to look into. But why him? He was as sure as he could be that they'd never met before, although ... there was something familiar about her that he couldn't quite place. He studied her intently, hoping he didn't look too obvious about it as he tried to work out what it was. An old girlfriend or fling from years back?

'Did you get in touch because you have some concerns about your mum's death and think I might be able to help?'

'No.'

That knocked that on the head then. Harry came to a decision. 'Look, we could stand out on the street all night saying nothing to each other, or you can come in and have a coffee while I eat this very unhealthy McDonald's I've bought – and tell me why you're here.'

She smiled, her manner relaxing a little. 'Okay.'

He led the way into the house, and she looked around curiously as he led her through the hall and into the kitchen. 'Nice place,' she commented.

'Thanks. Sorry it's not as tidy as it could be.'

He scooped yesterday's paper off the kitchen table and offered her a seat. 'Tea, coffee, or something else?'

'Tea. Thanks.'

She sat down at the table and Harry gave her some space, busying himself making the drinks and tipping his food onto a plate. All the while, his mind was ticking. What was she doing here? He pulled a tin from one of the cupboards. 'Biscuit with your tea? I'll feel guilty scoffing my food when you've got nothing.'

'No... thanks ...' she added awkwardly, perhaps realising how abrupt it had sounded. She sat stiff as a board, her expression terrified.

Harry took the seat opposite and looked at her calmly. 'Okay, so how about you tell me what this is all about? You look as if you're about to pass out at any moment and you're even giving me the jitters.'

It was true, all sorts of scenarios were whizzing around his head, some of them quite alarming if he took in the ex-girlfriend possibility. What if she was about to tell him he'd fathered a child?

'I probably shouldn't be here, and you may hate me afterwards for coming. But I had to see you.'

His sense of foreboding deepened. 'Okay, I think we've established that. Now tell me why.'

She stared at him for a long moment. Then, taking a deep breath, said quietly.

'Because you're my brother.'

CHAPTER EIGHTEEN

'So, what are your thoughts on the case so far?' Geoff asked Beth as they tucked into their pizzas at her kitchen table.

She shook her head. 'Difficult to know, isn't it? It's not looking good for Finn Abara, I'd say, despite what his foster mum says about him being a reformed character. Why lie and leave the scene if you've got nothing to hide? There wasn't anything to suggest foul play on first impressions, so why wouldn't he have called an ambulance?'

'Perhaps because he's mixed race and has a criminal record? Put yourself in his position. It's obvious he doesn't trust "us lot", and with his background, even if he was innocent he'd be terrified we were going to pin it on him. And who can blame him? Let's face it, we do have him marked as our number one suspect.'

'But only because he knew her; he was there and was the last one to see her alive – he ticks all the boxes, Geoff. It's got nothing to do with the fact he's mixed race or has a record.'

'Doesn't it? Oh, not the mixed-race part, I agree with you there – though I doubt he would. But the fact he has a record? Of course, we're leaning more towards him because of that. Just like we are with those other two sleaze balls he hangs around with. But we need to keep an open mind and not let it blind us to other factors. That's where I have so much respect for Harry. He doesn't jump to conclusions. The pressure might be on him to make an arrest and prepare a case for the CPS, but he won't do it until he's sure he's got the right person. And that's good news for people like Finn Abara'.

'I guess. Our Harry certainly likes all his ducks in a row and hats off to him for that.'

'Yeah. We could do a lot worse than have him as our boss. Did you call your sister by the way?'

'Not yet.'

'Have you decided what you're going to do?'

She sighed. 'I don't want to go. I don't want to see my brother Mitch, or my mum. I've been much better off since I cut them out of my life, and I don't need the hard time they'll give me. But Isi obviously feels we should go and how can I leave her to handle it on her own?'

'Maybe they wouldn't be as hard on her as they are on you.'

'No, they won't be, but they'll manipulate her, make her feel guilty that she's not there supporting Mum.' She shrugged. 'Part of me thinks she's an adult and can make her own decisions...'

'And the other part?'

'Thinks I owe it to her, for deserting her like I did.'

'I could come with you if you like. It might act as a cushion between you and them?'

'I couldn't ask you to do that.'

'You're not. I'm offering. Just like I suspect you'd do for me if things were on the other foot.'

She nodded, acknowledging the truth of his words, and much as she hated admitting her weakness, it was a temptation. Mitch intimidated her, and he knew it and played on it. With Geoff there he'd be more likely to hold back, although she suspected he'd make his views on the police abundantly plain. She hesitated. Did she really want anyone else witnessing what a bloody nightmare her family was?

'I'd need to run it past Harry,' Geoff said, 'but who knows, if we pull our fingers out we might have this case sewn up by the end of the week.'

She made up her mind. Geoff could handle her family. 'I'm ashamed to admit it, but it would be good to have some support.'

'That's settled then.'

'I warn you though, Mitch and my mum won't make it easy for either of us.'

'It's a couple of hours – we'll survive. I'll see what I can do about taking the time off.'

CHAPTER NINETEEN

The following morning, Harry climbed into Beth's car with leaden legs, fighting off the headache and nausea that had plagued him from the moment he'd woken up.

'Thanks for picking me up.'

'No worries. Geoff ended up on my sofa bed again last night, but luckily for you, we had our own cars. You look shit if you don't mind me saying. Sure you're well enough to come in?'

'I'm fine.'

It was a lie. He was reeling from what Angela Kemp had told him and after she'd left, he'd buried himself in a bottle of wine and now had the mother of all hangovers, despite knocking back two paracetamols and two mugs of black coffee this morning. Yet in some ways, why should it come as such a shock after what he'd learnt at his gran's funeral about his father's affair? It was undoubtedly a possibility, especially when Angela had confirmed her date of birth, which was only fourteen months after his own and fitted perfectly with the timings his mother had given him. And if what Angela claimed was true, then his father had always known of her existence – had even paid maintenance support for her right up until she'd left university. But he'd never told his wife. And Christ, where did Harry go with that one?

'Heavy night?' Beth chuckled.

'Leave it, Beth, will you?'

It wasn't like him to snap and out of the corner of his eye, he saw her throw him a surprised look. But for once, he didn't care. How the hell was he going to handle this? His parents were landing tomorrow and there was no way he could keep silent.

But just the thought of bringing it out into the open made him want to dive straight back into that bottle again.

***

'Right.' Harry stood in front of the board in the incident room and looked around. A third cup of coffee seemed to have done the trick and he was beginning to feel a bit more normal. 'Any updates from yesterday? Who wants to go first? How about you, Dave? How did you get on checking Barbara Harding's finances?'

Dave Freeman skimmed his notes. 'So ... the routine for several years has been for the housekeeper to withdraw up to a thousand quid a month on her behalf, to pay for food, the gardener, window cleaner and any other miscellaneous expenses. For the last few months, however, Mia seems to have taken over that role and the bank confirmed that the account was recently changed to a joint account in Barbara and Mia's names, with an extra five hundred pounds a month being transferred to Mia on a regular basis. Geoff spoke to Mrs Mancini, who said she questioned Barbara about that when she saw it on some statements she was filing away, and Barbara admitted that she was gifting it to Mia to help her save for her own flat. The bank has given me the serial numbers of the stolen notes, in case we find those, and I also noticed that two withdrawals of five hundred pounds each, were made this week, *after* Barbara's death. One on Monday evening and the other, the following morning.'

'That's worth following up. While we're on the subject of money, do we know what her will says?'

'We found a copy in the safe with her other financial papers,' Beth said.

'Who knew how to unlock that?'

'I think it was Mia who told the forensic guys where the key was, but it was in Barbara's desk drawer, so anyone could have accessed it.'

'And what does it say?'

Beth checked her notes. 'It was written not long after her husband died. One hundred thousand to Elena Mancini, one hundred thousand to charity, twenty-five thousand each to three friends, and the balance to Mia – which going by the value of the house alone, is not an insignificant amount of money.'

'But you said one of her friends mentioned she'd talked recently about changing her will? Give me the name of the solicitor and I'll check it out.'

Beth nodded. 'One other thing ... while I was back at the house yesterday I noticed something else that I don't know if you'd already spotted. There's a gate tucked away in one corner of the back garden, behind the shed, that leads out onto the woods and a footpath. The path runs along the bottom of the gardens and can be accessed from both ends of the road. It means that whoever murdered Barbara, could have entered and left the premises from the rear, where they would have been less likely to be seen. There's no lock on the gate, it just has a bolt.'

'Yeah, I did see that. No cameras covering the footpath, I suppose?'

Beth shook her head.

Harry turned back to Dave. 'Anything else from you?'

'Interestingly, when I was checking Mia Carroll's Facebook account, I noticed one of her recent posts from last Sunday, shows her with some friends and she's carrying a Louis Vuitton handbag. I thought you might want to talk to her about that, bearing in mind the bags that were stolen?'

'Definitely. Beth, can you do that?'

'Sure. She told me yesterday that forensics have finished at the house, so she'd be there if we needed her.'

'Good. Now, as far as immediate friends and families go, is there anyone still to be spoken to?'

'I called on Mia's boyfriend last night. I think he was the last,' Beth said.

'And?'

'Don't think I got much more out of him than you did. He works in advertising. Mia was there with him, and I noticed they'd got several estate agent details of houses for sale – all in the million-pound bracket. They both looked a bit embarrassed when I commented on it.'

'Spending auntie's inheritance money already, then?'

'Looked like it. Providing she hasn't cut Mia out now, of course.'

'Well, narrowing it down, I think our two main options still apply. It's most likely either someone that she knew who had motive to kill her, or it was a burglary that went wrong – and we can't rule out Finn and his friends for that. But bearing in mind the gate onto the footpath, we also can't rule out that it was just a random attacker, either. We know there have been several burglaries in the area so let's compare MO on those and get as many details from uniform as we can. Any fingerprints they might have collected would be useful to compare, too. Have we got CCTV yet for the top end of the road?'

'We've requested it,' Dave said.

'Good. Nothing from the house search on Abara, I assume, linking him to the other burglaries in the area?'

'No.' It was Geoff who spoke. 'But that's not surprising really. If he and his mates did do them, chances are they're storing the stuff elsewhere.'

'Dave, check out local storage facilities – see if you can track any back to them. It'll be like finding a needle in a haystack in that area, but you never know, something might flag up.'

'Will do. One last thing ... forensics rang through first thing this morning to say they'd run the fingerprint check on the arm of the settee, and they've lifted three sets; Elena Mancini, Sylvia Carroll and one other, person unknown.'

'Okay, useful to know. Right.' Harry clapped his hands in a motivating gesture. 'What are you all standing around for? Let's see if we can break this case by the weekend.'

CHAPTER TWENTY

Elena Mancini looked tired and drawn as she answered the door to Beth. There was a mop and bucket at the bottom of the stairs and as she followed Beth's gaze, she said with a sigh. 'I know your people have cleaned the area, but I keep seeing all that blood when I found her.' She shrugged. 'I need to clean it myself if you can understand that? Sylvia and Mia have just arrived. They are in the lounge if you wish to speak to them.'

'Thanks,' Beth said, pulling a photo out of her pocket. 'But before I do, can you tell me, was this one of Barbara's collection of handbags that Mia is wearing?'

The woman frowned. 'Yes, I think so.'

'Did it go missing on that day with the others?'

'That I do not know.'

'Okay.' Beth turned and headed for the lounge.

'Have you got any news for us,' Sylvia asked, looking up. She was sitting in one of the chairs and opposite her on the sofa were Mia and Paul.

'Sorry, nothing new but I've got a few more questions.' She turned to Mia. 'Can you explain this recent picture of you on Facebook? Is that one of Barbara's handbags that you're wearing?'

Mia studied the photo a flush of pink rising to her cheek. 'Yes it is, she gave it to me last month for my birthday. Actually, she wanted me to have all her handbags as she no longer used them herself, but I felt uncomfortable with that, so she said she'd give me one for my birthday.'

'I can confirm that,' her mother said.

'So can I,' Paul added quickly.

'And you?' Beth asked, turning to Elena, who had followed her into the room.

The woman shrugged. 'I can't say. Barbara never mentioned it to me.'

'Well, why would she? You're only staff,' Sylvia remarked coolly. 'And not for much longer,' she added. She turned to Beth. 'Elena will be finishing here on Friday. We have no further need of her services.'

Elena looked shocked. 'You cannot do that. It is part of my contract that I am given three months' notice.'

'But that contract was with Barbara, who sadly is no longer with us. Mia and I have discussed this. We will pay you a further month's salary and you'll finish on Friday.'

'I will finish on Friday, but I will see a solicitor about my contract,' Elena retorted, tight lipped. She turned back to Beth. 'Was there anything else you wanted to ask me? If not, I have work to get on with.'

Beth had listened to this exchange with interest but before she could respond, they were interrupted by the sound of the doorbell.

———

On the doorstep, where Dave had deposited him, Harry sifted through the information he'd just acquired at the solicitors. It had been interesting. So, Barbara had changed her will that very Saturday she'd been murdered. Had the murderer known she was planning to do that?

In the lounge his gaze encompassed them all. 'I've just had a conversation with Barbara's solicitor. Were any of you aware that she'd changed her will the morning she died?'

A shocked silence greeted his words, but he didn't miss the quick look that passed between Mia and her mother. Then Sylvia said. 'We all knew she was thinking about changing her will, but I wasn't aware she'd done it.'

'Apparently, she arranged for her solicitor to come round Saturday afternoon with the necessary two witnesses, but then for personal reasons on her solicitor's side, that appointment was brought forward to the morning. Changes were made – all above board and legal.'

'Is that whose car was parked in the drive?' Sylvia asked.

Harry nodded. 'Yes, that's one mystery solved. He drives a white BMW.'

'So, what does the will say now?' It was Paul who broke the silence. 'Is it significantly different?'

'That's not for me to disclose. You'll need to speak to her solicitor or the executors about that.'

'One of the executors is coming over this afternoon, to start going through her paperwork,' Sylvia said. 'I suppose we can ask him.'

'She did not trust you,' Elena said with a malicious smile. 'She told me she thought you and Mia were just interested in her for her money.'

'Well, that's simply not true. And anyway, you know how neurotic she'd become, she said that about everyone, including you.'

'No, that is not so. She knew she could trust me. I have worked for her for twenty years. But you ... she was always suspicious of how your first husband died. She said it was very convenient for you.'

'How dare you. You know nothing about me or my first husband. It was a tragic accident and very upsetting for everyone at the time. I think it best that you don't wait until the end of the week before you leave. You can stay while we speak to the executor but after that you can pack your things and go. Mia and I will be moving in tomorrow and staying until the house is sold, and we can manage on our own.'

'I'd prefer it if no one stays here overnight for the time being, at least until we've established the motive for Barbara's murder,' Harry said. 'I'm not saying the perpetrator will come back but we can't know that for certain.'

'I thought there was a police guard on the house?'

'There has been, but resources are tight, he'll be withdrawn now that forensics have finished their investigation.'

'I'll be staying with them,' Paul said, not seeming to notice Sylvia's frown at this intervention. 'There's a good alarm system with a couple of panic buttons. I'm sure I can defend them if necessary.'

'And I don't think it's a good idea to leave a house like this empty, especially with the number of burglaries they've had in the area,' Sylvia added. 'We've already discussed it and Mia and I have agreed that we'll move in tomorrow. However, in the circumstances, Paul, if you wish to join us I have no objection.'

'It's your decision, of course,' Harry said. 'All I can do is advise. Now, while I've got you all here, I do need to ask you to consider again, if there's anything you can think of that's happened recently that could have triggered the attack on Mrs Harding? No matter how small or insignificant it might have seemed at the time?'

'Only as I said before, those other men coming – pretending they were sorry when you could see they were not the sort to be sorry for anything,' Elena said. 'Barbara did not trust them. She did not let them in past the hall because she did not want them to see the house.'

Beth dived into her pocket and pulled out the mug shots. 'Were these the men you saw, do you remember?'

Elena stared hard at the photos, then nodded. 'Yes, I remember the taller one had that scar on his cheek.'

'We're following up with them,' Harry said. 'But nothing else happened? No-one else called or visited?'

She frowned. 'Only the window cleaner. I remember now, he came on Wednesday, but he comes every month and has done so for the last six months, since the last one retired. Also, a couple of weeks ago she had all the carpets, sofas and chairs professionally cleaned. She was very fastidious and said that even though she could no longer see the dirt she would not let her standards slip.'

'And I suppose you regularly clean the wooden frames of the chairs and settee?' Harry asked.

'Of course. They get cleaned and polished with everything else.'

Which was good, because it meant that those fingerprints on the arms were recent, he thought with satisfaction. Still, they'd need to try and get prints off whoever had done the cleaning and eliminate them if necessary.

'We'll need to speak to both those contractors if you've got their numbers?'

'Of course, I will get them for you.'

'One other thing. It seems a thousand pounds has been withdrawn from Barbara Harding's account since her death. We'd like to clarify who did that and why. It obviously wasn't Barbara.'

They all looked embarrassed, and it was Sylvia who spoke. 'We took a joint decision to withdraw some money to cover any unexpected expenses over the next few weeks in case Barbara's bank account was frozen and couldn't be accessed.'

'I thought it was a joint account in her name and Mia's?' Harry said.

'It is.'

'Well, in that case there shouldn't be a problem, although obviously the bank needs to be notified of her death, which I assume you've done?'

'Yes, we've done that now, but we took the money out before we spoke to the bank, just to be on the safe side.'

'I see. Well, if you could get me that number for the window and carpet cleaners, Mrs Mancini? And while you're doing that, I'll just take a quick look at the back gate access to the property and then we'll be off. You've all got one of my cards if you think of anything.'

CHAPTER TWENTY-ONE

F inn Abara sighed as he clicked his phone off. Christ, anyone would think he was applying to be a security guard, not a bloody gardener the number of questions they'd asked. And he could tell it was a no-go the minute he'd given his name, though why that should surprise him in a posh area like Hadley Wood…

He turned to the next job vacancy he'd circled. A gardener for a crematorium. Not much to get excited about but a job was a job and at the rate he was going, beggars couldn't be choosers.

The number was engaged and as he gave it a few minutes, he found himself staring at the date on his phone. 3rd December. His heart gave a jolt. Tomorrow was the anniversary of his parents' death, and even though it had been over twelve years now, he still felt the shaft of pain rip through him almost as sharply as it had done that day his mum's best friend had told him about the accident – a train derailment that had taken only three lives; two of which had been his parents.

He hadn't cried, hadn't shown his shredded emotions externally. Not once. People thought he was being strong, they talked about what a brave little boy he was; they hadn't seemed to see that inside it felt like he'd died with his parents. When they'd taken him and his baby sister to the children's home, he'd clung tightly to her little hand, terrified to let go – screaming whenever they were separated, even if it was just to change her nappy. They told him that he'd be fine; that it took time to accept the reality of a tragedy like that. But they were wrong. He understood straight away that he'd never see his parents again; that Alyssa would be taken away from him as well, and that life as they knew it had ended. They tried to comfort him, encourage him to talk, but they just didn't get it. Talking about things just brought back the memories, like the last conversation he'd had with his mum over the breakfast table, that day she was killed.

'I don't like to hear you're misbehaving at school, Finn. We're a decent family and I want you to remember that and grow into the sort of man your dad and I can be proud of. There's lots around here will try to change you – want you to do things you know are wrong – and it takes a strong boy to fight against that. But you are strong, and you need to fight it,'cos your dad and me we're working hard to give you and Alyssa a good start in life – the start we never had – and you have to help us do that by working hard at school and getting a good education.'

He'd nodded carelessly as an eight-year-old does, dismissing her words almost as soon as they'd left her mouth. He knew his grandfather had come over from Uganda in search of a new life after his wife had died, bringing Finn's dad with him as a young boy,. And how hard it had been for them. He knew also how hard his mum and dad worked: his dad, working all the hours he could as a station porter. None of it seemed relevant to him.

But later that day, when she wasn't there waiting at the school gate, when they'd told him about the accident, her words had come back to haunt him, and he'd sworn there and then that he'd become the sort of son they would have been proud of.

The next month had been vicious. Alyssa had been fostered out with a couple where the woman was mixed race like them, while he'd stayed in the home. He'd screamed when they'd taken her away. It felt like his soul had been ripped from his body. Despite his good intentions, he'd become difficult and aggressive, testing their patience, making it difficult for them to place him with a family.

And then, what he now knew was nothing short of a miracle had happened. The people who'd taken Alyssa had offered to take him as well. They could be together.

'But you'd better behave yourself more than you do here,' the social worker who took him, warned him. 'Or you'll be coming straight back to us and your chance to stay with your sister will be gone. You understand that?'

He'd nodded, a lead block forming in his heart, as he vowed that he'd control his feelings no matter how awful his new life might be and do whatever was necessary to stay with Alyssa. She was his responsibility now, and she was the only thing that mattered. As long as they could be together, he could pretend that life was normal.

And then he'd met Marigold Lamb – AKA, Goldie – and her husband Kev. And suddenly, a shaft of light had flickered in his dark world.

He let out a sigh, coming back to the present. He and Alyssa had been dealt a lucky card the day they'd been placed with Goldie and Kev, no doubt about that. They'd loved them as their own and when Kev had died seven years later, it had hit Finn hard.

On Sunday, the three of them would visit the cemetery as they always did for the anniversary of their parents' deaths. Goldie would have a bunch of flowers to take, and he and Alyssa would equip themselves with a trowel and fork to tidy the small area around the memorial stone, paid for by Goldie and Kev so they'd have somewhere to go to remember them.

His thoughts turned to Barbara – another minor miracle in his life – and the circumstances of her death. Who would have wanted to kill her, and why?

He cast his mind back to last Saturday, as he'd done so many times, racking his brain. He hadn't noticed anything unusual or out of the ordinary, but why had Conn been there later that day? Why had he wanted Finn to say he'd borrowed his car? Could Conn and his mates have broken in and killed her for some reason and then gone back to loot the place later? He wouldn't put it past them – he was under no illusions as to how dangerous Conn had become. His power had grown hugely over the period Finn had been in prison. It was more than just petty theft and the odd dabbling in drugs now; it was organised crime – and how did Finn protect his little sister and Goldie from that?

There was only one way ... to move ... and that wasn't going to happen in a hurry, even assuming he could persuade Goldie to do it. Her work in the community centre, giving kids like Alyssa somewhere to go, was her passion. She wouldn't easily be talked into giving it up. He couldn't see a way out of it all and the realisation swamped him.

He did what he always did when he felt he was losing the plot. He went upstairs to his keyboard.

<hr />

'Alyssa, hold up.'

Alyssa turned to see her friend Hayley crossing the road to join her.

'Why didn't you wait for me after school? I thought we were going over to Conn's.'

'I can't go. I gotta get home.'

'Why?'

Alissa shrugged. 'My brother – he's being a pain. Says he doesn't want me going over there. That Conn's trouble.'

'But we said we'd go, and you know Conn. He won't like it if we don't turn up.'

'I know. But ... maybe Finn's right. Those packages we delivered ... Finn says they could've been drugs. I don't want to get caught up in that sort of stuff. Do you?'

'No, but...' her friend shrugged. 'Everyone does it, don't they? It's not like we're making them take it. It's their choice.'

'I know, but ... some of the stuff my brother told me ... maybe we should just lie low for a bit, keep out of Conn's way. Until Finn gets off my back.'

Her friend looked worried. 'But what if Conn comes looking for us? I don't want to get on the wrong side of him.'

Their conversation was interrupted by a voice from behind them. 'Well, look who it isn't. Alyssa and her little ginger-nut friend.'

Alyssa didn't need to turn round to know who it was. Vanessa and her cronies. 'Keep walking,' she muttered to Hayley. 'Ignore them.'

'Oi, Alyssa, I'm talking to you.'

"Yeah, well I'm not talking to you,' Alyssa threw over her shoulder. 'So, get lost and leave us alone.'

'Well, now, that's not very nice.'

The voice was right behind her now and before Alyssa knew what was happening, she felt a foot thrust between her ankles, bringing her crashing down to the ground.

'Oh dear, are you okay?' Vanessa mocked, looking down at her. Then, quick as lightning, she snatched Alyssa's school bag and was off. 'Come on guys, let's see what we got in here,' she laughed.

'Hey, bring that back.' Alyssa shouted, jumping to her feet.

'Catch us if you can,' Vanessa taunted over her shoulder.

They were headed for the park, and once there, they veered left, racing past the swings and zip wire, to the small copse that lay beyond. A hundred yards or so into the woods they suddenly stopped, swinging round to confront the two girls chasing them.

'Right, get her.' Vanessa shouted, and before Alyssa knew it, the three girls were on her, wrestling her to the ground and pinning her down, smearing mud in her hair and on her face.

Hayley leapt in, trying to defend her, but Vanessa grabbed her by the hair and yanked her back. 'If you know what's good for you, you'll piss off,' she screamed into the other girl's face.

'Leave her alone, you bitch. What's the matter with you? She ain't done nothing to you.'

'Yeah, well if you don't want the same treatment you better get out of here.'

'What's going on?'

It was a man's voice, and four pairs of eyes swung round in shock.

'I said what's going on? Get off her, now. Help her up.'

It was Connor Stephens and there was only the slightest of pauses before the girls sheepishly did as he said.

He looked at Alyssa. 'You okay?'

She nodded as she clambered to her feet, brushing herself down and pulling mud and twigs from her hair and mouth.

'Right, you two...' he indicated to Vanessa's two friends. 'Clear off ... now.' He shouted, as they looked uncertainly at Vanessa. 'Your friend's staying here with me. I said, go.'

They went, and Conn turned his attention to the remaining girl.

'So, what's this all about? I don't like people messing with my friends. Bullying them. What you got to say for yourself?'

Vanessa hung her head, saying nothing.

'Would you like it if the boot was on the other foot? If my boys here knocked you to the ground and started having a bit of fun with you and shoving mud in your mouth? Shall I get them to do that now? Shall I?'

He nodded in the direction of two of his mates and they started forward.

'No.' Vanessa cried out in alarm. 'Please. I'm sorry.'

'It's not me you need to say you're sorry to. Let me hear it.'

The girl looked at Alyssa and hesitated.

'I said apologise,' Conn screamed, closing the space between them.

'I'm sorry,' she shouted at Alyssa.

'And you won't bother her again.'

'And I won't bother you again.'

'Cos if you do, you'll have me to answer to. You got that?'

The girl nodded, terrified.

'Now get out of here, and if I hear from either of these girls that you've been hassling them...'

Vanessa fled.

A smile curved Conn's lips as he turned back to the two girls. 'That's that sorted. Good thing I was here, looking out for you, eh? No one messes with my mates. Now, come with me, I got something I want to talk to you about.'

'I've got a lot of homework to do,' Alyssa said quickly. 'I promised Goldie I wouldn't be late tonight.'

'And you won't be. It'll only take half an hour.'

He led the way back to his car, a large 4x4 Toyota, and opened the passenger door to let them in.

'Where are we going?' Alyssa asked nervously when she realised they weren't heading back to the estate.

'I'm meeting some mates at Ali's. You girls fancy a kebab?'

'Goldie'll be cross if I'm back late, and I haven't got any money.'

'No hassle. The kebabs are on me and no worries about Goldie. She'll be fine, I'll have a word with her if you like?'

Alyssa shook her head quickly. 'No, it's alright.'

Fifteen minutes later they pulled up outside a Turkish restaurant and takeaway in Hatfield. Alyssa and Hayley got out of the car and followed Conn inside.

'Hey, Ali,' he greeted a man behind the counter. 'You got some nice food for me and my girls here?'

'Of course, Connor.' He eyed the girls. 'Shish kebabs for you two if I remember right?'

The girls nodded.

'Just thought I'd bring them out for a treat. Shall we go through to the back?'

'Yes, my friend, I will bring your food through to you. You have my money?'

Conn tapped his pocket. 'All here. You got my goods?'

'Sure. Berat is in there. He will give them to you.'

In the small back room, three men were seated around a table playing cards and a fourth, younger man, was in a chair, snogging a girl on his lap. He winked at Alyssa over the girl's shoulder, and she turned her gaze away, embarrassed.

'You might want to clean some of that mud off your face,' Conn said to Alyssa. 'You know where the toilets are. Then if you wait a few minutes while I conduct a bit of business, we can have a chat about a little job I've got for you both, where you can earn yourselves a bit more pocket money.'

Alyssa headed for the bathroom, her mind in a spin. Finn and Goldie would kill her if they knew she was here. It had been so much easier to get away with stuff while Finn was in prison, but he wasn't an idiot, and he'd soon start to guess that something was going on. But the trouble was, she didn't know how to change things even if she wanted to. Conn and his mates had become their friends, and it felt cool having someone like him as a friend. He was important around here and while he had their backs, people like Vanessa wouldn't dare mess with her and Hayley. Look how he'd stepped up for her today.

She dried her face and went to join Hayley on the settee. They watched in awe as Conn withdrew a huge wad of notes from his pocket and handed them over to one of the men. The man counted it and then gestured to some boxes in the far corner. 'The drills are there, fifty in all.'

Conn nodded and turned to his mate. 'Start loading them into the car. Red'll be here soon, and he can take any that don't fit. Ah, great, food. Come over here, girls, and tuck in.'

They got up and moved over to the table.

'You can sit on my knee, if you like,' one of the older men offered with a toothy grin, patting his knee.

Alyssa tried to hide her revulsion. 'I'm all right standing.'

'If you were a gent, Berat, you'd offer her your seat.'

'Of course,' the man said standing up. 'Be my guest.'

'And you can sit here,' one of the other men said to Hayley, also getting up. The girls sat down and took some of the proffered food.

'Fancy a bit of wine?" Conn asked with a grin, picking the bottle up from the table.

'I'll have some,' Hayley said. Alyssa hesitated, remembering the last time when she'd ended up quite drunk. Finn and Goldie weren't stupid.

'Just half a glass,' she said, and rolled her eyes when Conn filled both glasses to the top.

'So,' he said, helping himself to a kebab and directing a keen gaze at Alyssa. 'How are you girls doing, all good?'

They nodded nervously.

'Good, 'cos I've got another little job for you both on Friday, if you're interested. I'll pay you a hundred quid each. What do you think to that?'

Both girls stared at him, their eyes almost popping out of their heads. 'What sort of job?' Alyssa asked, Finn's warnings coming back to haunt her.

He laughed. 'No need to look so worried. It's just that it involves a bit of travelling, so I reckon I need to be more generous paying for your time. I'll give you the money for the train tickets on top, of course, and it will involve staying in a very nice country house overnight, that I'll also pay for. There's a spa there and everything.'

'Overnight? No way Goldie will let me do that.'

'Then don't tell her. You just skive off school on Friday and come home on Saturday. Couldn't be simpler and lots of kids do it don't they? Skip a day or two off school here and there? It's all part of growing up and becoming more independent. Parents expect it. And it's good money – where else you gonna earn money like that for Christmas? So ... are you in?'

The girls exchanged glances. Already, the wine was going to Alyssa's head, and somehow the thought of Goldie and Finn's anger didn't seem as scary now, as it had. She felt a stab of excitement. A country house with a spa? How posh was that?

'Is there a swimming pool?' she asked.

'You bet and I'll throw a couple of beauty treatments in for you both too.'

'I'm in,' Hayley said without hesitation. She looked expectantly at her friend, and it didn't take Alyssa long to come to a decision. So, what. There'd be murder to pay with Finn and Goldie afterwards but ... a hundred quid. She could buy them great Christmas presents with that much money.

'Okay,' she nodded, grinning.

～ 〰 ～

'Where have you been?' Goldie asked sharply when Alyssa walked into the house an hour later.

'Over at Hayley's doing our homework together.'

'You should have let me know. Dinner was ready half an hour ago. Finn and I have already had ours.'

'Sorry. My battery died.'

Goldie looked at her. 'You're not lying to me, are you?'

'No. Phone Hayley's mum if you don't believe me.' Her tone was aggressive. It didn't feel good lying. She held her breath, praying that Goldie wouldn't take her up on that. She also hoped Goldie couldn't smell the alcohol on her breath and clamped her mouth firmly shut.

'No, I trust you, Alyssa. I know you wouldn't lie to me.'

Which made her feel a hundred times worse.

'I'll just go and wash my hands,' she mumbled, fleeing from the kitchen. She felt like crying and didn't know why.

CHAPTER TWENTY-TWO

H arry made himself a coffee and walked back to his desk. He sat down and flicked his screen on, to continue reading.

'How's it going?'

He looked up to see DCI Murray looking down at him and leaned back in his chair with a sigh. 'Considering how few suspects we have, not that well. I've been trying to think various possibilities through, but at the end of the day, we have either a random burglary and killing, or someone who had a motive. And the only obvious motive we have is the fact that she'd talked about changing her will, which she did the morning she was killed.'

'So, who does that narrow it down to?'

'The housekeeper, who's worked for her for twenty years, a cousin and a niece she wasn't close to, their partners, and three friends who are mentioned in her will. We're checking them all out. It's still possible it could have been Abara and his friends. The other burglaries in the road started after he began working for Barbara, and we know his mates knew where she lived. She could have realised who it was had broken in and they decided they had no choice but to silence her. We'll hopefully know more when we get detailed CCTV from the top end of the road and hopefully from the other break-in dates, if uniform collected it.'

'I doubt that somehow.'

'Yeah. Meanwhile, the housekeeper more or less accused Sylvia Carroll of killing her first husband today. Said Barbara had always been suspicious of her. I'm looking into the details of his death at the moment.'

'And?'

Harry flipped his screen around so that Murray could see the old headline he'd dug out. *"Ex-wife quizzed in man's house fire death."*

'A verdict of misadventure was recorded, but there does seem to have been an element of uncertainty surrounding it. He was nearly thirty years older than her, and they'd recently separated. They reckon he'd been drinking heavily, and the blaze was thought to have been started by a cigarette that slipped down between the cushions before he took himself off to bed. He was already dead by the time they got to him. Sylvia Carroll inherited a lot of money from him. According to his sons and ex-wife, in their statements at the time, he'd made an appointment to see his solicitor to change his will, but he died before he could do that.' Harry shrugged. 'It rings rather similar. I've requested the archived file.'

'Stick with it,' Murray said, turning back to his office. 'Something will break. It always does.'

Harry picked up his phone and looked at his messages. Claire had texted him two hours ago, asking if he was dropping round later, but he didn't feel ready to share what was going on in his personal life yet, and he wouldn't be good company. Anyway, Angela had said she'd drop round later with some photos of her with his father when she was younger and he felt he needed to get as much of a handle on the situation as he could, before his parents arrived tomorrow.

'Sorry, really tired and not feeling my best. Early night for me,' he texted back. 'My parents arrive tomorrow, but how about we go out for a meal on Friday?'

Her response was instant, and he swallowed his guilt. 'Sure, no worries. Sounds like you need a bit of TLC! Hope you cheer up soon, and Friday sounds good. xx'

On television when people did these family reunion things, long lost relatives waiting to meet each other usually looked eager, hopeful – excited by the prospect of new opportunities opening to them, but as Harry waited for Angela's arrival that evening, he didn't seem to be experiencing any of those emotions. Numb, was the best word to describe how he was feeling, and now that he'd had time to absorb his new situation, it felt overwhelming – an insurmountable problem that he didn't want to have to deal with.

Now, as he looked at his watch for the hundredth time, he jumped as the doorbell rang. Seven o'clock and she was bang on time.

'Hi.' She stood awkwardly on the doorstep, and for the first time, as he looked at her, he saw the similarities between them. Same light brown hair, same eyes – was that why she'd looked familiar when he'd first seen her yesterday? Because he'd been used to seeing that similar reflection in his mirror every morning?

'Come in,' he said, opening the door wider. 'Here, let me take that bag, it looks heavy.'

'It's just a couple of my mum's albums, but there are some photos of your dad – our dad, in there.'

'Can I get you something to drink?'

'No thanks. I just want to get this bit over with so that hopefully, you'll know I'm telling the truth and we can decide where, if anywhere, we go from here.'

In the lounge, Harry sat on the sofa and Angela took the chair next to him. She said nothing as he flicked through the pages, but her eyes were anxious when, finally, he looked up to meet her gaze. He shook his head slowly, still trying to absorb what he'd just seen. Pictures of his father with a tiny Angela in his arms, more at various stages of her life, getting fewer, the older she got. The latest ones were when she must have been about twelve or thirteen. After that, nothing.

'When did you last see him?'

'Just after my thirteenth birthday.'

All these years, his father had led a double life. It was insane.

'We argued, because, by then, I was only seeing him maybe once a year, usually around my birthday, and the whole situation was messing with my head. It didn't feel like he wanted to see me, more a duty visit, and I thought what was the point. Mum could see how it was affecting me, so she wrote to him and told him no more visits unless he was prepared to openly acknowledge me and see me more frequently. He didn't argue the point, which says it all, really, although he did send me a birthday card every year. I kept those. Don't know why.'

Her eyes misted up and it tugged at Harry's heart strings. He couldn't begin to comprehend what she must have gone through, the sense of rejection. How could his father have done that?

'I don't know what to say. This has come as such a shock. I had no idea.'

'Maybe you're the lucky one. It's not been easy knowing I have a father out there who wants nothing to do with me. And a half-brother who I assumed had no idea I existed.'

'You assumed right.'

'My stepfather died three years ago, and I wanted to get back in touch with Dad then, but Mum didn't want it. No point raking up old wounds she said, and hadn't Frank been a good enough dad to me? And he had. He'd been a brilliant one, so I left it. But now...' there was the faintest trace of emotion in her voice, and he could see her mouth working. 'Now I realise that your father – and you – are the only family I have apart from my mum's sister. It's a scary feeling.'

It also felt a responsibility to Harry. One that sat uncomfortably on him, and he felt ashamed of himself for that. 'But friends ... your parents must have good friends, and presumably you do too?'

Her stance stiffened, as if sensing that he was trying to distance himself from her. 'Yeah, of course we do, and they've been great since Mum died. I'm not trying to force myself on you. If you want me to walk out of here and never see me again, that's fine. I just decided you had the right to know I exist. What you do with that information is up to you. I also wanted my father to know that both my parents are dead now. I don't know why, really. He's been pretty crap as a dad up to now, so I'm not expecting miracles, but again, I'll leave it to him to decide what happens next. Oh, and by the way...' She rummaged around in her handbag and pulled out an envelope. 'Just in case you want proof, this is a copy of the paternity test they had done when I was born, proving to your dad that he was my father.'

She rose from her seat and handed him the envelope. 'I can see you're feeling very uncomfortable about all this, and so am I. It's the hardest thing I've ever done and maybe it's a mistake but keeping silent just didn't feel like an option. I'll take myself off now. My mobile number's in there if you want to get in touch, but if I don't hear from you again, have a good life.'

She was already walking into the hall, her back ramrod stiff, and Harry jumped up and sprinted after her. 'Wait. Don't go like this. I'm sorry if I've reacted clumsily. It's just been a shock. And my parents are arriving from Egypt tomorrow and I don't know what I'm going to say to them.'

She opened the front door and turned to face him on the doorstep, her eyes glistening.

'It doesn't matter. It was naive of me to think you'd react any differently. You were hardly going to greet me like a long-lost friend, were you? I'm an embarrassment who's going to cause problems in your nice cosy little family unit. That's the reality of it.'

She turned away as if to walk down the path and Harry grabbed her hand, pulling her back towards him.

'Don't go. I'm sorry, I just need a bit of time to get my head around it all. Please, come back in.'

She hesitated and he took advantage of that to put his arm around her and draw her firmly back into the house. He was ashamed of himself. It couldn't have been easy for her to do this ... approach him when she couldn't be sure of his reaction.

'Come on,' he said, 'you can talk me through some of those photos. Looks like you had some fun birthday parties when you were younger.'

A hundred yards down the road, Claire's steps faltered. The attractive young woman leaving Harry's house was clearly upset and she watched as Harry reached out and took her hand, preventing her from leaving. It was obvious, just looking at them, that it was a highly charged moment and there was some sort of history between them. She watched in disbelief as Harry drew the girl into the circle of his arm and led her firmly back into the house.

The Indian take-away dangled limply in her hands. Just for a moment, she toyed with the idea of knocking on his door to find out what was going on, but she decided against it. Wrangling on doorsteps wasn't her thing.

She turned and headed back to her car.

CHAPTER TWENTY-THREE

E arly next morning, Harry stood outside the rather swish detached house in Hampstead and couldn't help wondering what he was doing there. It was probably a wild goose chase following up on the death of Sylvia Carroll's first husband, but for the sake of completeness it needed to be done. The door was opened by a man who looked to be in his early forties.

'Detective Inspector Harry Briscombe,' Harry said, showing his card. 'I've got an appointment with Mrs Hart?'

'Yes, come in. I'm her son, Mark. My mother rang to say you were coming. Sorry we had to make it so early, but I've got a meeting. I hope it's not a problem for me to be here. Mum's over eighty and can get a bit confused sometimes.'

'No worries. I'll try to keep things as brief as possible.'

'I don't get what this is about,' the man said, leading the way through to where his mother was waiting for them in a small TV room. 'Mum mentioned Sylvia, but we haven't seen her in thirty years or more. Not since my father's death. Mum, this is Inspector Briscombe.'

Mrs Hart was a short, frail looking woman who looked as if she'd blow over in a puff of wind, but there was a steeliness to the gaze she directed at Harry that belied her fragility.

'What can I do for you, Inspector? Please, take a seat. You said you had some questions about my first husband's death. Am I to take it, after all these years, that you're finally taking my allegations seriously?'

'Not exactly, Mrs Hart, but I would be interested to know what grounds you were basing your accusations on? Was there anything specific?'

'Only that Sylvia knew that Eric was going to change his will to make sure she was cut out, and she was the last person to see him alive that night. I was still in touch with my ex-husband because of the boys, and he told me that she was going around to discuss the terms of the divorce and that she wouldn't be pleased because, even though it was unusual in those days, she'd signed a prenup agreeing to a one hundred thousand pound pay off should the marriage last less than five years, and he was going to hold her to that. Of course, a lot of people would be quite happy with a pay off like that for a meagre five years' service, but Sylvia knew how much Eric was worth and she was going to fight it all the way to the top. That night...' she looked at her son, and then back at Harry. 'Eric had a drink problem, no one's denying that. But he hadn't smoked a cigarette or touched a drop of alcohol, in over a month. The boys were seeing him regularly over that period because he was quite distressed about the break, so we knew how well he'd been managing to stay off the drink. It's our belief that Sylvia somehow got him started on the alcohol again, and after that, there would have been no stopping him. When they did the post-mortem, they reckoned, had he lived, that he would have suffered from severe alcohol poisoning the levels in his blood were so toxic. We can't prove it was her that actually put the cigarette down the cushion, but frankly, I wouldn't put it past her. She was a mercenary bitch.'

For someone over eighty and apparently prone to confusion, she wasn't doing too badly, Harry thought. In fact, she rather reminded him of his grandmother, who'd been on the ball with a mind of her own, right up to the end.

'Were your concerns investigated at the time?' he asked.

'They said they were, but I'm not sure how thoroughly. They said they couldn't find any evidence and eventually a verdict of misadventure was given. But why are you digging this up now? Has she done someone else in?'

'Mum, you can't say that.' Her son looked shocked, but there was a wry twist to his lips.

'Yes I can. They haven't completely banned freedom of speech yet, as far as I'm aware. Even if she didn't set fire to the sofa herself, she's got a lot to answer for, driving him to drink like she did. He may not have been the easiest of men to live with, and he liked his drink, but he didn't have a problem when he was with me. So ... what's all this about?'

'I can't say too much, I'm afraid, just that in the course of our enquiries, the nature of Mrs Carroll's relationship with your ex-husband is being looked into. Is there anything else you can tell me about that night?'

'No. I wish there was. The boys had gone round to visit him that evening and when I went round to pick them up it was around eight thirty and she was already there.'

She looked at her son. 'I remember you were in a foul mood in the car, saying that they'd been arguing all evening out in the kitchen.'

'I don't remember much about the details, just Dad saying she'd only married him for his money, and that he was going to make sure she didn't get any more of that than she was entitled to. I remember the atmosphere was toxic.'

'So, what made you think she might have had something to do with his death?' Harry asked the old woman.

She shrugged. 'I just wouldn't put it past her. She told the police she knew nothing about him wanting to change his will, but that was a lie because he told me he'd told her. And she's hard as nails, that one. If she wants something, she'll go for it.'

'Well,' Harry stood up to take his leave. 'Thanks for seeing me, that's been helpful. I hope I've not raked up too many negative memories for you.'

'Not for me you haven't, but it was worse for the boys at the time. Eighteen and sixteen – difficult ages and hard not knowing exactly what had happened with the fire. It affected them badly.'

Mark shrugged and gave a tense smile. 'It was all a long time ago. It would have been nice to get all the answers neatly tied up, but you learn as you get older that life's not like that. You have to roll with the punches.'

His words reverberated in Harry's brain as he walked back to his car. Was that what he needed to do with his parents and Angela? Roll with the punches? Could it be that simple? He knew the answer to that even before he'd finished thinking it. No, it couldn't. A can of worms had been opened and it wasn't going to close in a hurry. He'd had ups and downs with his parents before and though he tried not to, he knew he harboured resentment that they'd farmed him off to boarding school and not even bothered to see him every holiday. Even though his mother had explained to him about the affair, how it had made her paranoid about not letting his dad go on his archaeological trips solo, it didn't explain why they hadn't made more effort to see him in the school vacations. So, if he felt angst over that, then he totally got the sense of rejection Angela must be feeling.

He climbed into his car and on impulse, decided to pay Sylvia Carroll a visit.

She was alone when she opened the door to let him in – a luxury flat in Stanmore overlooking parkland. She led him through to a modern lounge and indicated a chair.

'How can I help you, Inspector?'

'A few questions if you don't mind? You understand we must look into all angles in a murder enquiry like this, and sometimes our investigation might feel intrusive, but I wanted to ask you about your first husband, Eric Hart?'

'What about him?'

'He died in a house fire, I understand?'

'Yes, it was very sad, but he had a drink problem, and they reckoned he was drunk and a cigarette dropped onto one of the cushions and started to smoulder.'

'You were the last person to see him alive?'

'Apparently so. I'd gone round that night to discuss our divorce settlement. It was stressful, which is why I think he drank more than he should have.'

'He was an alcoholic?'

'Yes, and once someone like that starts...'

'Did you try to talk him out of drinking alcohol?'

'That was no longer my responsibility, thank God. I probably made some comment, but he wouldn't have taken any notice.'

'Were you aware that your husband was going to change his will later that week?'

She shrugged. 'He may have mentioned it, I don't remember. And I know where you're going with this, but I did nothing to hasten my husband's death. It was a difficult conversation, I'm not denying that, and yes, we had a drink or two. But there's no law against that, and I can't take responsibility for what happened after I left.'

Her gaze was totally devoid of emotion as she looked at him. 'Is that it, or do you have any other questions for me?'

'And Barbara Harding? You knew that she was going to change her will, too?'

She gave a derisive little snort. 'She loved taunting us with that one. And I never had expectations of inheriting anything from her. She'd always made it perfectly clear that she had no time for me.'

'But you had expectations for your daughter?'

'I hoped she'd inherit something, of course. What mother wouldn't want that for her daughter?'

'So, if you thought Mia was also being cut out?'

'There would have been nothing I could do about it. Barbara was free to do as she wanted with her money. So, what?' Her laugh was dismissive. 'You're saying I killed my first husband for his wealth and now I've killed Barbara for hers?'

'No. We just need to gather the evidence so that we can get a clear picture of what's gone on. And obviously we can't ignore the fact that Barbara's death happened after she'd been talking about changing her will. On the very day she was seeing her solicitor, in fact. It was fortunate for her that she managed to do that before she was attacked.'

'Well, we may not have got on, but even I wouldn't have wished that on her. And I certainly wouldn't have pushed her down the stairs to kill her. No murderer could guarantee that would work.'

'We've now ascertained that it wasn't the fall that killed her.'

'Oh?'

'No. It was an action taken after the fall, that I'm not at liberty to disclose yet.'

She looked shaken at this revelation. 'Right ... well, if I'm on your list of suspects, I'd point out there are others, equally as likely.'

'Such as?'

'Elena for one. She certainly had as much of a motive to kill her as me, even more so, I'd say. A hundred thousand pounds she'll be getting – it's a lot of money. She wouldn't have been happy at the thought of being cut out of the will.'

'It's a lot of money for sure, but nothing like the millions Mia was expecting.'

She regarded him coolly. 'Do I, or my daughter, need a solicitor?'

'No. There are still a lot of loose ends to tie up and I'm just fact finding. I'll let you know if anything changes. Thanks for your time.'

'Well, I won't say you're welcome. I'm heading over to Barbara's now if you need to speak to me about anything else.'

'Thank you. Hopefully that won't be necessary again today.'

An assumption that was busted the moment he climbed into his car and his phone rang. It was Beth. 'Harry, where are you?'

'Just finished questioning Sylvia Carroll at her flat in Stanmore.'

'Can you divert? A call's come in saying that a body's been found and ... wait for it ... it's in the woods at the back of Barbara Harding's house. Me and Geoff are heading over there now.'

'Any idea who it is?'

'Nope, all we know is that a jogger put the call into uniform.'

'Right. On my way. I'll be about half an hour.'

When Harry arrived at the scene, it was already a hive of industry, with a significant area sealed off in the woods, covering several houses either side of Barbara Harding's property. Through the flap of an open tent, he could see Simon Winter bent over a body, and the only other person on that side of the tape was the photographer, angling his camera this way and that, to get the best images. Beth and Geoff were talking quietly to themselves several yards away on the footpath, but as soon as they saw Harry, they made their way over to him.

'It's Elena Mancini,' Geoff said without preamble, handing him a protective Tyvek suit to put on.

'*What*?'

He nodded. 'Got a glimpse of her before CSI moved in and erected the tent. Beth and I were just talking about who should be the one to go and tell the husband. We're thinking it should probably be her as she's already met him.'

'Agreed. And no point delaying it if you're sure it's her. We don't want him hearing it from anyone else.'

'I'll go now,' Beth said. 'Catch you later.'

Harry donned the protective suit, gave his name to the police constable guarding the scene and moved around the perimeter of the tape until he was close enough to catch Simon Winter's attention.

'Am I okay to come in?' he called.

The pathologist looked up and then over at the cameraman, who was taking photos outside the tent. 'How are you doing, Graham? Can D I Briscombe come in?'

'As long as he stays close to you and sticks to the footplates.'

Harry lifted the tape and approached the tent cautiously. It was about thirty yards from the main trail.

'The body wasn't that obvious from the path, but the jogger apparently just caught sight of her foot. He was in a bit of a state by all accounts.'

'Not surprised. Geoff says it's Elena Mancini?'

'Afraid so. There doesn't appear to have been anything taken from her bag. Her phone and purse were still in there.'

Harry looked at the corpse. There was a transparent bag over her head, presumably preserving evidence from an open gash on the side of her head, and her hands were also bagged. But it was her. 'So close to the house. I saw her here yesterday, with Sylvia and Mia Carroll. What could have happened between then and now to warrant this? Was she killed here, do you think?'

'Can't say at the moment.'

'Estimation on time of death?'

'Well, going on pretty basic analysis, the body's cold and stiff and if you saw her yesterday, then that narrows it down. It takes between eight and twelve hours for the muscles to become fully stiff like this, and they stay that way for a further twelve to twenty-four, so I'd say latest time of death was probably around two o'clock this morning and earliest could have been any time after you saw her yesterday. I might be able to narrow it down a bit more back at the lab.'

'How was she killed?'

'Again, difficult to be precise, but she's certainly been struck hard in the face, and she's got a deep gash here on the side of her head which could have been caused by some sort of weapon or possibly an injury if she fell and banged it.' He peered out of the tent as the heavens suddenly opened. 'We'll need to get her back to the mortuary. Not much more I can do here and its bloody freezing. I'll update you when I've got more info.'

Harry raised the collar of his jacket and ran back to where Geoff was sheltering under a tree. He removed his protective coverings and shoved them into a bag that someone held out to him.

'Has anyone been to the house yet? Do we know if anyone's there?'

'There was a mini parked in the drive that we think is Mia's, but we thought we'd wait for you before telling them. We didn't want news leaking out prematurely. Uniform are already on the house to house though.'

'Good. Okay, we'd better go see who's there and hear what they've got to say for themselves. Find out the last time they saw Elena alive. There was no love lost between them all yesterday, that's for sure.'

It was Mia who opened the door, and she looked at Harry warily.

'Mind if I come in? Is your mum here yet?'

Mia looked over his shoulder. 'Looks like she's just arrived. Why?'

Harry turned and waited for Sylvia to join them.

'That was quick,' she remarked with some asperity. 'More questions already?'

'I'm afraid so.' He turned back to Mia. 'I don't know if you've noticed the police activity in the woods at the bottom of the garden?'

She frowned. 'No. What ... now you mean?'

He nodded and followed her into the kitchen where Paul Cunningham was seated comfortably at the table reading the newspaper. Mia walked over to the window and peered out.

'Right. I can see signs of activity down there. What's happening? Why are they there?'

'I'm sorry to have to tell you this, but it looks like Elena may have been murdered.'

He watched their reactions carefully. They all looked shocked, but who was to say how genuine those reactions were.

'Oh my God,' Mia gasped. 'Who would do that?'

'Can you tell me what time she left here yesterday?'

They exchanged glances, and it was Sylvia who answered. 'It was a little after four if I remember rightly. We allowed her to stay until the executors had been.'

'And were they still here when she left? Did they see her go?'

'No. She went to pack her belongings so that she could come back with her husband at the weekend to pick them up. She probably left an hour or so after them.'

'And nothing unusual happened while she was here?'

Mia looked at her mother, who shook her head and spoke. 'No. Obviously, she wanted to know if she was still in the will, so she sat in on the discussion with the executors. As it happens, she did better than all of us as I'm sure you know. A hundred thousand pounds. For the cleaner!'

'She was a bit more than that, Mum,' Mia said. 'She'd worked for Aunty Barbara a long time and, to be fair, she did a good job. She was more like family to her.'

Her mother sniffed. 'That's as maybe but she told you she was leaving you over a million and you get a paltry fifty thousand. Whatever happened to proper family ... blood being thicker than water, and all that?'

'So, she left about four, you say? Did she walk? Take a taxi?'

'I gave her a lift to the station,' Paul said smoothly. 'She was upset, and it didn't feel right sending her off in a taxi.'

'Where did you drop her and what time?'

'Barnet station. I don't remember the exact time. Around four-twenty or four-twenty-five?'

'Did you return here afterwards?'

'Not straight away. I went back to my flat and did some work from there. Then I came back here about seven for supper, and Mia and I headed back to mine sometime after ten. There was a lot to talk about as you might imagine.'

'The fact that Mia only got fifty thousand pounds and not a million?'

'That was part of it, yes. It was obvious Barbara was losing her marbles; she'd become very forgetful and vague these last few months, and somewhat paranoid; although she did have odd days when she seemed quite normal. She originally told Mia she was leaving her more than a million pounds. Mia's lived with her here, helped her out as much as she could. She deserves that inheritance. It's not as if Barbara couldn't afford it. I've told Mia I think her mother's right, she should contest the will.'

'There's no need to go into this now,' Sylvia cut in firmly. 'Have you got any other questions, Inspector?'

Harry turned back to Paul. 'What did Elena talk about in the car? Did she say where she was going?'

'Very little was said. She wasn't exactly happy with her situation. I assumed she was going home.'

'Where exactly did you drop her?'

'On the main road, a little up from the path to the station. There was a big traffic jam going down the hill, she said it would be quicker for her to walk from there.'

'Okay, thanks.'

Harry looked at them all. 'In view of what's happened I can only advise you that I still think it safer for you not to stay overnight here. Obviously I can't force you, but it would be my strong recommendation.'

Sylvia gave a shudder. 'Don't worry, I wouldn't stay here now if you paid me. What do I care if it gets broken into? None of it's coming our way. It's all going to be sold or auctioned off, with the proceeds going to charity. Did you know that she left the bloody gardener twenty thousand pounds? I mean, we were beginning to suspect she was losing it, but for god's sake, she's only known the man a few months. I've already contacted my solicitor about challenging her will. Her memory wasn't good, and her sanity was clearly compromised.'

'Her solicitor seemed to think she was of perfectly sound mind.'

'And she could be. She had moments of lucidity but a lot of the time...' She shrugged. 'It was quite sad to see.'

'Where will you all be if we need to contact you again?'

'Mia will be at mine,' Paul said, and Sylvia glared at him.

'I'm not sure that's a good idea. We've got a lot to organise, and it would be better if she stayed with me, certainly for the time being.'

'Why don't we let Mia make her own mind up?' Paul said, looking at Mia.

She looked uncomfortably from one to the other, then said quietly. 'I'll go back with Paul, but I'll call you, okay?'

Her boyfriend smiled his satisfaction and rose from his seat. 'I'll just put our cases back in the car. Are you coming, Mia?'

Sylvia watched as Paul left the room, then stopped her daughter from following him with a touch on the arm. 'I wouldn't put all your eggs in that basket,' she advised quietly. 'He's a chancer. Can't you see he's only after you for the money? Tell him you're not contesting the will and see how keen he is to stay with you then, once he hears you're not about to become the millionairess he was expecting. I doubt you'll see him for dust.'

Mia shook her mother's arm off and glared at her. 'That's a horrible thing to say. And you wonder why I don't want to come and live with you?'

She turned to Harry. 'You know where to find me if you need me and you've got my mobile number. I'm back at work tomorrow.'

'That's fine. I'll be in touch if we have anything to report.'

CHAPTER
TWENTY-FOUR

B eth watched helplessly as Lorenzo Mancini's legs collapsed beneath him and he clutched at the arm of a chair before sinking
into it. His shoulders crumpled. He was a large man, but he looked
totally broken as he buried his head in his hands and rocked back and
forth.

'It cannot be,' he said finally, tears in his eyes as he looked up at her.
'I only spoke with her yesterday morning.'

'I'm so sorry. Is there anyone I can call to come over and be with
you?'

'I ... uh ...' He fumbled in his pocket and pulled out a phone with
shaky fingers, speed dialling a number. 'My son. He will come.' As
soon as it was answered, he broke into Italian, the tears streaming
down his face.

This was the part of her job that Beth hated the most, and she
moved over to the window to give him some privacy. On the win-
dowsill was a photo of Elena with her husband and a younger man.
Lorenzo stood proudly between them, an arm encircling them both
and she felt an unexpected stab of envy at the family unity portrayed in
that picture – even if it was somewhat misplaced bearing in mind that

Elena and her husband spent most of the week apart. There hadn't been a single family photo exhibited in Beth's home. Her parents weren't into soft stuff like that.

"Elena and our son, Matteo,' Lorenzo's broken voice came from behind her. 'It was taken three years ago for our silver wedding anniversary.'

The tears streamed down his face again and Beth led him gently back to his chair. 'I'm so sorry, Mr Mancini. This has come as a terrible shock to you, I know, but I promise you we'll do our best to find out exactly what happened to your wife. Can I get you a drink of some sort? Tea, coffee?'

He shook his head.

'I do need to ask you a few questions, I'm afraid. I'll keep it as brief as I can.'

He nodded.

'You said you spoke with Elena yesterday morning, but didn't you see her yesterday when she came home?'

He frowned. 'Why would I see her then? She does not come home until the weekend – Saturday morning.'

'She didn't call you then, yesterday afternoon, to tell you she'd been fired from her job?'

He looked shocked. 'No.'

'I'm afraid the family told her they didn't need her anymore. We were there yesterday, and she was waiting to see the Executors for the will, after which it was our understanding she was coming home. It's possible things changed, but it seemed pretty final that that was her plan.'

'I knew nothing of that. And Elena did not deserve to be treated in such a way after so many years working for Barbara – although nothing that woman, Sylvia, does surprises me. She and her daughter only became concerned about Barbara after Roy was killed. It was obvious they were only interested in her money, whereas my Elena, she loved Barbara as a good friend.'

'So, just to get things clear, Mr Mancini, when was the last time you saw your wife?'

'Monday morning, when she left here as usual to go to work. The last couple of days when the police were checking the house, she stayed with our son in Cockfosters, because it's nearer than here and she was determined to return to Barbara's house as soon as possible to keep an eye on things.'

Further evidence of a lack of closeness in their marriage? Beth couldn't help wondering. It was only a matter of a few miles difference. Yet the man's grief seemed genuine. 'There's a family liaison officer on the way,' she said 'She'll stay for as long as you need her, but I'll hold on now until your son gets here and speak to him about Elena's exact movements. Are you sure I can't make you a drink of something while we wait?'

He sighed. 'Perhaps a cup of coffee, black? There is a cafetiere near the kettle. Please make one for yourself, too.'

Beth took her time preparing the coffee and while she made it, she thought. The options seemed simple enough. Elena either left heading for home, her son's home or elsewhere.

Or maybe she never left at all.

She took the coffees through and watched as Lorenzo went to the cabinet and poured a generous measure of brandy into his cup. He offered the bottle to her, and she shook her head. 'I'm on duty,' she smiled.

It was some twenty minutes later before she heard a key being inserted into the lock.

'Papa?' The voice was urgent.

'Matteo, we are in here.'

A rather good-looking man, possibly late twenties, rushed into the room. He bent to embrace his father on the chair for a long moment, before straightening up and turning shocked eyes towards Beth.

'DC Mackaskill,' she introduced herself.

'What's happened? My father told me that my mother...'

'I'm very sorry,' Beth said. 'But we found your mother's body this morning in the woods at the back of Barbara Harding's house. We believe her death is suspicious.'

'No.'

His face crumpled as he turned back to his father and sat down next to him. Beth gave them a few minutes to console each other.

'They say she left Barbara's house yesterday to come home,' Lorenzo said to his son. 'But she never arrived.'

'I understand your mother was staying with you while the house was undergoing forensic examination?' Beth said. 'Did anything suspicious happen while she was there? Did she seem anxious or worried about anything?'

'Only the fact that Barbara had been killed. Obviously she was upset about that, but nothing else I can think of.'

'Were either of you aware that Barbara had changed her will?'

'No.'

They answered in unison.

'When was the last time you saw your mother, Mr Mancini?' Beth asked Matteo. 'Please be as accurate as possible.'

'Yes, of course, that's easy. It was yesterday morning. She'd given her number to one of the policemen guarding the house and asked him to call her when it was clear to return. She received a phone call on Tuesday evening, to say that she was free to return the following morning if she wanted to. She had breakfast with us yesterday, and I dropped her off at the bus stop at about nine o'clock.'

'And you live and work where?'

'Cockfosters. My wife and I own a restaurant there. We live in the flat above it.'

'And you didn't see or hear from your mum after that?'

'No.'

'You didn't know then that she'd been sacked?'

His eyes jerked towards his father, before he shook his head. 'Are you serious? Can they do that?'

'I can't comment on the legalities of it, but they did it.'

He shook his head in disgust. 'Barbara would be turning in her grave if she knew that. She never did trust them.'

Okay.' Beth got up from her chair. 'I'm sorry, but as I said, we're treating your mother's death as suspicious and will be launching a murder enquiry. We'll probably need to ask you some more questions, but I'll see if I can get someone over here to save you having to come down to the station. They'll take formal statements and your DNA and fingerprints, so that we can eliminate you from our enquiry. I think I already left you one of my cards, Mr Mancini, but ...' She handed another one to Matteo. 'Just call the number on there, if you think of anything else we should be aware of.'

Matteo took the card. 'Thank you. You've been very kind.'

'You find who did this to my wife,' Lorenzo said, his eyes misting over again. 'Please?'

'We'll do our best, I promise you.'

And they would, she thought, determination creasing her brow as she made her way back to her car. She'd liked what she'd seen of Elena Mancini, and the poor woman hadn't deserved to die like that. Life could be so cruel, and so random. Alive one day, dead the next. It didn't bear thinking about.

Forty minutes later, she was back at the station, perching on the edge of Harry's desk. He looked up from the file he was studying. 'How did it go with Elena's husband?'

'He was devastated. I hate giving news like that.'

'Did he have anything useful to say?'

She shook her head. 'He didn't even know she'd been sacked.'

'What?'

'She hadn't told him. She's apparently been staying with her son in Cockfosters this last couple of days while the house was sealed off. The husband hadn't seen her since Monday morning when she left and wasn't expecting her back until Saturday as usual. Maybe she was saving the fact she'd been fired to tell him in person.'

'So, she didn't go home yesterday. I suppose she could have gone back to the son.'

'Not according to him, she didn't. Mr Mancini phoned the son when I broke the news, and he came straight over.'

'What did he have to say?'

'Just that Elena had been staying with him while forensics were doing their stuff and left early yesterday morning once she was given the all-clear to return. He dropped her off at the bus stop and says he hasn't seen or heard from her since.'

'You believe him?'

'Who knows? No reason not to. He seemed genuine enough.'

'Make sure her phone records are being checked to see if she called anyone yesterday. She must have gone from Barnet to somewhere and the obvious place from that station would be Finchley, where she lived. If she didn't go there, we need to know why not, and where she went instead. Was it because she had a reason to go somewhere else or was she forcibly prevented from going home?'

'How did you get on with the Carrolls?'

'They seemed shocked by the news, but again, who knows? They weren't happy about the change of will and say they're going to contest it on the grounds of Barbara's soundness of mind. The mother was particularly put out by the fact that Finn Abara had been left twenty thousand pounds.'

Beth gave a low whistle. 'Does he know that, do you think?'

'Don't know, but if he does, it gives him an added motive for Barbara's murder. But it seems to me that they've all got motives. Finn because that would be a huge amount of money to someone like him; Sylvia and Mia because Mia was in danger of losing her potentially very large inheritance, and even Elena, for the same reason. It seems that Barbara wasn't slow in threatening all of them with disinheritance at one time or another, and if one of them got wind of the fact she was meeting the solicitor...'

'Except that we can rule Elena out now.'

'True. But what motive could there be for murdering her?'

'Maybe she found something out and had a hold over someone? Or, if Sylvia was sounding off about contesting the will ... Elena was very protective of Barbara. She wouldn't have made it easy for them to challenge it. Could have been a row that got out of hand and now they're all covering it up? How did you get on looking into the death of Sylvia's first husband?'

'It was interesting, and clear that his first wife and son suspected Sylvia of having something to do with the fire that started. But nothing concrete. I've written some notes on it here if you want to take a look. Then I think, hand them over to Dave, to dig deeper.'

She took the file from him. 'So, are we thinking it's definitely one of our little group?' she asked.

Harry sighed. 'Who knows? Most murders are committed by someone known to the victim, as we both know. However, we still have the added complication of the recent burglaries in the neighbourhood, and we could really do with getting an answer as to who's responsible for those. Maybe Elena had her suspicions about those and that's why she was silenced? Whatever, we need to speed up the background checks on everyone currently in the frame. Has everyone been DNA'd now?'

'I think so, but I'll check it out. I did wonder about Birdman across the road. We haven't given up on him, have we?'

'Definitely not, but there's no law against having a telescope in your room and we need something more concrete than that to bring him in. No harm adding him to the list for background checks though. In fact, I might look at him myself. Priority I think, is to check Elena's phone log and CCTV at Barnet station. We need to know where she went after Paul dropped her off – if he did. We're losing valuable time on all this.'

'Okay, I'll get onto that.' Beth hopped off the desk. 'By the way, you've remembered I've got my dad's funeral tomorrow? Geoff offered to come with me, but I feel bad dragging him away with all this going on. I'll tell him not to worry.'

'We can probably manage...'

'Don't worry about it. It's probably better I go on my own, anyway. I'll speak to him.'

CHAPTER
TWENTY-FIVE

H arry logged out of the search he was doing on Birdman and switched off his computer. Nothing much of interest, except that he'd once been accused of spying and taking pictures of a young couple making out in some woods. He'd said he'd been bird watching and had been let off with a caution. Not a lot to go on.

He looked at his watch. Seven o'clock. He couldn't put it off any longer. His mother had texted him two hours ago saying that they'd arrived safely and had let themselves into his house. 'Boeuf Bourguignon in the oven and will be ready for eight. Can't wait to see you.'

He felt sick to the stomach. He handled difficult situations every day, but how was he going to handle this one?

'I'm heading off,' he said to Geoff, who was poring over a host of newspaper articles on the Internet. 'Sorry you had to cancel going to Beth's dad's funeral.'

'No worries. You know our Beth. Independent with a capital I. Once she'd made up her mind that I was needed here more than there, it was a foregone conclusion. But she warned me I'd better not waste my time while she was gone, and that she expected me to come up with something ground-breaking by the time she got back.' He smiled, but his face showed concern. 'I must admit, I don't like the sound of her older brother.'

'She'll be fine,' Harry said. 'She's tough and from what she's told me, he's just a loud-mouthed bully. I'd back our Beth against him any day.'

'Yeah, you're probably right. See you tomorrow.'

Outside his house, Harry switched the engine off and took a deep breath. He looked at his surroundings, gaining a quiet comfort from them despite the heavy flow of rush hour traffic. The other houses lining the street, the convenience store across the road, the local church on the corner – all of it familiar to him in a way that gave him a sense of belonging he'd never experienced anywhere else. His parents had a house that they now rented out in Essendon and although he'd spent part of his early childhood there, it meant nothing to him. This was where his roots were, here in his grandparents' house, and he knew why. If it hadn't been for them stepping into the gap, he probably would have spent half his holidays at school with the other poor sods who couldn't go home for whatever reason. It had meant a lot when they'd left it to him.

He climbed reluctantly out of his car and walked up the path.

'Oh, it's so good to see you, Harry,' his mother greeted him with a warm hug, as he walked through to the kitchen. 'Dinner's ready, I'll serve it up now you're here.'

Harry braced himself as his father turned from the counter, where he'd been pouring himself a glass of wine. 'Harry. Good to see you. How are things? Busy as always, I'm guessing?'

Harry found himself stiffening as his father embraced him, unable to meet his gaze. 'Hi, Dad. Yes, things are pretty manic. How was your flight?'

'Good. Good.'

'Come on, you two. Ted, pour Harry a wine and come and sit down.'

'Not for me, thanks. I've got a non-alcoholic beer in the fridge. I'll have that in case I get called out.'

Harry poured it himself, making use of the time to compose himself. This was bad. He'd always got on okay with his father but now, he could barely look at him.

Somehow, he got through the meal talking trivia, but when his mother shooed them into the living room, insisting they have a bit of father and son time while she cleared up, he knew he couldn't keep quiet any longer. He was wondering how to broach the subject, when his father gave him the opening he needed.

'Everything all right with you? You've seemed a bit withdrawn since you came in. Work problems, or women problems? It's usually one or the other.'

'Not for everyone, it isn't, Dad. Though in your case, I can see it might have been.'

He heard the passive aggression in his tone. That wasn't good.

His father blinked at him. 'What's that supposed to mean?'

Harry looked him straight in the eye. 'I found something out this week, Dad...' He broke off and shook his head. He could tell from his father's expression that he had his full attention. 'How could you have kept quiet about it all these years?' he finished lamely.

For a long moment his father stared him out, before saying warily. 'What are you talking about?'

He knew, Harry could see it in his eyes, but he clearly wasn't going to come straight out with it.

'I'm talking about the affair you had, and–'

His father looked relieved. 'Oh, that,' he said quickly. 'Well, I don't know how you found out, but your mother knows all about it. I told her not long after it happened. It was a difficult period, but we came through it. Why would we tell you? You were only a baby at the time.'

'I'm not talking about the affair. I'm talking about the result of it ... Angela. My half-sister. Does Mum know about her too?'

He watched his father's face drain of colour.

'Who told you?' he finally asked.

'Angela. She turned up on my doorstep two days ago. How could you think it wouldn't come out one day?'

His father didn't answer.

'Did you know that her mother died recently?'

He could tell from his father's reaction that it was news to him.

'With both her parents dead now, she decided to get in touch with me. Can you imagine how that felt? For both of us? I'm still reeling.'

'Oh, God. I'm sorry, Harry, I don't know what to say – but we can't talk about this now. Mum will be in any minute and she can't know about this. It would break her.'

'Dad! What planet are you living on? This isn't something you can keep to yourself. You've got a daughter out there who needs you. You can't pretend she doesn't exist.'

His father looked harrowed. 'And I won't. I'll meet up with her, of course I will – and make sure she's okay. But you don't understand ... if your mother finds out now ... after all this time.'

'And whose fault is that?' Harry demanded angrily. 'If you'd been completely honest with her at the time–'

'I didn't know Rosemary was pregnant when I told Mum, and she was so devastated about the affair, that I just couldn't make things worse for her by adding that complication in when I found out. You mustn't tell her, Harry.'

Harry's body stiffened. 'You expect me to hide it from her? Be complicit with you and live a lie for the rest of my life?' He shook his head. 'I won't do it. She has a right to know, and Angela has the right to be fully acknowledged, not tucked away like some dirty little secret you're ashamed of. It wasn't her fault she was born.'

'Harry, you don't understand.' His father's eyes were desperate. 'It was weak of me not to tell Mum at the time, I know, but if she finds out about Angie now, it will be the end of our marriage. Is that what you want?'

Harry's mouth tightened. It jarred, his father using the softened version of his sister's name. It showed familiarity – confirmation, if it was needed, of the relationship that had existed between father and daughter.

'Of course it isn't,' he snapped, 'but you have to do what's right. That's what you've always told me. That we must face the consequences of our actions. And, if this isn't a prime example of that, I don't know what is. Angela and I intend seeing each other and I won't do that behind Mum's back. You need to tell her the truth.'

'Tell me the truth about what?' His mother's voice interrupted from the doorway. 'What's going on?'

Both men swung around in horror, and for a moment no one spoke. Then Harry said. 'I'm sorry, Mum, you need to talk to Dad about this and it's better I'm not here. I'll head off to Claire's for the night and give you some privacy'. He looked at his father. 'I'm sorry it's come out like this, but you need to deal with it and maybe it's for the best. We'll talk tomorrow.'

As he passed his mother, he dropped an awkward kiss on her forehead. 'I'm sorry to ruin your homecoming but we can get through this, all of us, if we keep our heads.'

'I don't understand.' She turned bewildered eyes on her husband. 'Ted?'

Harry squeezed her hand, reining his own emotions in. 'Just hear him out.'

Five minutes later, he'd shoved a couple of things into an overnight bag and was heading out. He could hear heated voices coming from the living room and felt bad walking away, but he hardened his heart. It was their discussion to have, not his.

His mind was full of it as he headed over to Claire's. He thought about calling her to warn her he was coming but it wasn't the sort of conversation anyone wanted to have over the phone. He just hoped she was in.

'Hey.' She looked surprised as she opened the door to him, and not that pleased. 'Have I missed something here?'

'No. Sorry to dump myself on you like this, but there's drama going on at home with my parents and I needed to get out from under their feet. I hope I'm not intruding?'

She hesitated, then opened the door wider. 'No. Come in.'

Her manner was offhand, and he hesitated. Something wasn't right. 'Are you sure this is okay? I don't have to stop if it's inconvenient. Or if you've got visitors?'

She shrugged and stepped back. 'It's fine.'

But she didn't sound fine.

'Hey, what's up?' He stepped over the threshold and dropped his bag, making to draw her into his arms, but she resisted him.

'Come into the kitchen and I'll get the kettle on. We can talk there.'

He waited while she went through the process of filling the kettle and switching it on, noting her set features, and when still she said nothing, he prompted, 'Claire? What's the matter? Have I done something to upset you?'

She turned to face him. 'I don't know, Harry. Have you?'

He frowned, trying to read her face. 'I don't think so.'

'I dropped round to yours last night. I thought you sounded a bit flat on the phone and thought I'd cheer you up with a takeaway. You were in deep discussion with some girl on your doorstep and then you put your arm around her, and you both went inside. It looked pretty intimate to me.'

The tight knot of tension that had balled in Harry's stomach dissolved in an instant, his face breaking into a relieved smile. 'Oh, God, is that it? It's the reason I'm here and it's a mess, but it has nothing to do with you and me. I needed to get away so my parents could deal with it.'

'Right.' Her expression was still frosty. 'So, who was she?'

'You're not going to believe this, but ... she's my sister.'

'What?'

Harry nodded and ran a hand through his hair. 'You can't be more surprised than I was. Gobsmacked is putting it mildly. Her name's Angela, and that woman ... the one whose funeral details I received? That was her mother.' He shook his head. 'It seems she and my father had a fling after I was born, and Angela was the result. I knew nothing about her, but now both her parents are dead I think she wanted to end all the secrecy.'

'So, it was her who sent you the obituary notice?'

'Yes. I'm still not sure why she chose to do it like that. Unless she suspected I already knew about her, which I didn't. At least ... I knew about the affair, but it came as a massive shock to learn I'd got a sister.'

'God, I bet it did.' All traces of Claire's anger had dissipated as she looked at him. 'What's she like?'

'Difficult to say after two meetings, but...' He shrugged. 'A bit lost losing both her parents, I think. I feel sorry for her.'

'You said you needed to get away so that your parents could deal with it?'

Harry nodded. 'Yeah. Mum knew about the affair but not about Angela. She overheard me tackling Dad about it. I told him I wasn't prepared to live a lie and that he needed to tell Mum – but I don't know, maybe that was the wrong decision. I'll feel terrible if this breaks up their marriage.'

'I don't see how you could have said anything different. He must have known it would come out one day.'

'I don't think he let himself think about it. I'm sorry you had to find out the way you did, though.'

Claire sighed, then grinned. 'Well, I'm just glad it wasn't an ex, deciding she'd made a big mistake breaking up with you.'

'Were you jealous then?'

'No.'

'Liar.'

'Big head.'

She laughed and moved over to the oven. 'Well, I didn't feel like eating the curry last night, so I was about to have it now. I know you've eaten, but do you mind if I scoff this lot in front of you? And I've got an open bottle of wine here if you want to pour us a glass.'

He watched as she pulled the dishes from the oven.

'I reckon I could force myself to help you out with some of that. I didn't eat much at mine, I was too worried about the conversation I knew was looming with Dad.'

'In that case, make yourself useful and lay the table. And try not to dwell on it. They'll have their conversation and what will be, will be. It's their problem to solve, not yours. Let's just hope they can work it out.'

He closed the gap between them and relieved her of the dishes, placing them carefully on the worktop. Then he pulled her in for a hug. 'Thanks, Claire.'

She succumbed for a moment, before drawing back and angling him a look. 'What for?'

He dropped a kiss on the tip of her nose. 'For being you.'

She poked him in the ribs. 'You just want to get laid.' But he could see she was pleased.

And he meant it. He'd had numerous girlfriends over the years but none of them had penetrated his outer skin like Claire had done. She was solid as a rock, and from the very beginning, when he'd met her as his gran's carer, there'd been something about her that had set her apart from the crowd. He'd responded to her on a level he hadn't experienced before, and it was an eye opener. When he'd screwed up first time around, he'd kicked himself hard. He'd be eternally grateful that he'd been given a second chance – and while it was still early days, he resolved that if things didn't work out it wouldn't be because of him. He'd had numerous relationships stall at the starting line because of his commitment issues, but Claire was living proof that he was as capable as the next person of forming a solid relationship, and for that knowledge alone, he could kiss her a thousand times.

'Of course, I want to get laid,' he grinned, heading for the cutlery drawer. 'But first things first. I know better than to come between a girl and her food.'

CHAPTER TWENTY-SIX

Alyssa was sitting up in bed, unable to sleep, looking at the phone Conn had given her. She must only use this phone for calls to him or for anything to do with him, he'd said. Did that mean she could use it to call Hayley if it was to do with the job they were doing tomorrow? She didn't know, but she was getting more and more anxious about what they were about to do. She kept remembering how Finn had said Conn was a drug dealer. What if it was to do with drugs, this job he had for them? She needed to speak to her friend.

She put the phone down and picked up her own mobile.

'Hello?' Hayley's voice was thick with sleep.

'It's me. We need to talk.'

'What about?'

'Tomorrow. I don't want to go through with it. I keep remembering what Finn said about the drugs. I don't want to get involved in that sort of stuff.'

'Alyssa, we can't back out now. Conn'll go mental.'

'I know. But he can't force us to do it. I'll phone him if you like and tell him.'

'No. We're getting a hundred quid for this job. Have you ever had as much money as that? Cos I haven't. Think what we can buy with it.'

'It won't be any use to us if we get caught and go to prison.'

'That ain't gonna happen.'

'How do you know? It could.'

'Conn's too clever. And anyway, we don't even know that it is drugs. It could be anything. He didn't say what it was.'

'It just feels *wrong*.'

'A hundred quid though. We've never had that sort of money. Look, do this one job and then if you want to stop afterwards you can. But you know what? I'm not sure I care if it's drugs or not. If people are stupid enough to want to take them that's their problem. What chance have we got of making money like that anywhere else? And Conn's our mate, look how he helped you with Vanessa – he's important around here and he'll look out for us.'

'Yeah, well that's not what my brother says. He says we should steer clear of him, or we'll get into big trouble, like he did.'

'Oh, Lyssa. Please don't back out now. I've never done anything like staying away before and I'd be scared doing it on my own. We've always been there for each other, haven't we? Just do it this one time. Please?'

'Goldie and your mum will kill us when we get back. They'll be really worried about where we are. I'll probably get grounded for a week.'

'Me too, but it will be worth it for a hundred quid. Just think about that. And we can always text them that we're okay.'

There was a long silence before finally Alyssa gave a big sigh and spoke. 'All right, but just this once, and I mean it. Then I'm done.'

'Yay! We can go shopping at the weekend. What are you going to buy with yours?'

Alyssa tried but couldn't work up any excitement at the prospect. She couldn't shake off the premonition that something awful was going to happen to them. But she'd committed herself now.

'I'll see you tomorrow,' she said. 'Did Conn give you the train tickets?'

'No, he's giving them to us in the morning when he takes us to the station. Don't say anything to anyone, remember.'

'Yeah, yeah.'

Alyssa clicked off her phone. Just this one time, she told herself.

———

The next morning, she silenced her alarm and lay there for a moment looking up at the ceiling. She tried to ignore the knot in her stomach that told her quite clearly she shouldn't be doing what she was about to do. Stevenage wasn't somewhere she knew. It felt so far away and alien, even if it was only a few stops on the train. The knot twisted. What if they missed their stop? Or what if they didn't get picked up at Stevenage when they got there? Her thoughts were running away with her, and she was grateful for the distraction of her phone ringing.

'Just checking you're all right?' Hayley said.

'Yeah. I feel nervous though.'

'Me too, but we'll be fine. We'll be together and if the worst comes to the worst, we just phone home.'

'Yeah. You're right. Finn and Goldie would be cross, but they'd always come and get us.' The knowledge comforted her. 'I'll meet you at the end of Park Road in an hour then. That's where Conn said he'd pick us up, isn't it?'

'Yeah. You will be there, Alyssa? You won't let me down and not turn up?'

'Course not. I wouldn't do that. I'll be there. Promise.'

She disconnected and threw back the bedclothes. Well, that was it, then. There was no going back now; she couldn't break her word. So, she might as well try and look on it as an adventure.

Half an hour later, Finn walked into the kitchen as she was eating her breakfast. 'Why aren't you wearing your uniform?'

She looked up from her Cheerios. 'Dress-down day,' she said breezily.

'Oh right, they still have those?'

'Course they do.'

She felt bad lying, but not as bad as she had when she'd lied to Goldie about doing her homework over at Hayley's. Did that mean she was getting better at it? It wasn't a nice thought. 'Are the police leaving you alone, now?' she asked.

'I hope so. But I'll tell you something for nothing. Once you get on the wrong side of the law, they never leave you alone. Just you remember that.' His look was penetrating. 'Everything all right with you? You've seemed a bit down this last couple of days.'

'I'm fine.'

'Good. But I'm here, you know that, if you need me? I remember what it was like being your age. Lots of pressure from different areas, but there ain't nothing we can't solve together. Just remember that.'

'I'm fine,' Alyssa repeated, resisting the urge to tell him everything. She wanted to tell him, knew he'd sort it, but Hayley would be mad at her, and she was frightened of what Conn might do if she didn't turn up. He was their friend, but she knew from other people that he didn't like being messed around. And what if Finn took it on himself to have things out with Conn and his mates, and they turned on him? She wished she'd never got involved with the gang, but it was too late to undo it now. She'd stick to what she'd decided … she'd do this one trip with Hayley and no more.

'I'm off now,' she said, scraping back her chair before she could change her mind. 'I'm meeting Hayley.'

'That's early.'

'It's her mum's birthday coming up. I'm gonna help her choose a present.' *Another lie.* 'See ya later.'

'See ya, kid.' Her brother ruffled her hair as she walked past him. 'Have a good one.'

Fifteen minutes later, she and Hayley were climbing into the back of Conn's car and heading for Hatfield station. Alyssa was subdued, the guilt of knowing how worried Goldie and Finn would be when she didn't come home, sitting heavily on her.

'I've put a rucksack each on the back seat for you both,' Conn said. 'They got drinks and a snack in'em, as well as your train tickets and a couple of packages I want you to give to Jake when he picks you up. He'll take you to the hotel and the rest of the day is yours to do what you want with. I've booked you a couple of treats - haircuts and a makeover – and you'll find some different clothes in your room for you to wear tonight. There'll be a few of my mates there, relaxing and having a bit of fun before a business meeting we're having tomorrow. You'll meet them at lunch time, and they're not from round here so be nice to 'em, and at dinner tonight, you can dress up and act like my hostesses. Reckon you'd enjoy that?'

Alyssa frowned. 'What will we have to do?'

'Nothing to get nervous about, just chat with my mates and get to know 'em a bit better. There'll be a couple of older girls looking after you. You'll have a great time. How old are you? Thirteen, fourteen? And I bet everyone still treats you like kids. Well, you ain't kids. You're growing up and there's a great life for the taking. Much better than being stuck in school for the next few years, I can tell you. Right, here we are...'

He swung the car into the station forecourt and jumped out.

'Just look out for Jake when you get to Stevenage, and I'll see you later this afternoon.'

'Why couldn't we have gone with him later, in his car?' Hayley asked, as they made their way to the ticket barrier.

'Dunno. Maybe the packages had to be delivered before then.'

Or maybe he didn't want to be caught with them in his possession, she found herself thinking.

Hayley's eyes met hers, her own anxiety reflected back in that look. 'What's in 'em, do you think?'

Alyssa shrugged, feeling uneasy again. 'Dunno and I ain't opening them to find out.'

CHAPTER TWENTY-SEVEN

B eth climbed into the taxi and gave her mother's address in a small village just outside Newcastle. It was late morning, and she was knackered. The funeral was at mid-day, and she'd been up since the crack of dawn to catch the train. She sank back in the seat and made herself do the deep breathing techniques she'd been practising. It angered her that just coming home could have such a negative effect on her. Familiar landmarks and sights in the countryside flew by, and she felt nothing – just an enormous sense of relief that she'd moved away. Soon she'd have to face her mother and older brother. She could do this. She was her own person, and they had no control over her now. She wondered if her younger sister, Isi, was already there and hoped she was. It would help with the balance of power. She closed her eyes and allowed sleep to catch up with her and next thing she knew, she was pulling up outside the small council house she'd grown up in.

Even though she still had a key, she rang the bell. It was Isi who answered it, and they stared at each other for a long moment before Beth's face softened and she reached out to pull her younger sister in for a hug. There was a moment's hesitation before she felt the returning pressure.

'How's it going?' she whispered.

'Nightmare. I got here an hour ago and Mum was already pissed. I reckon she's been on the booze since breakfast. We've got an hour to sober her up before the hearse arrives. Mitch is brewing some coffee now.'

Beth walked through to the living room, where her mother was sitting in her usual chair smoking a cigarette. She looked at Beth dispassionately. 'You've put on weight.'

'Hi, Mum.' Beth sighed. 'I had a medical. They told me I was too thin, so yeah, I've been trying to put some weight on.' She didn't add that being underweight had been a side effect of the anxiety she'd grown up with. That now she'd moved away, despite the pressures of her job, she'd found it only too easy regaining her weight.

'Coffee, Beth?'

She looked up as her older brother, Mitch, walked into the room, two mugs in his hand. He held one out to her, his expression impassive.

'Thanks.'

'Good of you to turn up for the funeral, even if you couldn't make it to see your pa when he was ill and dying.'

'No one told me he was dying. And anyway, he wasn't. Isi said it was a massive heart attack and unexpected.'

'Yeah. But you'd have come if you'd known he was dying, right?'

She shrugged.

'He was your father,' her mother shouted. 'Does that mean nothing to you?'

'He hated me.'

'You're talking rubbish, girl.'

'I'm not, and you know it. How many trips to the hospital did I have because of him? From when I was a little lass right up to when I was seventeen? That was the last time he raised a hand to me, because

I swore to him then that if he ever touched me again, I'd report him to the police.'

'It weren't his fault, it were the drink. You know what he was like when he'd had a few. And you pushed all his buttons, you did. You and your uppity ways – right as a little girl, you looked at us as if we weren't good enough for you. It wound him up, so it did, and me too. Toffee-nosed little brat. Listen to you now, with your posh London accent.'

'Mam, this is not a posh London accent. And that was just how I dealt with stuff. It was bad enough him beating me up, but worse that my own mother didn't stick up for me. Or my older brother,' she added, looking at Mitch.

He looked right back at her. 'Right chip on our shoulder, haven't we, pet?'

'No. But I've realised I don't need this shite in my life, and that's why I've settled down in London. I'm happy there.'

'Well, as long as our Beth's happy, that's all that matters, eh?' her brother replied. 'Don't matter what's going on up here with your poor mam, cos good old Mitch'll sort that one out. Isn't that the way of it?'

'I don't know how I'm going to manage,' her mother wailed into her tissue. 'He didn't leave a pot to piss in as far as savings goes. What am I supposed to do?'

Get a job?

For a horrible moment, Beth thought she'd said it out loud, and almost wished she had. It would be worth it just to see the shocked expression on her mam's face. She'd never had a job and had worked the system all her life. Beth couldn't help feeling that doing an honest day's work would be a tonic for her.

'Oh, for Christ's sake, Mam, shut up and drink your coffee. You need to sober up before the car gets here.' Mitch's patience was obviously running thin.

'Is someone doing a eulogy or something?' Isi asked.

'Yeah, me and Beth,' Mitch answered. 'I'm doing the reading and she's doing the eulogy.'

'No way,' Beth said.

'It needed two people and as bloody Ryan's not made the effort to come, you're next oldest.'

'I don't care. I won't be a hypocrite. Isi can do it.'

'Your name's on the Order of Service now.'

'Well, you had no right to do that without speaking to me first.'

'Oh, yeah, lass. Like you'd have picked up, if I'd called you.'

'Mitch, I'm not arguing with you about this – and, believe me, no one would want to hear what I'd have to say about him.'

Mitch threw his hands up in the air. 'Jesus Christ, okay, you do the reading then and I'll do the eulogy. Though Christ knows what I'm going to say.'

'I'll say something,' their mother slurred. 'I should speak because he was my husband.'

Beth doubted her mam could even stand on her own, let alone deliver a speech. She shook her head in despair. It was like a scene out of a TV sit-com, except there was nothing funny about it.

'Fine. I'll do the reading and you do the eulogy,' she said to Mitch. 'Only, for God's sake, write something down and read it out. Don't make it up on the spur of the moment. I can't believe you haven't already done that.' She turned to her sister. 'Are you happy with that? If you want to do the reading...?'

'No way. But can we just sober our mam up? She can't go to the crematorium like this.'

Somehow, Beth got through the next three hours, but if ever she'd needed a reminder of why she'd made her life elsewhere, this was it. There hadn't been many people at his wake, maybe thirty or so, but the class of person there had spoken volumes about the company her father and Mitch kept. She'd take a bet that nearly every one of the men there had a criminal record, and their wives looked just like her mum ... downbeat, downtrodden, crushed by years of knowing their place and learning to turn a blind eye. They'd taken the mickey out of her no end, saying how good it was to have friends in high places, and who knew when they might need them one day. And she suspected they weren't joking, which unsettled her. As for her mum, despite trying to sober her up before the funeral, she'd hit the bottle again as soon as she could after it, and Beth experienced the same tightening of stomach muscles and anxiety she'd always felt seeing her mother like that. She couldn't get out of there quick enough, staying the bare minimum she had to, before taking her leave.

'You off already? I suppose it'll be another few years before we see you again,' Mitch sneered, lounging against the exit and stopping her in her tracks as she headed for the car park. 'Mam's funeral probably if you can be bothered to turn up for that one.'

'You don't want me here, Mitch, any more than I want to be here. We're different animals.'

'Yeah, well I might be a load of shite but at least I've looked out for Mam and Dad these last few years, which is more than can be said of you, pet. And no doubt it'll fall on me again to look after our mam now she's on her own.'

Beth's conscience pricked despite herself. 'If I thought I could be of any use I'd help, but our lives are polar opposites – you and Dad told me you'd never speak to me again if I joined the police and the few times we've met, you've done nothing to suggest you've changed your mind. I got the message loud and clear.'

'Yeah, well, if you can't help out on a personal level, pet, maybe you can help out financially? You must be earning a decent bob or two and Mam's a mess, you can see that. No savings to rely on now that Dad's gone.'

'She'll get a widow's pension and she's worked the system well enough up to now. Doubt that'll end in a hurry. And she's fifty-four – there's no reason why she can't go out and get a bloody job like everyone else. You get her to agree to do that and stop drinking, then maybe I'll help but I'm not throwing money at her just so she can drink herself to death. I need to hear it from her that she wants help, and it'll be practical help, not just financial.'

'Yeah, well she's not going to agree to that, the state she's in at the moment, is she?'

Beth sighed, knowing she'd regret every word of what she was about to say, but letting her guilt push her into giving it one more try.

'Speak to her. If she wants help sorting herself out, then get her to ring me and I'll see what I can do. But make sure she knows I'll only help her clean up if she wants to do it herself. If she feels she's being pushed it won't work.'

She turned to look back at the function room in the pub. 'How much did this lot cost?'

'The whole thing's set me back nearly three grand.'

'Okay, send me the bills, and I'll split it with you. But not a penny more for Mam unless she gets her act together.'

CHAPTER TWENTY-EIGHT

H arry sat at his desk and ran his hand through his hair. He looked at the various scribbled notes he'd written and the increasingly bigger file on the Barbara Harding case and didn't know what to tackle first. His email pinged and he clicked on the message. It was from Simon Winter, the pathologist. 'Still working on Elena Mancini, but thought you'd want to know that she wasn't killed on site. I reckon she was moved there. There were what looked like silk carpet fibres in her hair and in the wound. So, you're probably looking at a room with a coloured silk rug where she fell or was rolled up in carpet, if that's any help.'

It wasn't much, but it was something. Harry didn't remember seeing any silk rugs at Barbara Harding's house, but it was worth checking out.

He called across to Geoff. 'You busy?'

'Is that the trick question of the day?'

'Ha ha. Reckon you could take another look at Barbara Harding's house to see if there's a coloured silk rug there? They found carpet fibres in Elena Mancini's hair that would suggest she was killed somewhere else and then taken to the woods. The Harding house was the last known place she was before she died.'

'Will do. I've just had something interesting in from Dave. If you remember, we saw Connor Stephens' car on CCTV driving along the main road near the bottom end of Barbara Harding's road, the afternoon of her murder. He's now found images of two men getting out of the car up on the main road, at the top end of Beechwood Way, at seven-fifteen pm. They've both got holdalls and they return to the car at seven fifty-seven, which would tie in well with the neighbours' burglary that night. Dave's checking to see if uniform have got any CCTV for the previous burglaries in the area, but if they haven't, we should still be able to get hold of the most recent one before it gets over-written. I was about to go down to the incident room to see if I can recognise anyone from the images.'

'I'll come with you.'

But in the incident room the images were disappointing. 'Bloody hoodies,' Harry muttered, straightening up. 'And it's too dark to see anything properly. Could be anyone. But speak to Connor Stephens again – see what he's got to say for himself. And check that part of the road for earlier in the day, around the time Barbara was killed. They could have parked up there, walked down the footpath to her house and got in through the back garden, so whoever was driving that car is still very much in the frame for her murder.'

He looked up as Penny, from reception, popped her head round the door. 'Harry, I just took a call from a guy called Elliot Frith? He wanted to speak to Beth and said he had something suspicious to report about the Barbara Harding case. I told him she wasn't in today and offered to put him through to you, but he said it could wait. He'd rather speak to her.'

'Did he say what it was?'

'No.'

Harry sighed. 'Well, I could do with stretching my legs, I'm fed up sitting round here getting nowhere. Was he calling from home?'

'He didn't say, but I'd guess so, because he started off by asking if Beth could drop round to see him.'

'He's unemployed,' Geoff said, 'so chances are he'll be there.'

'Right, well I'll go and see him now and while I'm there I'll do that check of Barbara Harding's house for the carpet fibres. Let everyone know we'll have a team briefing at 5.30 pm sharp.'

***

Finn looked up from preparing his lunch, as Goldie walked into the kitchen, looking worried.

'What's up?'

'The school just rang. Alyssa's not gone in today and she bunked off yesterday afternoon too. They wanted to know if I knew.'

Finn frowned. 'Stupid girl. What's she playing at? She told me it was a dress-down day.'

Goldie sighed. 'I don't know. I'm worried about her. She's been different these last few days. Where the hell is she?'

'I'll call her.' But when he dialled her number, it went straight to voicemail.

'Hayley didn't go in either,' Goldie said. 'I've got her number, I'll try her.'

She pulled her phone from her pocket, but before she could look the number up, it rang. 'Oh, hi Sandy ... I know, I've just had a call too. They're not with you, then? We tried calling Alyssa but she's not picking up. I don't know, but I'm sure they'll be back ... of course. And you ring us too, if you hear anything?'

She hung up and looked at Finn.

'I'll go and look for them,' he said, getting up from the table. 'If you hear anything, call me.'

'Mr Frith?' Harry held up his card to the man who had answered the door. 'DI Briscombe, Hertfordshire police.'

The man squinted at Harry's card, then opened the door wider. 'Your sergeant couldn't come then? I felt comfortable with her.'

'She's not in today. Hopefully, you'll feel comfortable with me too. Can I come in?'

'I suppose so. My mum's resting, so come into the lounge. We won't disturb her there. Can I get you a drink of anything?'

About to say no, Harry noticed a multicoloured rug in front of the fireplace. 'A glass of water would be good, thanks.'

He waited until the man had left the room before quickly moving over to take a closer look. He was no expert on rugs and couldn't tell if it was silk or not. He hesitated. It would be so easy to pull a couple of threads to get them checked out, but it would be inadmissible as evidence without a search warrant. He'd just have to log it for future reference.

'So,' he said, when Frith returned. 'You have some information for us?'

'Just thought it was odd, you know? And the more I've thought about it, well ... thought I should give you a call.'

Harry waited.

'It was Wednesday night. Well, early hours of Thursday morning really. I'd got up because mum wasn't sleeping well and after I'd dealt with her I thought I'd take a look at the stars. It's a new hobby of mine and the sky was clear, which it often isn't. When I looked out of the window, I noticed a dark coloured car in Barbara's drive. It was parked up to the side entrance with the boot up. I waited, and a few minutes later some guy in a hoody comes back, closes the boot, and drives off. That's it.'

'Definitely a man?'

'Well, now you ask I couldn't say for sure. I assumed it was but could've been a woman I suppose.'

'Why didn't you call it in yesterday?'

'I was round at a friend's all day and only heard about Elena last night, when my mum told me. Terrible business. Was she murdered as well?'

'We're waiting for forensics to confirm cause of death.'

'Too much of a coincidence for it not to be, surely? And it happened right under your nose. Doesn't say much for you lot, does it?'

The smirk on his face was designed to wind Harry up and succeeded. He took a breath and counted to five before moving the conversation on. 'A dark car you say. Could it have been the same car you saw parked in the road on other occasions?'

'Couldn't say for sure, but it was similar. They were both hatchbacks.'

'And just one person?'

'As far as I could tell.'

'When was the last time you saw Elena Mancini?'

That wiped the smirk off his face. 'Why are you asking that?'

'Routine. Answer the question please.'

'Wednesday morning, when she came back to the house. We had a few words, that's all. She seemed fine.'

Another quick glance at the rug, and Harry headed for the door. 'Well, thanks for calling it in. If you remember anything else...'

'I'll call you of course,' the man said smoothly. 'I feel a responsibility now to keep a bit of an eye on the place. I hope you pull your fingers out and find whoever's doing all this. I won't be leaving my mum alone again for a while, that's for sure.'

'Very sensible,' Harry said.

He exited the house and nipped across the road to speak to the policeman standing guard.

'You're back on duty then?'

'Just keeping an eye on it for a day or two.'

'I'm going in to check something out. I won't be long.'

In the house, he went into every room, but nothing remotely resembling a silk rug could be seen. Barbara's bedroom was large and dual aspect, and he looked out of the window onto the back garden. It was a straight line from the side entrance down to the garden gate. It wouldn't have been that difficult to shift a body down there. Especially one as tiny as Elena Mancini. It wouldn't even have been impossible for a woman to have done it. Which did nothing to narrow their options down.

Outside, he pulled out his phone and called Geoff. 'Have you got hold of Connor Stephens yet?'

'We haven't been able to contact him. Someone went round to the house, and he wasn't there, and he's not answering his phone. I've left a voicemail asking him to contact us urgently to answer some more questions about his whereabouts last Saturday. We've also circulated his numberplate to uniform to pick him up if they see him.'

'Good. I've just seen Elliot Frith and he reckons he saw a car parked by Barbara Harding's side entrance in the early hours of Thursday morning, not dissimilar to the car he observed parked on the road. It could be that was when Elena Mancini's body was dumped in the woods. I'm going over to the mortuary to see if Simon's got anything more for us. I'll catch you later but let me know if you hear from Stephens.'

Simon Winter was working on Elena Mancini's corpse when Harry walked in. He replaced an instrument in the tray as Harry approached.

'Anything?'

The pathologist pointed to a vicious gash on the rear side of the woman's head. 'That's what killed her, and it's difficult to say whether it was deliberate or not. She could have been struck with some sort of weapon – although she'd also been struck by a fist first, I'd say, from the look of that bruise on her cheek – but she could just as easily have fallen from that blow and caught her head on something with a sharp edge. There's some red colouring in her hair that isn't blood, so I've sent it off for analysis. Could be paint or some sort of similar substance. There'd have been a lot of blood at the scene of the crime, that's for sure, so a lot of clearing up to do.'

'One of the neighbours saw a car parked up to the side entrance of Barbara Harding's house very early hours of Thursday morning,' Harry said. 'Any idea how the body got to the woods?'

'I'd say the three most likely possibilities are via Barbara's garden, or either end of the footpath. And of the three, I'd favour the garden route. It just seems too risky manoeuvring a body a significant distance down the footpath, even at that time of night. She's tiny though. A man could have just slung her over his shoulder to carry her.'

'Yeah, and I'm thinking even a woman could quite easily have dragged her there, which doesn't help much.'

'CSI went through the house again, but didn't come up with anything suggesting she was killed there. They're still working on the garden. I'm trying to process the most relevant information first, to see if we can get something really concrete for you. One thing I have noticed ... there are some older signs of injury. Her right arm has been broken as well as her left tibia and two ribs. I'd say they date back quite a while, but it might be worth checking her GP records to see if there's anything on file to say how she got them.'

'Domestic abuse?'

'It's a possibility. Worth checking out.'

'Okay, that's interesting, thanks. You know where I am if you need me.'

'Sure.' Simon was already turning away and reaching for his instruments. 'Don't hold your breath that anything's going to happen in a hurry, though. You're not the only one breathing down my neck.'

CHAPTER TWENTY-NINE

Alyssa and Hayley stood side by side, staring in awe at their reflections in the large mirror in their bedroom.

'Wow.' Alyssa said, turning sideways on to view her reflection. She was wearing a short, figure-hugging knitted dress in cream, with a low rollneck, that made her look far older than her fourteen years. 'I'd never think to buy something like this, but it looks cool doesn't it?'

'You look great,' Hayley agreed admiringly.

'And you do, too. I reckon we'd pass for at least eighteen, don't you?'

They giggled. 'All those clothes to choose from,' Hayley said. 'But weird we have to dress up for lunch. Especially when we're going for a swim and sauna afterwards. It's all so posh.'

Alyssa grinned. 'Yeah, it is, and we're gonna enjoy it while we're here. What time did Jake say our appointments were?'

'Three thirty, and he was coming to get us for lunch at one fifteen.'

Alyssa looked at her watch, and at the same time, there was a smart rap on their door. 'That'll be him now,' she said, feeling suddenly fidgety. 'Is this dress too short?'

'It's fine. Longer than mine,' her friend laughed.

Alyssa moved over to open the door, and Jake gave a low whistle when he saw her. 'You look fab, babe,' he said, his eyes running over her from top to bottom. 'You sure you're only fourteen?' He laughed and winked at her, and she felt the colour rise in her cheeks. He was fit, even if he was a lot older than her – mid-twenties, she guessed. But there was something about him that unsettled her.

'You girls ready to eat, now?'

Downstairs, in the smart lounge, she tried not to look too overwhelmed. But really, she'd only ever seen places like this on the telly.

'That's our table over there,' Jake said in a hushed voice, pointing over to where four men and two women were sitting, tucked away in a corner, looking at menus. 'Conn'll be here later, but he wants you to be nice to them, you know? Give 'em a bit of chat.'

Alyssa looked terrified at the prospect. They were old – in their thirties or forties at least. What on earth could she find to talk about that would be interesting to them?

'Don't look so worried,' Jake laughed. 'You'll be fine. They like young girls to cheer 'em up. Just smile and be polite —they'll do most of the talking. All you need to do is go along with what they say and keep 'em happy. One of them's come all the way from Devon 'cos Conn's hoping to spread his business further afield. Think you're up to helping him?'

Both girls nodded, but Alyssa battled a sense of unease as she felt Jake's hand in the small of her back, pushing her forward.

***

Finn let himself into the house, his anxiety spiked to a new level. He'd spent two hours scouring the neighbourhood for Alyssa and Hayley, with no sign of them at all.

'Any luck?' Goldie asked, coming into the hall.

He shook his head. 'I've tried everywhere. All the places I used to hang out. Nothing. And she's still not picking up.'

'Hayley's mum said she'd tried ringing Hayley's phone and heard it ringing upstairs in the bedroom. So, she hasn't even got hers.'

'There's not much more we can do,' Finn said. 'We'll just have to wait it out, but I'm telling you now, I don't care about upsetting her, she's going to get a right talking to when she gets back.'

'You and me both,' Goldie said grimly.

Finn's phone rang and he snatched it from his pocket. Conn.

'You alone?' Conn asked.

'Yeah,' Finn replied, walking up the stairs to his bedroom.

'Good. Cos listen, I need a favour. The cops left me a message saying they want to talk to me again about seeing my car last Saturday, and I need you to go in and confirm that you borrowed it that day and it was you in the car, not me.'

'I told you, I ain't lying for you again.'

'I think you will, mate, if you don't want anything to happen to that lovely little sister of yours.'

Finn's blood ran cold. 'What do you mean? Where is she? Is she with you?'

'Not yet, but she soon will be, and I can either choose to look after her ... protect her ... or let some not very nice stuff happen to her. Know what I mean? Young girl, very attractive, just on the verge of womanhood. Sort of thing that might appeal to some men.'

'You bastard. Where is she? If you hurt a hair on her head–'

'Calm down, Finn. It don't need to happen, mate. It's up to you, and you know what you gotta do. Think on it and call me back.'

The line went dead, and Finn stared at his phone, feeling sick. If Conn was in the room with him now, he'd kill him. But he wasn't, and the reality of the situation hit him hard. He had no idea where Alyssa was, or how to begin going about finding her. That left him no choice. The very thought of what they might do to her...

He called Conn back. 'I want proof that you know where Alyssa is before I do it. Where is she?'

'I ain't that stupid I'm gonna tell you that. But okay, I'll get someone to send you a picture. I'll tell him to make sure it's a real nice one.'

Quarter of an hour later, Finn made the call to DI Briscombe's office. The picture of Alyssa sitting on the knee of some fat bastard, in her swimsuit, had made his skin crawl, and he felt a raw fear for her, not knowing what she might be going through right this very minute. He knew his sister, and although she'd been trying to smile, she'd looked deeply uncomfortable – and he was powerless to help her.

He opened WhatsApp and sent her another message. 'Urgent, call me. You're not safe. Where are you? Wherever you are, get out of there now and I'll come and get you.'

He looked at his watch. The cops had wanted him to go straight in when he'd called, but there was no way he was doing that before he tried looking for Alyssa some more. He'd told them five o'clock to get them off his back. And if that clashed with him having to pick Alyssa up, then they'd just have to wait.

'You girls are doing well,' Jake said, escorting Alyssa and Hayley from the swimming pool back to their room. 'The boys all like you and that'll please Conn.' He looked at his watch. 'Come on, better get a move on. Mustn't miss the makeup and hair appointments. I'll take you up there. Who's got the card for the room?'

Hayley pulled it out and opened the door, and Jake settled in one of the chairs. 'Come on, then, chop chop, get them swimsuits off, and here...' He got up again and reached for the two towelling robes on the back of the bedroom door. 'Wear these with just your undies on. No one will know ... except me.'

He gave a wink and a smile that made Alyssa's stomach turn. She didn't know how she'd thought him fit. She thought about how he'd made her sit on that horrible man's knee down at the swimming pool. She could still remember the feel of the man's hands spanning her waist, stroking his fingers up and down her spine, telling her how lovely and soft her skin was. It made her want to puke just thinking about it. And Jake had just laughed – even taken a photo of them. He'd taken other pictures too of her and Hayley in their swimsuits. He was a creep and she wanted as little to do with him as possible.

She went to the wardrobe to pull out some clothes. 'It's alright, I've got a track suit here. I'll be back in a minute,' she said, heading for the bathroom. 'You coming?' she threw at Hayley, over her shoulder.

'Yeah, okay,' the other girl muttered, not looking at Jake and grabbing some clothes of her own.

Inside the bathroom, the two girls looked at each other. 'I don't like this,' Alyssa said in a low voice. 'Those men ... touching us like that and drinking all that alcohol at lunch. What are they gonna be like tonight, over supper, if they're like that already? What if we can't control them? We should never have come.'

'Conn'll be here tonight. He'll look after us.'

'But what if he doesn't?'

'He will. He's our mate. And you know what he's always saying about sticking by his mates. It'll be fine once he's here.'

That calmed Alyssa a bit, but she still said. 'I could phone Finn. Him and Goldie would come straight away to get us.'

'No you can't. We're not allowed to use those phones except for contacting Conn or Jake.'

'I know that, but I didn't do like they said. I didn't leave my own phone at home. I brought it with me. Didn't you?'

Hayley shook her head, but her expression cleared. 'That's all right then, isn't it? If we're not happy later, we can call your brother.'

A sharp rap on the door had them both jumping out of their skins. 'Hurry up in there, or I might just have to come in and get you. You'll miss your beauty slots if you're not careful.'

CHAPTER THIRTY

Harry got himself a coffee and made his way to the incident room, where several members of the team were busy compiling information and working their way through the seemingly endless log of things to be done.

'Anything on Connor Stephens yet?' he asked Geoff.

'He finally called back – said he was at a business conference if you can believe that and repeated that he didn't drive the car at all that day, it was Finn Abara. He said he'd talk to Finn and get him to call us, and that if we still wanted to see him after we'd spoken to Finn, then he'd come in. The good news is that Abara rang and admitted it was him driving the car. He volunteered to come in at five and I went along with that, but we've already got someone picking him up, on the pretext they were in the area and thought he might like a lift. Hopefully, he'll comply as he doesn't have a car himself.'

'Good thinking. We need to get this car business sorted.'

'I agree. By the way, Murray said he wanted to see you as soon as you got in.'

Harry sighed. 'Okay, I'll go now, but give me a shout when Abara comes in.'

Outside the DCI's office, Harry took a moment to gather his thoughts, then rapped smartly on the door and opened it.

'Ah, Harry. Come in and give me an update. I'm being chased, and it feels to me like things have stalled.'

'You know what it's like, Gov. We're still trying to piece everything together, but we've had a bit of a break-through in that Finn Abara has admitted to borrowing Connor Stephens' car, which was observed near Barbara Harding's road the afternoon she was killed. It was also picked up on CCTV that evening, on the main road up the other end of Beechwood Way. Two men in the car, both seen returning to it with rucksacks which could have contained goods stolen from a house that was burgled a few doors up from Barbara's. I want to get to the bottom of all that if I can.'

'So, Connor Stephens is out of the frame then? Well, that's good because I've had word from upstairs that we're not to touch him.'

'I don't think we can rule him out completely yet, Sir. He's a slippery customer and the second person in the car has yet to be identified. We can't tell from the CCTV exactly who it is in the car.'

'Be that as it may, my instructions are not to go anywhere near Connor Stephens. Apparently, the NCA are monitoring his activities, and to put it in their terms, they don't want us buggering up their investigation.'

'Well, I'll do my best to steer clear of him but if we begin to find evidence that clearly links him to one or both murders–'

'You'll tell me, and I'll make sure that anything you have is passed on. I know how annoying these situations are, Harry, but you need to toe the line on this one. You hear me?'

Harry sighed. 'I hear you.' His phone bleeped and he pulled it out. '*Call me.*' It was from his mother.

He scraped back his chair. 'Better get on – I want to check that CCTV again before I interview Abara. I'll keep you posted.'

Back at his desk, he looked at his mother's text again and hesitated. He couldn't deal with this now.

'Really tied up at work, but I'll see you later. Can we chat then?'

'*No*,' the response came straight back. '*I need to talk to you now.*'

He bit back an expletive and walked out to the fire escape off the main corridor. He dialled her number. 'Mum ... what's so urgent it can't wait?'

'My marriage, Harry. Remember? Do you really have to ask?' She'd clearly been crying. 'Or maybe it's no big deal to you?'

'Of course, it is–'

'Well, it doesn't seem to have mattered much to your father, does it? How could he have lived such a lie all these years? And what about you? Did you know about this ... this half-sister of yours, as well?'

'No, I was as shocked as you are. She only tracked me down after her mum died.'

'I don't know what to do.' She was sobbing down the phone, and Harry felt useless. He couldn't think of a thing to say to console her. 'Mum, it's a terrible shock for you, I know, but I'm sure it can be sorted. I'll try and help you work your way through things, but not now. I'm in the middle of a murder investigation, and ...'

'Oh, God forbid a small family matter like this gets in the way. When have I ever asked you for help, Harry? Surely there are times when family comes first?'

Harry reined in his frustration. In this job, nothing short of death qualified as a reason for that, but he didn't think telling her that would go down well. 'I'm sorry, Mum, I really am, but I have a suspect to question. Two people murdered – I can't just up and leave. I promise I'll come home as soon as I can.'

'Fine. I'm here at the house. Your father's moved into a hotel.'

Oh, crap. 'Okay, I'm sorry about that. I'll see you ...'

But he was talking to himself as the line went dead.

He walked back into the office.

'They've brought Abara in,' Geoff called out. 'He's in Interview Room One.'

'Good, he can stew for a bit while I check a couple of things out.'

He took his time, checking his notes and the CCTV, which he knew could be crucial to solving this case, before making his way unhurriedly up the stairs to the interview room.

He settled himself on the opposite side of the table to Finn and fixed him with a hard stare. 'So ... you have something to tell us?'

The man's returning look was equally hard, but there was something else in his expression too. Anger. He was controlling it, but it was evident from the tight draw of his mouth to the agitated jigging of his knee that it wouldn't take much to make him blow.

'Yeah, I've decided to come clean about the fact I was driving Connor Stephens' car. He did lend it to me that day.'

'And you lied, because...?'

'I ain't got a licence for cars. Only my bike.'

'Right, so let me just recap on what you've already told us. You turn up at Barbara's house first time around a little after two o'clock, on your bike, and find Barbara dead in her house. You panic and leave. But then, for some mysterious reason, you borrow Connor Stephens' car and return some three hours later. For what reason?'

'I'd calmed down a bit by then and started worrying I might have got it wrong and maybe she wasn't dead. I felt I needed to check.'

'And she was?'

He nodded.

'And then what?'

'I drove back to Conn's to return the car and went home.'

'You still chose not to notify anyone?'

Finn shrugged.

'Why did you borrow Connor Stephens' car rather than use your own bike? Was it so you could nick some of Barbara's stuff and stash it in the car?'

'No. I didn't nick anything. I just borrowed the car 'cos it was quicker than my bike.'

'And you then returned the car to Connor.'

'That's right.'

'So, perhaps you can explain this.'

Harry turned his laptop around so that Finn could see it. 'That's CCTV footage taken of Connor Stephens' car parked up on the main road at the top of Beechwood Way later that day. It shows two people leaving the car at 7.15 pm, and this bit ...' he fast forwarded '... shows the same two people returning to the car forty-five minutes or so later. Is that still you, and if so, who's that with you and what's in the bags?'

Finn didn't reply.

'There was a burglary in Beechwood Way around that time. It's possible you could have waited until the people left and then burgled them. Was it you and this unknown person who broke into the house?'

Finn shrugged.

'Is that a yes?'

'I don't want to say no more.'

'Or talk about what goods you stole?'

'No comment.'

'Or where those goods are now?'

'No comment. I borrowed the car and that's all I'm prepared to say.'

'But did you? You see, I'm not so sure that you did. I'd say that both those guys look a bit broader than you, and if I had to put a bet on it, I reckon the driver looks more like Connor Stephens.'

'It weren't him. I'd bulked up with extra layers because it was cold.'

'Right. Well, the tech guys are taking a closer look at these pictures, and we'll see what they come up with. But if it was you, then what were you doing there? Where did you go when you got out of the car?'

'There's a Costa's further up that road. We went to get a drink and a snack.'

'Who's we?'

'No comment.'

'We'll get to the bottom of this, you know. We'll go back now, trawl more CCTV, see if we can get pictures of you going into Costa's. Clearer pictures probably than the ones there. Why don't you just save us all a lot of time and tell me exactly what you were doing and who you were with?'

Finn gave him a considering look. 'I'll tell you when the time's right. But I got other things to do now that are more important. Can I go? I done what you wanted. I came in and admitted to borrowing the car.'

'But you've not given me much else, have you?' Harry's stare was penetrating, before he switched it to look at some papers on the desk. 'There's one other thing. Did you know that Elena Mancini was murdered yesterday?'

'*What*?'

He certainly looked stunned.

'Her body was found in the woods at the back of Barbara Harding's house. Where were you between the hours of around 4 pm Wednesday evening and early hours of Thursday morning?'

'Shit, you can't think that was me, as well, man? I was down the community centre with Goldie, helping out. She does a session there

Wednesday nights for the local kids. Plenty of people will have seen me.'

'Until what time?'

'Finishes at ten and then we clear up. I probably got home around 10.30.'

'Did you leave the house for any reason after that?'

'No. Ask Goldie, she'll tell you.'

'I'm sure she will.'

Finn shook his head. 'Elena murdered? Who'd want to do that? It gets crazier and crazier. She wouldn't hurt a fly.'

'Well, if you're not involved, then I suggest you put your thinking cap on and think who might be. I don't know what's going on, but I know something's not right. This business with the car. Does Connor Stephens have some sort of hold over you? Is that why you're protecting him? Or is it just because he's a mate?'

'Connor Stephens ain't no mate of mine.'

'So, he has some sort of hold over you?'

Finn clamped his mouth firmly shut and didn't respond.

Harry sighed and shut his notebook. 'Okay, Finn. You can go for now. But keep your phone handy. We'll want to talk to you again.'

CHAPTER THIRTY-ONE

J ake was waiting for Hayley and Alyssa as they exited from their appointments.

His smile was friendly. 'You girls alright? Haven't you tarted up well?'

Alyssa's hand moved self-consciously to her head. She'd never had her hair styled before, thinking it was a waste of time because her hair was curly, but the hairdresser had known exactly what she was doing. She'd taken some of the curl out, which made her hair look longer, and she loved it. And the way they'd done her makeup looked really grown up.

'We need to get you back to your room and changed into your posh gear again, and then we can join the others for some tea and cake. Here...' He pulled a bag of sweets from his pocket. 'Fancy a couple of these? They're just like Haribos.'

'Is Conn here yet?" Alyssa asked, taking two from the packet and popping them in her mouth.

'No. But he'll be here any time now. Everyone's just relaxing and getting to know each other before the more serious business stuff starts. And don't look so worried. You were both great earlier, the guys liked you. Carry on like that and Conn'll probably give you a bonus payment for keeping them happy. Cos that way, you see, they'll be more likely to agree to his terms.' He gave a wink and pressed the button for the lift.

Fifteen minutes later they came to a halt outside the Diamond Suite. Alyssa felt sick with nerves, her sense of unease refusing to budge. She tapped the little bag she was carrying for reassurance. At least she'd managed to grab her phone and slip it in without Jake noticing. If they were at all unhappy, she'd call Finn.

'Don't look so worried,' Jake said, offering them both another sweet before tapping on the door. 'They ain't gonna eat you. And I wouldn't let anything happen that you guys weren't happy with, okay? Just be yourselves and act nice.'

The rumbling in Harry's stomach reminded him that he hadn't eaten since breakfast, and it was going to be at least another half hour before the briefing finished and he could nip down to the canteen. He rummaged in his drawer, pulled out an ancient, half-eaten Twix bar and headed to the vending machine for a coffee. Then he made his way to the incident room where the rest of the team were waiting for him.

'Everyone here?' he asked, looking around.

'Except Beth,' Geoff said. 'She rang in about half an hour ago to say she's on her way back and the train gets into Hatfield around six-fifty.'

'She doesn't need to come in.'

'From the brief word I had with her, I think it's been a crap day and she wanted to come in for a bit of light relief.'

Harry grimaced. 'Fair enough. Right, so what have we got. Who's going first?'

'I dug deeper into the background behind Sylvia Carroll's first husband's death,' Dave Freeman said. 'Nothing concrete. We already know that the former family suspected foul play, but there was no evidence to support it. I went through the whole file, and I think the most we could pull from it, is that she was complicit in watching him drink himself into a stupor and, I suppose, it's possible she could even have actively encouraged that. I spoke to his solicitor, who confirmed he was going to change his will, but he died before it happened, and while that may have given her a motive, unless we were to come up with new forensic evidence, we can't prove the fire was anything other than an accident. I'll keep on it.'

'Okay. I'll leave it with you. Finn Abara has come forward saying he was the one in Connor Stephens' car on Saturday afternoon. I'm not sure I believe him, but with the CCTV footage of the same car up on the main road that evening, I think there's enough circumstantial evidence to impound it for forensics and see if we can link it to either the burglary that took place the day of Barbara's murder, or Barbara or Elena Mancini's deaths. At the very least, we should find some of Finn Abara's DNA if he did borrow it, which would help confirm things one way or the other. Geoff how have you got on?'

'I had a call from Barbara Harding's solicitor. She'd heard about Elena's death and wanted to let us know that if we needed a copy of her will, she had one in her office. It seems Barbara insisted Elena make a will a few years back and took her along herself, to do it. I asked what it said, and everything goes to her son, apart from five thousand pounds which she's left to her husband.'

'Only five thousand? I wonder if he knows that. And that's interesting because I saw Simon Winter earlier and he raised the possibility that Elena might have been the victim of domestic abuse. Check it out with her GP, see if there's anything in her records that they were aware of? It might explain why she's left everything to her son.'

'I've also been looking at the Mancini's,' Dave said. 'It seems Matteo had some behavioural issues as a child and was under a child psychologist. I've requested the full notes but the bits I've seen suggest his problems stemmed from an over-authoritative and aggressive father. There could be a pattern emerging here.'

Harry moved over to the board where each of the possible suspects had a column to their name and scribbled some notes under Lorenzo Mancini's name. Then he stood back and surveyed the list.

'Okay, so let's face it, it's looking more and more likely that it's one of these people that we're looking at.'

'Are we giving up on person unknown?' Geoff asked.

'Not completely. It's possible it's still a burglary that went wrong for Barbara's murder, and also possible none of these people are the culprits but, the sighting of Connor Stephens' car puts him and his mates firmly in the frame for the burglary, as well as Finn Abara. I can't see what motive they'd have for killing the housekeeper, though.'

'Could have found out something incriminating?' Dave Freeman suggested.

'It's possible.' He studied the names again. 'We're building quite comprehensive pictures on most of these people, but we're still quite light on Mia Carroll and her boyfriend. Can someone dig deeper into them? Sylvia made a very pointed jab at Paul while I was there, suggesting to Mia that he was only with her for the money he thought she'd inherit.'

'Brutal, but that wouldn't give them a motive to get rid of Elena,' Geoff said.

'Unless they were worried about her defending Barbara's mental capacity if they were going to challenge the will. It's all too vague though, we need facts and evidence, and we haven't got either. In fact, it feels like we've got bugger all, in the words of our esteemed boss.'

'I'll look into Mia and Paul,' Dave said, 'and I've got one other thing to add. Elena's phone records show she made three phone calls the afternoon she was fired. One to her son, one to you, Harry, and one to someone who we've just traced as a Mrs Capello. I tried calling the son, but he didn't pick up.'

'I thought the son told Beth he hadn't heard from her,' Harry said. 'We need to follow both those leads. But also, why was she calling me?' He dug out his phone and scrolled back to Wednesday. 'This must be it. I had an unidentified missed call at 16.54.'

'So maybe she'd found something out that she wanted to tell you,' Geoff said.

'There's no message left.'

'She might have lost signal, or been interrupted. Someone could have stopped her?'

Harry looked at his watch. It was five fifty-five. 'This Mrs Capello,' he said to Dave. 'Where does she live?'

'She's an accountant. Works and lives in Enfield.'

'Fine, give me her details. I've got a few things to finish off here and then I need to drop back to mine for something. I'll call on her after that.'

'What about the son?' Geoff asked. 'He's probably at the restaurant getting ready for tonight. I can question him about the phone call if you want?'

'Or maybe call Beth and let her do it as she's already met him, it'll give her something to concentrate on when she gets back. But gather everything you can on him and his father in the meantime.'

CHAPTER THIRTY-TWO

A s soon as Finn entered the house, he walked into the kitchen where Goldie was getting supper ready. 'What did they want?' she asked anxiously. 'Any news of Alyssa?'

He shook his head. 'Just a few more questions. You've not heard from her, then?'

'Nothing. What are we going to do, Finn? It's past 6 o'clock. This isn't like her. She could have been abducted or anything. Maybe we should tell the police?'

'No.' Finn's tone was abrupt, and he tempered it. 'She hasn't been abducted.' He hesitated, then said with a sigh. 'I know who she's with, I just don't know where she is.'

'What do you mean? Who's she with?'

'Connor Stephens.'

'Oh, no. What's the stupid girl thinking? We've warned her so many times about him.'

He sighed. 'It's tempting when you're a kid that age. The promise of money; feeling like you belong. Conn's good at that – sucking people in. I found that out good and proper, didn't I?'

'What you gonna do?'

'Not much I can do without knowing where she is, and Conn's not picking up. I'm going out again, looking for him. And when I find him...'

'Don't you get into trouble, Finn. We don't want you back in jail. That won't solve anything and he's not worth it.'

The memory of Alyssa sitting on that bloke's knee came back to him. No point worrying Goldie with that one, but the way he felt right now, he'd kill Conn if he got the chance. And it would be worth going to jail for.

He walked over to the sink and downed a quick glass of water. 'If I find her, I'll call you, and you do the same if you hear anything.'

***

Alyssa sat perched on the edge of the sofa, listening to the men talk about turfs, county lines, elders, runners ... none of it meant anything to her, but that didn't matter, she was intrigued by it all. She looked around in awe. This suite was so much bigger than her and Hayley's room – and it was dead posh, with two bedrooms, two bathrooms and a separate lounge. There were two other older girls in the room, Daisy and Holly. Alyssa vaguely remembered them from school, but they'd left last year if she remembered right. She worked out that they were probably about seventeen, but they looked and acted so much older than her and Hayley, flirting with the men, even doing a sexy little dance to the music that was playing in the background.

'You like them sweets, do you?' a man called Sam asked from her side, as she took another one from the packet Jake had given her. He was about forty and sitting a bit closer than she was comfortable with, but she didn't like to make a fuss. She nodded. 'Yeah, they're alright.' In truth, she was only eating them for something to do, something to take her mind off what she was doing in this room with people she couldn't help feeling were dodgy.

'That's good, 'cos I sell 'em see, and maybe you could act as my runner up this way?'

'What do you mean?'

'Well ... sell 'em around your school and the like, and I'll pay you a commission. Ten percent of everything you sell. Easy way for you to earn some money.'

'Really?'

Alyssa chewed on the sweet more thoughtfully. They weren't bad, but she wasn't sure she'd go out of her way to buy them over other sweets she liked.

'They got a funny taste,' she said.

'That's 'cos they got natural, herbal stuff in them – good for re-laxing kids when they're doing exams and the like. Or even if they're feeling worked up about something – calms 'em down.'

It was true, she realised. Because she'd been feeling really anxious when she'd first got here, but she felt fine now ... relaxed even. That was cool.

'I'd have to check it with Conn,' she said.

'Sure. How long have you worked for him?'

'I don't. We just hang out with him sometimes.'

'Ah, I see. Well, he's a good bloke. He'll have your back. And we all need someone like that these days. Ah, talk of the devil...'

Alyssa looked up as Connor walked over. 'How are you guys getting on? Alyssa looking after you alright?'

Sam slid his hand on her thigh and squeezed it. 'Yeah, she's been doing a grand job. I reckon we'll be up for a bit of fun later; won't we love? Play some games maybe.'

'But before that, we've got some business to settle,' Conn said. 'Alyssa, Hayley, Holly, Daisy ... you girls go in the bedroom and watch some TV while we talk. I'll call you when we're ready to go down for dinner.'

Alyssa jumped up from her seat and gave a little squeal as Sam's large hand landed on her rump. 'Good arse you got there,' he said with a grin. 'Sorry, I couldn't resist.'

In the bedroom, Alyssa tried to catch Hayley's eye, but she was out of it, laughing and giggling with the two older girls as they grappled with the television remote. It hadn't taken long for the tea and cake to make way for beer and wine, and although Alyssa had tried to take just small sips from her glass, remembering how ill she'd felt the last time she'd got drunk, it was difficult to keep check on how much she'd had, with Jake topping her up on a regular basis. And Hayley, she was sure, hadn't been watching what she was drinking. That Sam had made her feel uncomfortable, rubbing her thigh like that and smacking her bum.

She moved to the cabinet next to the television and poured out two glasses of water, downing one completely before refilling it and taking the other one to Hayley. 'Here, drink this,' she said, 'or you'll feel bad later. I read that you should have a glass of water for every glass of alcohol you drink.'

'God, I need about ten then,' Hayley giggled, taking the glass from her. 'This is so cool don't you think? My mum would kill me if she knew what we was doing, but this place is amazing. That Ed, said that Conn's hired a private room for our dinner tonight. He must be rolling in it.'

'He is,' Daisy said. 'And if you do what he wants, you will be too. He's very generous to his mates.'

'I don't like those men, though,' Alyssa said.

'I know what you mean, but...' Daisy shrugged. 'You get used to it, it's part of the job and if you keep'em happy, Conn'll reward you.'

'What do you mean, keep them happy?'

'Oh, you know, just let them touch you a bit if that's what they want to do. They won't hurt you. They just like pretty girls, and we've all been through it.'

'Been through what?'

The two older girls exchanged looks. 'You'll find out when the time's right,' Daisy said with a shrug. 'It ain't always very nice to start with, but you get used to it.' She downed the rest of her glass in one, as if taking comfort from it, and Alyssa watched her uneasily. She wasn't that innocent that she didn't know a bit about sex, and she had a gut feeling that that was what Daisy was talking about.

'Do you have sex with them? Is that what you mean?'

Daisy's eyes glittered into hers. 'I ain't saying no more. Let it drop babe and just concentrate on doing what Conn wants and not pissing him off. That's my advice. And I noticed that you ain't bin drinking as much as your mate here, but if I was you, I'd eat the sweets and drink the booze, cos it'll make the evening a whole lot easier for you.'

CHAPTER THIRTY-THREE

Harry parked outside his house and turned the engine off. For a few moments, he sat there trying to get into the right headspace. It felt like everything was crowding in on him. He hadn't spoken to his parents or Angela since all this had kicked off and truth was, he didn't want to, because he didn't know what to say. He felt angry with all of them for pulling the rug from under his feet, forcing him to become part of a club he didn't want to belong to. His family life may not have been perfect but at least up to now it had felt secure, a known entity. Now that entity had been blown apart. How many more secrets were waiting to come crawling out of the woodwork?

He opened the car door and climbed out.

His mother looked dreadful as she preceded him into the kitchen and fussed round putting the kettle on.

'How are you?' he asked, getting a couple of cups out.

'Terrible. This is the worst thing that's ever happened to me – and that includes when I found out your dad was having the affair. This feels so much worse. He's hidden it – her – from me, for all these years. What sort of man does that?'

'One with a guilty conscience, I suspect, who doesn't want to lose the woman he loves because of one stupid mistake he made. I'm not making excuses for him, Mum, but men are different to women. We tend to bury stuff, rather than get it out into the open and deal with it. It was a stupid thing for him to do because he must have known you'd find out. But maybe he hoped he'd be dead and gone by then, or that you'd have enough good years behind you, for you to forgive him. I don't know. You'll have to ask him. But for what it's worth, I've never doubted that he loves you. You'll come through this.'

'I don't know that we will, Harry.' The tears welled up in eyes that were already red raw from crying. 'I feel totally betrayed.'

He hesitated. He should put his arms around her, comfort her, but doing that didn't come naturally. They'd never been that sort of family. With his grandparents, maybe. Not his mum and dad.

But his grandparents were dead, and it didn't have to continue that way. He could almost hear his grandma urging him on.

He stepped forward and put an arm around her shoulder, and she sank into him for a long moment. Then ... 'He's coming round in half an hour,' she sniffed, drawing back. 'Will you stay?'

'I can't, I'm sorry. This murder investigation ... when we're in the thick of it like this, it's all hands on deck, right through the night if necessary. I'm on my way now to interview a witness.'

'I can't do this on my own, Harry.'

'You can,' he said gently. 'I'd only be a hindrance. You and Dad need to sort this out yourselves. I can't make decisions for you.'

'This girl, Angela. I can't meet her, you know. I don't ever want to meet her.'

'Mum, it's not her fault–'

'I don't care. I won't meet her. Please make sure she's aware of that.'

Harry felt his heart harden. 'I'm not getting involved, Mum and I'm not acting as a go-between. It's for you and Dad to sort out how you want to handle things. But as far as I'm concerned, Angela's my half-sister and I'm not going to turn my back on her and pretend she doesn't exist. I can't. I'm sorry.'

He looked at his watch. 'I need to go. I just wanted to drop by and check you were okay. Hear Dad out when he comes. I'm not saying you should welcome him back with open arms but let him have his say.'

He knew what his mother was like when she went off on one, and she didn't leave much room for anyone else to get a word in. Least of all his mild-mannered father who, in Harry's opinion, had been a bloody saint at times – although clearly not back in the day. Despite working in the job he did, where he heard the most atrocious stories, Harry was surprised at how hard his father's duplicity had derailed him.

Mrs Capello's house was a ten-minute drive from Harry's and, as he pulled up, he took heart from the fact that there were two cars parked in the drive. Looked like they were in.

'Mrs Capello?' he queried of the well-dressed woman who answered the door. He showed his card. 'DI Briscombe. I wonder if you could spare me a few minutes to talk about Elena Mancini. I'm hoping someone called you to say that I'd be dropping by?'

'Yes, come in. Terrible news, I still can't believe it.'

She showed him into a lounge, where a man in his mid-fifties was sitting watching television. He turned the volume down and looked at Harry.

'This is my husband. How can we help you?'

'You were a friend of Elena's?'

'Yes, we belong to the same Italian Club.'

'I believe she phoned you on Wednesday afternoon, and we're trying to pinpoint her movements that day. Did she call for any particular reason – and do you know where she was heading?'

'She was very upset. She'd just been fired from her job, and she'd had an argument with her son. She's usually quite private, but I think she needed a sounding board.'

Harry's ears pricked up at that. 'What was the argument about, did she say?'

She shrugged. 'She didn't go into details, but I think it was probably something to do with her husband. She said Matteo and she had argued at the beginning of the week while she was staying with him and Sophia because she'd told them that if Barbara had left her a decent amount of money, then she was going to leave Lorenzo. Matteo was upset about that and tried to talk her out of it.'

'What was her relationship with her husband like?'

'Well, you can see from that, that it wasn't good. He ruled the roost – or liked to think he did. She never said much, but she grumbled about him sometimes; said he was a lazy slob during the week when she wasn't there. He used to help out at Matteo's restaurant two or three days a week, but that stopped when they did some renovations last year and, as far as I'm aware, he hasn't started back on any regular basis yet. I think that annoyed her.'

'This is a difficult question to ask, and it's just your opinion that I'm interested in, but do you think there's any chance Lorenzo might hurt his wife?'

She blinked. 'I have no idea. Is that what you think?'

'We have to consider all angles.'

'Well...' She hesitated. 'Elena and I have known each other a long time but, as I say, she was quite a private person. She didn't always seem happy, that I will say, and sometimes I wondered if perhaps he ... you know, bullied her maybe. They had quite a fiery relationship, but...' She shrugged. 'That's the Italians for you. We're passionate people and Elena used to say it meant nothing.'

'And yet she was thinking of leaving him.'

'Yes.'

'Was Elena heading home when she called you?'

'That was my impression, but she didn't actually say that.'

'Thank you. I think that's everything. I'll leave you in peace now. If you think of anything else, this is my card. If I don't pick up you can leave a message and I'll get straight back to you.'

The woman took the card from him and shook her head. 'I can't believe she's gone. First her employer, now her. It's awful. Do you think there's a link?'

'We won't know until we get all the details. As I say, if you remember anything else...?'

'Of course.'

CHAPTER
THIRTY-FOUR

B eth pulled up outside A Taste of Italy in Cockfosters and got out
of the car. She could see through the restaurant window that
there were a few people in there. She'd had a quick catch-up call with
Geoff, and was now ready to tackle Matteo Mancini.

She walked into the restaurant and pulled out her card. 'DC
Macaaskill to see Matteo Mancini. Is he here?' she asked the young girl
who came to greet her at the door.

'Uh, yeah. Come up to the bar and I'll get him.'

Matteo joined her a couple of minutes later. 'I'm sorry, but this isn't
a good time. I've got a table of ten coming in at eight. I shouldn't even
be here with my mum only just passing, but I can't afford to pay for
more staff, and someone has to be here.'

'Sorry. It shouldn't take long but I need to ask you a couple more
questions about your mum.'

He sighed. 'Okay, how can I help?'

'You told us that the last contact you had with her was when she
left your house on Wednesday morning, but we've checked her phone
records, and they show that she called you around five fifteen on
Wednesday afternoon and you were talking for nearly ten minutes.'

'Oh, God, yes, I'm sorry, now you mention it, you're right. I was in such a state, I completely forgot.'

'Strange that. Especially when I specifically asked if you'd spoken to her about the fact she'd been sacked. Can you tell me now, what your conversation was about?'

He gesticulated towards a table at the back of the restaurant. 'Shall we sit?'

Once they were seated, he said. 'She was upset because that witch, Sylvia, had sacked her. After all the years she'd worked for Barbara.'

'And did she also tell you that Barbara had left her a hundred thousand pounds?'

There was the slightest of hesitations before he answered. 'Yes, she did mention it.'

'Did she come back here that afternoon?'

'No. When I spoke to her she was on her way home.'

'And what exactly did she say?'

He didn't answer.

'This is your mother's murder we're looking into. I'd have thought you'd want to help in any way you can.'

'I've already told you, she was upset about being fired and she'd also said she'd give me a call after seeing the executor, so she was filling me in on that.'

'We know she also called a friend after she spoke to you. Do you know why?'

'No. When we finished the call she just said she was going home.'

'And yet according to your father, she never went home.'

'No.'

'Do you think he's lying about that?'

He didn't answer.

'What was your parents' relationship like?'

'It was fine.' His tone was defensive. 'Why do you ask that? Their relationship was fine.'

'Just routine questioning. How's business?'

Matteo shrugged. 'Not bad. We closed for a couple of months for refurbishment, and it's taken a while to recover from that. Things are picking up a bit now in the run up to Christmas.'

'When was the last time you visited Barbara Harding's house?'

'God, I can't remember, it was so long ago. A year at least.'

'Did you know about the spare key she kept in the garden?'

'No. Why would I?'

'Your mum worked there a long time. I'd have thought that might have come out at some point.'

'Well, it didn't.'

'Where were you last Saturday between the hours of twelve thirty and three o'clock? I believe you haven't handed your statement in yet? Or your fingerprints.'

'No, because you only asked me for them yesterday and I've been busy today preparing for the weekend's meals. But it's an easy one to answer, I was here last Saturday, serving lunch to the few customers we had, then clearing up after they'd gone.'

'Can anyone back that up?'

He swept a harassed hand through his hair. 'Well, the customers I suppose, and my wife – but she's not well and is staying at her parents. Also, Luigi, our chef, and Marie. She helps out from Friday to Sunday.'

'Can you let me have their details? Are any of them here now? We'll need to speak to them.'

He pulled a pen out of his pocket, grabbed a serviette from the holder on the table and scribbled a few lines. 'That's my wife's number and her parents' address. Luigi and Marie are both here now, but...'

Beth followed his gaze to where a group of people had just entered the restaurant. The noise level rose immediately.

He turned back to Beth. 'Do you have to do this now? You can see how pushed we are.'

'I'd like quick confirmation, but we can get formal statements tomorrow.'

Matteo scraped his chair back. 'Seat them for me, Suzie,' he said to the woman who'd let Beth in. 'I'll be with you in a minute.'

He led her through to the kitchen, a large, modern area with shiny, stainless-steel surfaces and various pans simmering on the hobs.

A quick word with the chef and Marie was enough to confirm Matteo's alibi that he had been physically present over the lunch period the day Barbara died.

'We still need a formal statement and fingerprints. Please make sure you come down to the station tomorrow to supply those.'

'I'll be there,' he assured her. 'First thing in the morning. Thanks.'

Beth drove into the carpark at the same time as Harry, and he joined her as she got out of the car.

'Hey,' he said. 'How did it go today?'

'Much as expected.'

They headed into the building. 'You didn't need to come in. You must be exhausted.'

'I'd rather be here than moping around at home, mulling over what a crap family I've got.' She considered her words and grimaced. 'That's not fair. They're not all crap ... with my dad gone, it's about a 60/40 split now in favour of the good guys, but it's been a shit day none the less.'

'I spoke to Geoff; he said you were interviewing Mancini junior. How did it go?'

'He admitted that his mum called him, said he'd forgotten, if you can believe that. She was apparently upset because she'd been sacked, and she told him about the money she'd inherited. He reckoned she was on her way home and didn't have much else to add.'

'No mention of any argument between them?'

'No.'

'Then he wasn't being straight with you, because we know from one of Elena's friends that he and his mum argued. She reckoned it was something to do with his father. I need to check a couple of things and then I think we'll pay him another visit. He stands to inherit everything from her, bar five grand. That's a solid enough motive for murder in my book.'

Upstairs in the incident room, Harry took a quick look to see what had been added to the board in his absence.

'No real breakthroughs,' Geoff commented from his side, 'but I found out that Matteo Mancini's restaurant is in debt to the tune of fifty grand following renovation work that needed to be done. He apparently told the bank he'd be making a significant payment in the near future. And Elena's GP confirmed that she had suspected domestic violence in the past but could never get Elena to admit it. She also confirmed that Matteo had had some suspicious injuries as a child, but again no proof of anything. He apparently had anxiety issues as a teenager, which it was suspected were due to his relationship with his father. I spoke to his school earlier. The same headmaster was still there and said that he was threatened with expulsion in the sixth form for giving a fellow pupil a serious going over, after which he agreed to undergo anger management therapy and seemed to get his act in order. No reported incidents since then. It's all in here.'

'Thanks.' Harry took the folder from him and looked over at Beth. 'Are you okay to drive? Simon texted me to say he's sent me an email with something interesting in it, so I can check that and a couple of other things on our way over.'

In the car, Harry read through his emails, then shut them down and punched a number into his phone. 'Dave? According to Simon, Lorenzo Mancini's fingerprints are already in the system for an assault on a restaurant customer several years ago. Look into that further will you and run a check through Interpol to see if they've got anything on him while you're at it. You never know. I'll be back in about an hour if anyone's after me.'

He clicked off as Beth pulled up outside the restaurant. 'Now, let's see what Matteo Mancini's got to say for himself. You can lead as you were the last one to see him.'

CHAPTER THIRTY-FIVE

M atteo hurried to the door the minute they walked in.

'What the hell are you doing here?' he whispered angrily. 'You can't just walk into my restaurant when its full of customers. Do you have any idea what that sort of thing can do to a business?'

Beth's tone was uncompromising. 'I don't think it's that obvious to your customers who we are, but maybe you should have thought about that before you lied to me. Happy to talk somewhere quieter, and if you answer our questions quickly and to our satisfaction, we'll be out of your hair.'

He led them through the restaurant to a small room at the back, simply laid out with a desk, a couple of chairs and a television. No one sat down.

'What do you mean, lied?' Matteo said, rounding on them as soon as the door was closed.

'I asked you what you and your mum had talked about on the phone, and you omitted to mention that you'd argued.' She felt quite pleased with her terminology. She had Harry to thank for that; she'd never have used words like omitted before working with him.

'That was none of your business. It was personal.'

'Nothing stays personal in a murder enquiry, Mr Mancini. You need to know that. What did you argue about? Did you want some of her money to help clear your debts, which we understand are quite large?'

'No. We'd talked about that earlier in the week and I won't lie, I was upset when she said that whatever she inherited from Barbara she intended using on herself and not me or my dad. But on Wednesday, when she knew it was a hundred grand, she said she'd give me ten thousand pounds towards my debts, and I was grateful for that.'

At this, Harry chipped in. 'You can see why we wanted to talk to you, why it doesn't look good for you withholding important information. Especially when we hear you've been telling the bank that you'll be clearing your debts soon.'

Matteo shrugged 'I'm always telling them that to get them off my back. I think they'll be very pleased if they get ten grand.'

'Only now, of course, they'll probably get more as you seem to be the main benefactor of your mother's will.'

'I know nothing about what my mother's will says. I didn't even know she had one.'

'So, what did you argue about in that call, then?' Harry probed. 'Because we know that you did. Elena spoke to a friend after she spoke to you and told her that you'd argued and that she was upset about that. Did she come back to your flat that afternoon? Maybe to try and clear the air?'

'No, she didn't. She was going home.'

'We'll be checking the CCTV out.'

'Fine.'

'So, what was the argument about?'

For a long moment he appeared to be struggling to come to a decision. Then he looked at Beth and sighed. 'You asked me earlier what my parents' relationship was like. It ... it wasn't great, and Mama told me that now she had a decent amount of money of her own, she was going to leave my father.'

Now they were getting somewhere. 'Okay. And did he know that?'

'I don't know. But I did know that if she threw him out, he'd expect to come and live with me and Sophia – and there's no way my wife would agree to that. We've got a baby on the way and it's a small flat. But he helps in the restaurant sometimes, and it would be hard to refuse him if it came to it.'

'Shelving that for the moment,' Harry said, 'we also know that you had significant anger issues when you were younger. Were nearly expelled from your school because of them, in fact?'

Matteo glared at him. 'Is that going to be held against me forever? So, I had some issues when I was younger. It was a long time ago.'

'You completely lost your rag, though, beat up one of your fellow pupils quite badly. It was a vicious attack, and it wasn't the first time you'd been in trouble for fighting.'

'No, I was a teenage boy and sometimes got into fights, but I had counselling and had to do an anger management course after that. These things take time, but it worked. I don't have a problem with anger now.'

'You told my colleague that you knew about your mother's inheritance from Barbara, before she was killed.'

'So?'

'So, were you worried when Barbara started talking about changing her will? That perhaps your mother might not inherit the money after all?'

'Not enough to kill her, if that's what you're suggesting.'

'You could have solved all your money problems in one go if your mother had agreed to cough up more.'

'Yes, but it was her money and as I said, I was grateful for the ten grand she offered me.'

He stared off into the distance for a short moment, as if remembering, then returned his gaze to Harry.

'Was there anything else you wanted to ask? Because, if not, I need to get back to my customers.'

Harry shook his head. 'That'll do for now. We're checking the area around you for video footage. If we find just one picture of your mother in the vicinity of your restaurant on Wednesday afternoon, we'll be picking you up quicker than you can blink. So don't go anywhere.'

Matteo shook his head. 'I'll see you out,' he said tersely.

'What do you think?' Beth asked as they made their way back to the car.

'I get the feeling he's still holding something back, and he's got motive if Elena shared any concerns about Barbara changing her will. But it's getting late. No point digging any further tonight. If you can drop me back at the office, we'll start again with fresh eyes, first thing tomorrow.'

'Harry?' Geoff called out as they entered the office. 'We've got some info come in on Paul Cunningham, Mia's boyfriend?'

'Oh?'

'Seems he's not as squeaky clean as he might like us to think. He was threatened with court action a few years back by the well-to-do family of a young girl who he'd apparently defrauded out of twenty-five thousand pounds left to her by her grandfather. He told her it was an investment opportunity that would pay her back fivefold, and if she lent him the money, he'd pay it back and split the profit with her. She paid up and he did a runner. The family dropped the action in the end because they didn't want the publicity.'

'So, Sylvia could be right saying he's only with Mia because of the money?'

'Could be.'

'Okay. Either you or Beth can take that one on tomorrow. Revisit him and see what he's got to say for himself. For now, I think we should shut up shop and get a good night's sleep.'

He took his jacket off the peg. 'See you both tomorrow.'

After he'd gone, Geoff looked at Beth. 'How was it today?'

She sighed. 'Not good.'

'Do you want to grab a bite to eat before you head home?'

'I'd love to. I haven't eaten anything all day, apart from a few nibbles at the wake.'

She didn't add that even then, she'd had to force the food down her throat.

Once they'd ordered, Geoff looked at Beth. 'Was it as bad as you feared?'

'Pretty much. My mam's a mess and though I know I shouldn't feel guilty, I do, even though she's never wanted anything to do with me.'

'What exactly do you mean, a mess? Grief stricken?'

'Doubt it – reckon he killed any feelings she had for him years ago.' She hesitated, then shrugged. 'It's the bottle's her main problem. She's always blown hot and cold with that, and it brought back memories today, seeing her pissed like that.' She took a sip from her wine. 'Anyway, enough of that, how do you think the investigation's coming on?'

'Slower than we'd like.'

'Do you think there's anything relevant in this new info on Paul Cunningham?'

'Could be. We know that Sylvia Carroll doesn't think much of him, and if he's something of a con artist and thought Mia was going to inherit a million or more, and then learnt she might not...'

'Sylvia's hardly a character reference to go by.'

'True. But he's a bit too comfortable in his own boots for my liking. Worth a more detailed look.'

'Do you want to question him tomorrow or shall I?'

'I've got a chiropractor appointment first thing, but I can do it after that.'

'Don't worry, I'll do it. Get another box ticked.'

CHAPTER THIRTY-SIX

All through the dinner, Alyssa was on hyper-alert. She was trying not to drink the wine, but everyone was encouraging her to step outside her comfort zone, break free of her inhibitions. They'd look after her, keep her safe ... and after a while, she found herself believing them, joining in the fun, giggling with Hayley, getting used to Sam whispering flirty things in her ear.

It was ten o'clock when they finally rose from the table and headed back upstairs to the suite Conn had booked. Hayley was all over the place, singing loudly as she danced her way to the lift, and Alyssa grabbed her arm, steering her in the right direction.

'Shut up you idiot, people are looking at us.'

'I just want to have fun,' sang Hayley at full pelt, and Alyssa shook her head, laughing. 'You're mad, you know that?'

'Right, girls, more wine or something a bit more exciting?' Conn asked, as one by one, people drifted into the upstairs rooms. 'I could mix you a nice little cocktail here, pineapple flavour. You like pineapple?'

'I love it,' Hayley said straight away.

'Put some music on, Jake, while I pour the girls a drink, and let's get this party going. You going to give us a little dance display, Hayley, like the one you did downstairs in the foyer?'

Someone turned the music on. It wasn't a song that Alyssa knew, but it was catchy and had a heavy beat, and it was all Hayley needed to set her off again. 'Show us a bit of sexy,' one of the men called out, and immediately, Hayley started to wave her arms around in the air and gyrate her body in a slow rhythmic movement. The man reached into his pocket and pulled out a small bag of white powder, one eye on Hayley as he cut it carefully into lines on the table, then snorted it. It was the first time Alyssa had seen anything like that, but she knew what it meant straight away.

Drugs. It was like a siren exploding in her brain.

It was what Goldie and Finn had been banging on about ... warning how people got sucked into doing them without even realising what was happening. And she was right in the middle of it. Others were queuing up now for their turn and one of the men got up and started to dance with Hayley, everyone else clapping and cheering them on. He had to be at least forty-five and something about the way he was dancing with Hayley, trailing his hands suggestively down her sides, as he laughed and gyrated with her, sobered Alyssa up instantly. As her eyes darted around the room her unease catapulted into fear. Daisy was snogging Sam, and even as Alyssa watched, another man paired off with Holly and led her from the room.

And that left Alyssa.

As if on cue, the other man in the party approached her. She remembered his name was Greg, and he seemed quieter than the rest.

'Want to dance?'

She shook her head.

'She's gonna dance with me, ain't you babe?' Jake chipped in, appearing at her side from nowhere. 'You like EDM?'

Even though she'd never been to a club, she knew what electric dance music was, and now it took on a whole new sinister meaning for her. She shook her head. 'Not really.'

'That's probably because you're not into it yet, but it's wild. And when you've got a bit of booze in your system and maybe other stuff, if you know what I mean ... man, you just lose yourself in it. Come on, let me show you.'

He went to take her hand to drag her off, but Greg stepped in smoothly. 'No, mate, I saw her first.'

His eyes locked with hers and he smiled. 'It's me or him. Your choice.'

She looked panic stricken from one to the other. She didn't want to dance with either of them, she just wanted to get out of there, but something about this man's quieter manner made her plump for him.

'Okay,' she shrugged, letting him guide her to the middle of the room, where Hayley was still gyrating. Her friend clapped her hands in approval. 'Lissa,' she called drunkenly, 'come and have fun.'

Alyssa started to dance, but her movements were wooden as she tried hard to get her thoughts together and work out how she and Hayley could get themselves out of there. From the corner of one eye, she saw her handbag perched on the back of a chair. If only she could get to her phone.

Sam and Daisy pulled up alongside her. 'How you doing babe?' Sam asked above the noise of the music. 'Do you like how those sweets make you feel? I can give you more if you like. Or perhaps you'd like to try a bit of the stronger stuff over there? Just a tiny bit, and I'll let you have it for free. It'll blow your mind like nothing you've ever known.'

Alyssa shook her head. 'I don't feel too good,' she mumbled to Greg. 'I think I need to sit down.'

'You alright?' He peered at her closely. He seemed to be genuinely concerned for her as he put an arm around her shoulder and led her back to the seating area, but she still had to suppress a knee-jerk reaction to shake him off.

Her bag seemed to glow like a beacon, as if shouting to everyone that her phone was in it. She resisted the temptation to grab it, turning instead to say, 'I think I need a glass of water. Can you get me one while I go to the bathroom? I feel a bit sick.'

'Sure.' He leaned in and lowered his voice. 'You know, I don't reckon you're cut out for all this. You have a think about things when you get home, eh? And whether you want to be doing this sort of stuff. Tell 'em you've got your period if things look like they're getting out of hand. I'll get you that water.'

She stared after him, frowning. What was she supposed to make of that? She waited until he'd got his back to her before picking up her bag, oh so casually, and heading out of the room.

'You okay?' It was Jake's voice behind her, and she jumped like a startled rabbit.

'Yeah, just going to the toilet.'

'Okay, but don't be long, we're gonna play a couple of games in a minute.'

As soon as she was in the bathroom, she locked the door and pulled out her phone. There were eight unread messages from Finn. She hadn't opened any of them because she'd been able to see from the first couple of lines what they said – all variations on the 'call me, where are you?' theme of the first message he'd sent. But the last one grabbed her attention straight away. 'You're not safe. Wherever you are, get out of there and...'

It didn't matter how he knew. She moved over to the far corner of the room and speed dialled his number. He picked up straight away.

'Alyssa, where the fuck are you? We've been worried sick.'

Just hearing his voice made her crack. 'Finn, I need you. Please come and get us. Me and Hayley are in a hotel room with Conn and some of his mates, and we just want to get out of here. Please come.'

On the other end of the line, she heard Finn draw a deep breath and exhale it. 'It's alright, calm down. Just leave. Walk out–'

'I can't. Hayley's drunk and acting really strange. I can't leave her. Anyway, they won't let me just walk out. They're doing drugs and everything. Please, Finn, come and get me.'

'Don't touch anything they give you, you hear me? Christ, Alyssa! What's the name of the place you're in?'

'I don't remember.'

'*Think.*'

'*I can't remember.*'

She was shaking violently, losing it and she took a deep breath, trying to calm herself. 'Uh ... we're near Stevenage. It's a new place someone said, called the Sandalwood something.'

'Sandalwood hotel and spa? Is that it?'

'I think so.'

'Okay, I know of it. I'll get Goldie to bring me, and we'll be with you in about half an hour. Can you hang on til then? Don't eat or drink nothing except water. If you're worried, you tell Conn that you've rung me and that I'm on my way and remind him that I done him a favour today. Tell him I'll drop him right in it if he harms a hair on your head. You got that?'

'Why would he hurt me?' Alyssa's voice was panicked.

'He won't. He needs me too much, and he knows if he does anything to you, I'd kill him.'

'Finn, don't talk like that. You're scaring me.'

A loud knock on the bathroom door made her almost drop the phone. 'There's someone at the door,' she said agitatedly. 'I've got to go. Just get here, please.'

'You all right, in there?'

It was Jake, and quickly ramming her phone back in her bag, Alyssa flushed the toilet and moved over to the sink.

'Just washing my hands,' she called. She took a steadying breath and moved over to unlock the door. Straight away, Jake barged in and closed it behind him.

'Who were you talking to?'

'No one.'

'Don't lie to me, I heard you. Give me your phone. *Now*,' he shouted, when she made no move to do as he said.

She opened her bag and handed it to him.

'Code,' he snapped.

'121209.'

He punched it in and looked at the call screen. 'You phoned Finn? Why?'

She lifted her chin mutinously. 'Cos I don't like those men, and I want to leave.'

'Conn told you not to bring your phone. He doesn't like people who disobey him. Has Hayley got hers too?'

Alyssa shook her head.

'Right, well she better not have. As for the men, they're harmless, they just like showing off in front of pretty girls. Get out into the bedroom and wait there while I get Conn. He ain't gonna like this.'

In the bedroom, she didn't want to go anywhere near the bed, so she sat huddled on a chair in the corner and waited. It wasn't long before they returned. Conn closed the door firmly behind him and turned on her, his face livid.

'What the fuck are you playing at? Didn't I tell you not to bring your phone with you? Didn't I?'

She nodded.

'So why did you disobey me? You're going to have to find out the hard way that I don't like people disobeying me.'

Alyssa shrank back into her chair.

'What did you say to your brother/'

'Nothing.'

'Don't waste my time, Alyssa.' He stormed over to the chair and yanked her out of it, ramming his face right into hers. He smelt of booze and something else, and she shrank from him.

'Now you tell me exactly what you said to Finn, or I swear I'll hand you over to those men out there and let them do what they like with you. Do you understand me? What did you tell him?'

'I didn't tell him nothing,' she cried. 'I just said I wanted to go home.'

'And what did he say?'

She hesitated, but frightened though she was, her wits were coming into play, and she knew she had to downplay the situation. 'He said he'd come and get me. That I'd be all right 'cos he was doing you a favour, and he'd talk to you.'

'Oh, he said that did he? Well, your brother's been a pain in the arse ever since he got out of prison, and I think it's about time he got reminded who's running things round here. I need loyalty from everyone on my patch, including him.' He looked at her thoughtfully. 'And I think I know exactly how I'm going to get it. In the meantime, I want you back out there, being nice to my friends. Jake tells me that you don't like ' em, but let me tell you how it's gonna be. These men are important to me – they're business contacts that I need – and this is your chance to help me, just like I helped you the other day. And if you do a good job, maybe I'll even help your brother. The cops are trying to pin the murder of that old lady onto him because they know he's done time and he'll be easy to stitch up, but I could help him – maybe even fix him up with an alibi so's they can't pin anything on him. But if you ain't cooperative now … well, things could go the other way, and I could drop him right in it, so he ends up serving a life sentence for murder. Is that what you want?'

'He didn't do it!'

'Maybe he did and maybe he didn't. But you know what? I don't give a toss and neither do the cops. He was there that day. That's all they need to know and without an alibi he's stuffed.'

Alyssa's heart sank. She remembered Finn saying that once you had a record, the police never let up on you. How could she be responsible for him going back to prison?'

'I don't want to do drugs,' she said defiantly.

'You don't have to. All you have to do is act friendly and be nice, like your friend's doing right at this moment.'

He waited, and when she remained silent, he added. 'Are we okay with this now?'

His eyes bore into hers until finally, she nodded. He loosened his hold on her arm and patted it. 'Good girl. Then let's get back out there and enjoy ourselves, shall we?'

CHAPTER THIRTY-SEVEN

Finn ended the call and jumped up from the kitchen table. 'Get your jacket, I need you to drive,' he told Goldie. 'She's at that new hotel in Stevenage.'

Goldie grabbed her keys off the hook and followed him out to the car. 'Who's she with? What's going on?'

'It's like I said, she's with Conn. If they're at a hotel, it's probably some sort of meet up with his business contacts.'

'Huh! What sort of business contacts does someone like him have?'

'You don't wanna know, Goldie. We need to get her out of there.'

'What exactly did she say?' Goldie asked once they were on their way.

'Just that she and Hayley are at that hotel with Conn and his mates, and she didn't like what was going on.'

'Stupid girl. They won't hurt her, will they?'

He could hear the anxiety in her voice and it spiked his own. 'Christ knows, but if they do...' His face was grim.

'Finn, we need to stay calm. Don't you do anything stupid.'

'She's my sister and if he's hurt a hair on her head, I'm telling you now, I'll kill him.'

'Finn–'

'Leave it, Goldie, I need to think.'

In the car, Finn brought the address up on Google Maps. 'It's showing twenty-two minutes,' he said. 'Think you can do it quicker?'

'Yeah, but put it on Waze, they show the cameras.'

They did it in eighteen minutes flat. Goldie swung into the car park and screamed into a parking slot, slamming on the brakes. 'What are we going to do now?'

'You ain't doing anything,' Finn said, releasing his seatbelt and opening his door. 'We'll both go in and I'll see if they'll give me Conn's room number. You wait for me in the bar and if I'm not back within twenty minutes, you call the police.' He pulled a card out of his pocket and handed it to her. 'This is that Inspector's number. You make sure you speak to him if you need to call. Tell him what's going on and say that if he helps us, I'll tell him the truth about Connor Stephens' car.'

Inside the hotel, Finn parked Goldie in the bar where she'd be out of sight and walked up to the desk. 'I've got a mate of mine staying here, Connor Stephens? Can you tell me what room he's in?'

The clerk flicked his finger down the register book. 'Ah, yes, here he is, Diamond Suite. I'll need to call him and let him know you're here. Your name?'

'Finn Abara. I just need the gents. I'll be back in a minute.'

In the bar, he spoke quickly to Goldie. 'They're in the Diamond Suite. Remember, if we're not back down in twenty minutes, you call the number on that card. Got it?'

Goldie nodded. She looked sick with worry. 'You be careful, lad. You and that sister of yours mean a lot to me. Don't you go doing anything stupid.'

He squeezed her arm. 'Get yourself a drink so you don't look out of place. I'll see you in a bit.'

He walked back to the reception desk. 'Someone's coming down to take you up,' the clerk said. 'You can take a seat over there.'

Two minutes later, Jake appeared. 'Conn ain't happy you turning up like this when he's entertaining business clients,' he said, leading the way to the lift.

'I'm not looking for trouble, I've just come to get my sister and her mate. Then I'll be out of his hair.'

'He won't like it, Finn. It'll look like you're undermining his authority and you know what he's like.'

'My sister's only just fourteen years old, she's too young to be hanging out with you lot at this time of night. Conn must have known how I'd react when I found out.'

'He was banking on it; he just didn't think you'd find out as quickly as you did.'

'What do you mean, he was banking on it?'

'Mate, you have to realise he's gone up in the world since you were put away and anyone who don't accept that and fall in with his plans is heading for big trouble. Seriously, he's had people wasted for less.'

'I just want to take Alyssa and her friend home. I'm not out to pick a fight.'

'But maybe he is, and I warn you, you're not going to like what you see.'

They'd exited the lift and come to a halt outside a door and Jake wrapped smartly on it. 'Don't expect anyone here to back you up, you're on your own,' he said as the door opened.

Inside the room, a swift glance around confirmed the presence of half a dozen men, a couple of older girls and Alyssa and Hayley, sitting on settees and chairs around a small coffee table. Alyssa's scared eyes flew to his as he looked at her in shock and took in the fact that she and Hayley were sitting there in camisoles and not much else, with the men and the other girls also sitting in various states of undress.

'What the hell's going on?' he demanded of Conn, who was down to his trousers and bare chest. 'Alyssa, get your clothes on, you're coming home with me.'

'Alyssa's going nowhere,' Conn said. 'We're in the middle of a game of strip poker. You remember how it is, Finn. Join us.'

'They're fourteen years old,' Finn shouted, closing the gap between them in three strides. But before he could get his hands on Conn, he was grabbed from behind by Jake and another man, his arm pinned up his back before he knew what was happening.

'Get off me,' he yelled, struggling. 'You leave those kids alone. I swear, Conn, you don't let me take them home now, I'll kill you. And that's no empty threat.'

'More likely I'll kill you first,' Conn said, nodding his head in the direction of one of the bedrooms to Jake. 'Take him in there. We'll just finish this game to see who's the first to lose all their clothes, then I'll be in to deal with him.'

'No, don't hurt him,' Alyssa cried, jumping up. 'I'll do whatever you want, only don't hurt him, please.'

'Very touching,' Conn said. 'But I don't have no sisters or brothers meself, so it don't mean much to me. I warned you, Finn, that life had moved on while you was in jail. You need to be taught a lesson to toe the line – there's a lot more at stake now, and I ain't gonna let a jumped-up little prick like you mess things up for me. First off I think you need a personal lesson to show you who's boss, and then maybe...' His gaze shifted to where Alyssa was still standing, looking terrified at what was going on. 'Something a bit more subtle – to show you exactly how powerless you are.'

'You bastard.'

'Get him out of my sight,' Conn said to Jake. 'You got some rope?'

'Yeah, you know me, always prepared. It's in my holdall.'

'Good man. Get it now.'

'No wait!' There was desperation in Finn's voice as his eyes flicked to Alyssa and then back to Conn. His shoulders slumped and he ceased his struggles. Who was he kidding, thinking someone like him could rise above their circumstances and lead a normal life? The odds had been stacked against him from the minute he'd walked out of that jail, and no amount of wishful thinking was going to change anything. He was an ex-con, with a record, who couldn't even get a job as a gardener. He'd made a promise to his dead parents that he'd take care of Alyssa and now he'd do whatever it took to protect her.

He looked at Conn unflinchingly; saw into the depths of evilness in those eyes and knew there wasn't a shred of empathy. He needed to convince him.

'I'll do it. I'll come back on board and do whatever you want, I swear, just leave Alyssa out of all this.'

'You ain't in any position to lay down terms, Finn.'

'I know. But you do that for me, and you'll have my gratitude and loyalty always.' He almost choked on the words but ploughed on. 'I worked well for you before; I'm a grafter, you know that. I'll take the rap for you about the car, I'll do whatever you ask. Just leave my sister out of all this.'

Conn stared at him thoughtfully. 'Can't let you get away with dissing me like you did.'

'Do whatever you need,' Finn said desperately.

'Oh, don't worry, I will. Tie him up,' Conn said to Jake. 'And then sit him down in the corner over there where he'll get a good view of what's going on in the game. Now, where were we?'

Downstairs in the bar, Goldie tapped her foot nervously on the floor, and checked her watch for the hundredth time. It was ten fifteen. Twenty minutes he'd said, and twenty minutes was up. She looked at the card he'd given her. Should she do it now, or give him a couple more minutes?

She pulled out her phone and dialled the number.

CHAPTER THIRTY-EIGHT

H arry walked into Claire's hall and retrieved his jacket.

'You sure you want to go?' she said. 'You can stay if you want?'

'No, it's been good to have a breather, but I messaged Mum that I'd be back tonight. Might as well go back and face it. Has to be done sometime.'

'Poor you. It's horrible for you.'

It was, and he didn't fully get why. He was thirty-four years old, hardly in need of parenting anymore and they'd never even been a close-knit family. So why was it hitting him so hard?

'It's worse for them,' was all he said. 'They've had their ups and downs over the years, but I never thought for one minute they'd separate. I'm not sure I can see them resolving things in a positive way.'

'They might. It's a lot of history to throw down the drain.'

As he got into his car, Harry's phone rang and he answered it, noting the unknown number on the caller display. 'DI Briscombe.'

'It's Marigold Lamb,' an agitated voice said without preamble. 'I used to be foster parent to Finn Abara and I still foster his sister, Alyssa. They're in trouble. They need help.'

Harry frowned. 'What sort of trouble?'

He listened as Goldie filled him in, and when she'd finished, she said urgently. 'What are you going to do? If things were alright, Finn would've let me know. But he hasn't, and I'm worried. That Conn's a nasty bit of work. Finn said if you help, he'll come clean about the car. Please, it's urgent, you must help us.'

'Give me the details of where you are ... okay, I know it. You stay put; we'll be there as soon as we can.'

'No, I'm going up,' Goldie said. 'I can't sit here doing nothing – that's my baby up there and I'm not letting anyone hurt her.'

'Mrs Lamb, please don't do that. I strongly urge you–'

But it was too late. He was talking to thin air as she disconnected the call.

DCI Murray clicked his tongue impatiently on the other end of the line.

'Harry, you heard what I said ... ERSOU are working with the NCA investigating Stephens and his gang and we can't just blast in there.'

'I know that, Sir, but those girls are only fourteen years old. We can't stand by and do nothing.'

'That's exactly what we do have to do, Harry. I'll pass the information on, and they'll act on it, but after that it's over to them and no longer our responsibility.'

'With respect, Sir, of course it's our responsibility. We know what's going on and it would be criminal not to intervene. And Finn Abara said if we help him, then he'll give us intelligence on Stephens. That's got to be worth something to them. Those girls are underage and in danger.'

'And they'll take that into account. Once we tell them, I'm sure they'll go in as soon as they can –'

'And that could be too late. Finn Abara could be dead, and those girls' lives ruined. Do you want that on your conscience?'

'Jeez, Harry–'

But Harry knew he had him. His boss let out a heavy sigh and Harry could almost hear his thought process as he went through his options. 'Okay. I can't override a direct order – and neither can you. We've been told not to go anywhere near Connor Stephens, but I'll call the SIO heading up the investigation now and get back to you. Don't do anything until you hear from me. You got that?'

The line clicked and as Harry tapped the hotel into his satnav, he resolved that if he hadn't heard back by the time he got there, he was going in anyway. End of career or not, he wasn't going to have something like that on his conscience. He started up the engine. No point sitting around here waiting for that call.

Five minutes later his phone rang, and he answered it straight away.

'Sir?' But it wasn't Murray. It was an unknown voice.

'DI Briscombe?'

'Yes.'

'DI James Chambers, from ERSOU. Your DCI's been in touch, and I understand there's an urgent issue involving two young girls and Connor Stephens, who we're investigating.'

'That's right, the girls are underage, and I'd like your go ahead to carry out a raid tonight on a hotel room where we know he's holding them.'

'The Sandalwood Spa Hotel?'

'Yes.'

'We know he's there, and no you can't go in.'

Harry's frustration boiled over. 'Look, I've just had a call from the foster-mother of one of the girls, and she's extremely concerned about their welfare. We have a duty of care to–'

'I'm aware of that,' the other man interrupted, and Harry could hear the frustration in his voice. 'But this has been an ongoing under-cover investigation spanning two years, and we believe that tomorrow morning the man at the very top will be joining Connor Stephens and the others. He's the man we need to nail; responsible for millions of pounds worth of drugs flooding the market and lots of lives lost, including some of our own. If we go in now, we'll blow the whole thing apart and put lives at risk.'

'It's going to be blown apart anyway. The foster mother was already at the hotel when she rang, and she was adamant that she was going in.'

'*What*?'

'I tried to stop her, but–'

'*Shit!*'

Harry kept silent, allowing the man time to process it. 'Where are you now?' he demanded of Harry.

'On my way to the hotel'

Another silence, then ... 'Okay. We already have the place under surveillance. Main car park. Meet me there. What car are you driving?'

'A black Passat. I'll be as quick as I can, but I'm worried about what's going on meantime in that room.'

'It's a fucking disaster and no two ways about it, but I hear what you're saying. I'll need to speak to my boss. Meantime, we have someone in there and he'll be doing his best to protect the girls. Just get here as soon as you can.'

The line clicked and Harry hit the accelerator. He desperately wanted to call Goldie back but knew it was too risky. Instead, he rang Geoff.

'I'm just dropping Beth off,' Geoff said. 'Do you want us to meet you there?'

'It would be good to have the support.'

'Lucky for you we've finished eating, then. See you soon.'

CHAPTER THIRTY-NINE

As Goldie stepped out of the lift onto the top floor, she looked around her. The Diamond Suite, Finn had said. And there it was, a little off to the right.

She walked slowly forward. How was she going to handle this? She was under no illusions. Whatever was going on in that room, Conn was going to be livid at Finn, and then her, turning up and he wasn't someone to be messed with lightly. But her little girl was in there, and so was her boy, no way was she waiting until the police managed to get their act together.

She took a deep breath and rapped smartly on the door.

'Who is it?' a voice asked suspiciously, after a few moments.

'Room service.'

In any other circumstances, she might have smiled at how easily the lie dropped from her lips but not tonight. She clenched one hand tightly in the other as she waited. And then the door opened. She vaguely knew the man's face and noted his stunned expression with satisfaction. Before he even had time to speak, she pushed past him and stalked towards a room from where light was showing through the door and she could hear voices. She flung the door open, taking everyone by surprise as she burst into the room.

'What the ...!' Conn jumped up from his seat and stared at Goldie in disbelief.

The woman's face was uncompromising. 'I'm not looking for trouble. I've just come to get my girl and her friend. And Finn too.' Her eyes darted around the room, settling in shock on Finn trussed up like a chicken in the corner.

Her gaze swung back, locking in on Alyssa and Hayley. 'Alyssa Abara, you get your clothes on this minute, girl. You're coming with me.' She stormed forward, her face livid, but quick as lightning, two men grabbed her from behind.

She rounded furiously on Conn. 'What's going on here? How dare you involve her in your filth and dirt? You should be ashamed of yourself.'

Conn's lips twisted into an ugly grimace. 'Don't talk to me like that and if you don't want Finn or Alyssa to come to any harm, you'll shut up now.'

'You think I'm scared of you?'

'I think you should be.'

'Well, I'm not. And just so you know, I told them downstairs that I was coming to collect my daughter, so anything happens to me, or any of us, they'll know exactly where we are and who to look for.'

She told the lie without batting an eyelid, but inside she was quaking – whether from anger or fear she wasn't sure. She'd heard bad stories about Conn and seeing him like this banished any doubts she might have had that they weren't true. He was pure evil standing there, his expression ugly with outrage at having his plans thwarted. In that moment, she knew he was capable of anything. Including killing all three of them.

'This isn't good.' It was Greg who spoke from his seat next to Alyssa. He was looking at Conn, his manner belligerent. 'Looks to me like your security's been compromised. How many more people are going to come barging in here tonight? This was meant to be a quiet night of us getting to know each other but it's turning out to be a bloody fiasco.'

'It's fine. I can handle it.'

'Doesn't look that way to me. We can't afford to draw attention to ourselves, not with tomorrow happening. Maybe you need to contact your source and bring the deal forward to tonight.'

The shaking of Conn's head was instant. 'That's not how it works ... he contacts me, not the other way round. Not unless it's an emergency.'

'Well, what do you think this is, if not an emergency? We're exposed, and the longer we delay, the more danger there is we'll get caught. I'm not waiting until tomorrow to get my stuff. It's too risky. I want it tonight or I'm out of here.' The man's stare was hard.

'I'm with Greg,' Sam chipped in. 'We need to bring our plans forward.' His gaze fell on Goldie. 'And we need to get rid of her and the others. Permanently. They've seen too much.'

Conn's brows snapped together. 'I can't get rid of a whole fucking family. How the hell am I supposed to do that?'

'Your problem. Sort it. No witnesses and no loose ends – that's how I work.'

'Look, I know Finn, and I know how to keep him in line. He won't do anything that would compromise his sister's safety, and neither will she.'

He turned back to Goldie. 'You don't want anything nasty to happen to Alyssa, do you? And when I say nasty, I mean really nasty –

you know what I'm talking about – young innocent girl thrown to the wolves. I can do it, and I will if you take one step out of line.'

Goldie stared defiantly back at him – then at Finn, who was looking broken. 'And if I agree to keep quiet you'll let me take them home now?'

'I'm not that stupid. You'll stay here til it's all over and we'll agree the terms of your release before we let you go.'

'I'm telling you I don't like loose ends,' Sam snapped, and Goldie looked at Conn uneasily as he shrugged, his eyes not meeting hers.

'We can talk about that later. For now, you're right. We just need to do the deals. Jake, Mark, tie Hayley and Goldie up, gag them and don't let them out your sight. We'll come back for them later. Danny, you come with me. You can all get your hands on the cash?' He looked at three of the men individually and they nodded. 'I'll call my contact then.' He walked into an adjoining room and closed the door.

Three minutes later he was back. 'Okay, he's not happy about the change of plan, but this is how we'll do it. You follow me to one of my lock-ups and we'll meet my contact there. He'll have the stuff with him in a van. You can sample it, while he counts the money. If everyone's happy, deal done. We'll divide the gear up and everyone heads home.'

'How do you know we can trust him?'

'I've worked with him for five years. We can trust him.'

He looked over to where Jake and another man were dealing with Goldie and the girls. 'Leave Alyssa,' he said. He reached for her clothes and threw them at her. 'Put those back on, you can come with us. Just to make sure Goldie and Finn behave themselves while we're gone.'

Alyssa grabbed the clothes to cover herself up, but the look she threw Goldie as she dressed, was terrified.

Goldie looked at Conn. 'Take me instead. There's no need to put the girl through that. I'll come with you, that'll keep Finn and Alyssa in line.'

'It ain't up for negotiation,' Conn said. 'I'm taking Alyssa, and you put one step out of line, and you better believe that'll be the last you see of her.'

Goldie looked over to where the tears were streaming down Alyssa's face. 'It'll be alright,' the older woman tried to reassure her, as she felt her arms being grabbed from behind and tied behind her back. 'Just do as they say, and you'll be fine, alright? We'll see you later.'

It was the last thing she said, as a gag was thrust into her mouth, stifling further speech, and she prayed she was right. She felt like she was going to vomit and she choked back the bile. She didn't trust these men one bit. All that talk about getting rid of them ... as casually said as if they were discussing the weather ... what if they decided Alyssa knew too much? She fought back her own tears as she stared at the young girl who'd become like a daughter to her. *Dear God, look after her*, she prayed silently to herself. *Take me if you need to but spare her*.

'Right, I'm guessing you guys need to get the cash from your rooms?' Conn said. 'I'll meet you out in the corridor in five.'

CHAPTER FORTY

Harry's car pulled into the car park and almost immediately a dark shape stepped out from some bushes and directed him to a parking space. He climbed out of his car and another man got out of the car next to him.

'DI Chambers,' he introduced himself. 'James...'

'Harry Briscombe. What's happening? Has anyone gone in?'

'No. Can we get back in your car, we don't want to be seen. Tom, you keep an eye on what's happening and the minute you see them come out, let me know.'

'Yes, sir.'

Harry's heart plummeted as he got back in his car and the other man joined him in the passenger seat.

'I know what you're going to say,' Chambers said, before Harry could open his mouth. 'But things have moved on and I haven't got time to talk. We've got an undercover agent in there who's indicated that they're moving tonight instead of tomorrow, and the minute they make their move we'll be on their tail. There's nothing to suggest your girls have come to any harm and our guy would do whatever he could to protect them. Once Stephens and the big fry are out of there, you can move in. But please do nothing to compromise the scene and secure it as quickly as you can for forensics afterwards.'

His head jerked sideways as a car's headlights came on across the other side of the car park, highlighting some individuals as they got into it. 'I've got to go. Keep low, we'll touch base later.'

He slipped quickly out of the car and back into his own, and Harry lowered himself in his seat. The tension in his body was fit to burst. All he wanted to do was get up to that room and make sure those girls were okay and that no one had been injured. He pulled out his phone and dialled the station.

'Susie? It's Harry. I'm at the Sandalwood Hotel & Spa outside Stevenage. Can you get me some backup asap? Beth and Geoff are on their way, but we don't know what we're going to find, and we might need armed assistance. Tell them no sirens and to keep it very low key until they hear from you that they can come in. I'll call you as soon as I've got an update.'

'On it,' Susie said. 'Be careful.'

He looked towards the parked car that still hadn't moved. 'Come on,' he muttered impatiently. What were they waiting for?

Oh, no. His breath caught as his gaze was drawn to his driving mirror where fresh lights were appearing in the car park entrance. Straightaway, he recognised Geoff's grey Corsa. He'd be dead meat if DI Chambers realised it was more police compromising their investigation. Quickly, he dialled Beth's number. She picked up straight away.

'Keep driving straight up and whatever you do, don't head left to park,' he said urgently. 'When you get out of the car, don't look around, just make straight for the hotel as if you're a normal couple and wait for me in the reception. I'll be with you in a couple of minutes.'

'Right boss.'

He hung up and watched as their car drove past his and continued in a straight line until it got to the top of the car park. They found a space on the right and once they'd climbed out, Geoff put his arm around Beth's shoulders, looking like he was whispering sweet nothings in her ear, as the two of them sauntered unhurriedly towards the hotel entrance.

Harry's tension eased, a grin tugging at his mouth. He wondered whose idea that had been.

His eyes flashed sideways as more car lights suddenly came on. Three more. And then they were in motion, lining up behind the first car as it headed towards the exit.

He looked into the car next to him. DI Chambers was sitting in there hunched down, with three other people and the tension emanating from that car was almost tangible. But no movement yet. The other vehicles had all exited the car park before the engine was started and side lights came on. Should he have offered assistance? He quickly discarded the notion. They would have asked if they'd wanted help and undoubtedly had their own back up in place.

No, his concern was Finn and his family – and what was going on in that room right now. That was his priority.

He exited the car and made his way swiftly towards the hotel.

In the foyer, Geoff and Beth were waiting for him. 'That was close,' he greeted them, 'but fortunately, Connors and his gang have headed off somewhere, with the ERSOU team in hot pursuit. We need to get up to Connors' room though and see what's going on up there.'

He walked over to the reception desk and showed his card.

'What room is Mr Stephens in? Connor Stephens?'

'Uh ...' The man checked his computer. 'Diamond Suite, top floor, but he just went out.'

'Okay, are there any other rooms close to his?'

'Two other suites, further down the corridor, both currently occupied by members of the same party. But they just went out too.'

'Good. We're going up to take a look. Can you give me a key?'

The man hesitated. 'I don't know. I need to get permission.'

'We haven't got time for that. There's a potentially serious situation going on involving two underage girls. We need to get up there now and make sure they're alright.'

The man nodded, punching a key card and handing it to Harry. 'Okay. I should probably come with you.'

'No, that won't be necessary. How many lifts are there?'

'Two.'

'Stop people using them after we've gone up. Put an Out of Order sign on them or something. It should only be for ten minutes or so, then we'll ring down to clear it for normal use again.'

'Uh, okay. I really should inform the manager about all this.'

'Feel free. We'll need to talk to him later anyway. Just make sure no one comes up to the room until I say it's safe to do so.'

Harry pressed the button for the lift, and they waited impatiently for it to arrive.

'Come on,' he muttered.

There was a ping and the doors opened. Beth pressed the top button marked penthouse suites and they waited for the doors to close again. It seemed to take forever, and Harry groaned his frustration. Then, finally, they were heading upwards. The journey seemed incredibly slow, but eventually, with another ping, the fifth floor was announced, and the doors opened. They filed out in quick succession, splitting both ways to find the Diamond Suite.

'Over here,' Beth said in a low voice.

Harry and Geoff moved quickly to join her. 'Right,' Harry said. 'We need to catch them by surprise. Are you ready for this?'

He held the card to the lock and the mechanism gave a soft click. He quietly opened the door and peered around the frame. He was looking at a long, empty hallway with several closed doors leading off it. He entered the suite, beckoning the others to follow. From one of the rooms, he could hear talking. He took a deep breath and threw open the door. 'Police, put your hands on your head and don't move.'

There were two men sitting with their backs to them on a sofa and two teenage girls sitting opposite them. They all jumped up in shock.

'Remain seated,' Harry ordered, 'Don't move. We have armed back-up outside if we need it but we're trying to do this quietly.' His eyes did a quick flick of the room, taking in the two girls on the sofa. But neither of them was mixed race and they looked too old to be Alyssa Abara and her friend.

Without warning, one of the men leapt up from his seat and made a beeline for Beth, thrusting her out of the way and onto the floor, as he made a dash for the door. But Geoff was on him with an impressive rugby tackle that brought him crashing to the ground. The second man was also making a run for it, and this time it was Harry who headed him off at the door. They were grappling hard, and scrabbling up from the floor, Beth caught a glint of steel in the man's hand. She dived on him just as he drew his arm back to thrust the knife into Harry's side, catching him by surprise as she grabbed his arm and twisted it into an arm lock up his back. 'Oh, no you don't,' she shouted. 'Drop it. *Now!*' He cried out in pain as she twisted his arm higher up his back, forcing him to drop the knife on to the floor.

'Where's Finn Abara and his sister?' Harry demanded.

'Answer him,' Beth said, applying more pressure to his arm when he made no reply.

'In the bedroom,' the man gasped, jerking his head behind him to the right.

They manoeuvred the two men back onto the sofa and Beth rushed over to open the door he'd indicated. She stared in shock at the three people gagged and tied to chairs, before moving swiftly over to release their gags.

'Alyssa,' Finn gasped as soon as he could speak. 'They took her with them. We need to find her.'

'I'm telling you we need to go and find her, *now*.' Finn was on the point of losing it.

'And I'm telling you we can't,' Harry said. 'Another team's gone after them and if we intervene we could mess things up and make things worse for your sister. I know it's hard, but you have to be patient. As soon as I know anything, you'll know.'

Finn looked frustratedly at Goldie and she shook her head. 'There's nothing we can do, son. We just have to sit it out.'

'It's my fault they've taken her. If anything happens to her, it'll be my fault, and I'll kill him, I swear.'

'You need to come back to the station with us and make statements.'

'I ain't making no statement til I know my Alyssa's safe. And unless you're arresting me, I don't think you can force me.'

'I could do you for obstruction of an ongoing investigation.'

Finn glared at him, and Harry sighed. 'I know you're worried about your sister, and you want to find her, but we've got the best on that right now and if you go diving in as a one-man band you'll just make it more dangerous for her.'

'Man, I can't leave her to the mercy of those evil bastards. What would you do if it was your sister?'

Harry immediately thought of Angie. He hardly knew the woman, but was surprised to realise that, already, he felt a responsibility towards her.

His tone eased. 'Look, I know it's hard, and you want to help her but, as you said, they're dangerous people – and the chances of you successfully finding her and getting her out of there are next to zero. Put your trust in the police for once and let us do our job, eh? Let one of my team go home with you and stay until all this is over, so we can keep you up to speed with what's going on.'

He didn't add that it would also enable them to keep an eye on what he was getting up to.

He looked over to where Beth was quietly talking to Hayley while Goldie sat with her arm around the young girl, comforting her. They'd found the poor girl in her underwear with just a blanket over her – provided for her by Jake, he'd been quick to inform them. 'Felt sorry for the poor kid, you know? You make sure to put that in your report. That I looked after her.'

She was all over the place, incoherent and clearly the worse for wear from substance abuse.

'Beth, get her some water can you, and when the ambulance arrives phone her parents and let them know which hospital they're taking her to. Then accompany Hayley to the hospital and get a statement as soon as she's able to give one.'

Beth nodded.

His gaze shifted to where Geoff was standing guard over the two men.

'You okay to head back with Finn and Mrs Lamb once backup arrives, and stay with them until we can get a family liaison officer out there? I'll update you as soon as I know what's gone on.'

'Yes, boss.'

They all looked up as a loud knock on the door heralded the arrival of more police and the paramedics.

'Stop there, please,' Harry ordered. 'Paramedics only. We're waiting for CSI to come in. You head off with Goldie and Finn now, Geoff. I'll let you know as soon as I have any news.'

CHAPTER FORTY-ONE

Alyssa's hopes of calling out for help in the hotel reception had been crushed when Conn had said for everyone to take the emergency exit stairs out of the hotel. She'd tried to open her car door to make a dash for it when they'd first thrown her in there, but the child locks were on. Now she shrank into the corner of the seat to make herself as invisible as she could, keeping quiet as Conn ranted on about Finn and Goldie messing everything up.

'Your brother and that Goldie, they're idiots,' he said, turning round to look at her. 'They've put their lives in danger now. Don't know how I can get them out of that one. But you I can save. You want to live?'

No response.

'You want to live?' he shouted.

She shrank further back into her seat. Yes,' she whimpered.

'Then you do as I tell you. I need to know you're on board one hundred per cent. Cos when they tell me to get rid of you, which they will, I need to convince them that you're part of my team and won't rat on us. Can you do that? Can I trust you?'

She nodded in the darkness. She was shaking so much she had to clasp her hands together.

'Answer me,' he barked.

'*Yes!*'

'Even if Goldie and your brother get done in?'

'Don't say that. I don't want to hear it.'

'Grow up, Alyssa, and do it now. This ain't no game we're playing. If your brother hadn't interfered, none of this would've happened. It's his own fault.'

For a moment she wanted to believe him because it took the blame away from her. But she couldn't because she knew it was her fault, not Finn's. Her fault for not listening to what he'd been saying all along and then not asking him for help earlier. Whatever was happening back at the hotel, it was all because of her. Maybe Finn and Goldie were already dead and there was nothing could be done for them. She stifled a sob.

'You tell me if you're part of this team or not. If you're not, you won't see this night out alive. Simple as that. But if you are, I'll look after you and you'll have more money than you could ever have imagined. But you need to convince me I can trust you.'

She shut her mind off to the awful images flooding her imagination. Finn, Goldie and possibly even Hayley, lying dead, murdered. She didn't want to die. She hardened her heart, feeling a sudden, irrational anger against all of them – even her parents for dying. Where were they all now when she needed them?

She swallowed hard. 'Yeah, I'm part of your team,' she said, hating herself as she said it. 'I'll do whatever you want me to do. You can trust me.'

'Good. Then don't let me down.'

He turned to the man, Danny, who was driving the car. 'When we get there, Will said he'll have the stuff in a white van. He'll bring a sample into the lock-up for them to check and once the money's been handed over, we'll divvy up the goods as quick as we can and get out of there.'

'What'll we do with her while that's going on?'

'Bring her into the lock-up. Sit her quietly in a corner at the back. If she puts one step out of line,' he paused, 'finish her.'

Some fifteen minutes later they turned into an industrial estate in Hatfield and pulled up outside a large lock-up. Alyssa could see a white van parked in front of them and watched as Conn got out of the car to speak to another man, before moving over to unlock the unit. Then Danny got out and opened her door. 'Out. And remember. No trouble.'

Alyssa looked nervously around as she climbed out of the car. What they called the lock-up was a small warehouse on an industrial estate with a corrugated roof, a pull-up double door, and a smaller door to one side. Danny wasted no time, hauling her over to the smaller door that Conn had unlocked and pushing her through it. The unit was bigger inside than it looked, stretching quite a way back, and was filled with all sorts of miscellaneous crates and containers stacked against the walls. 'Sit on that crate back there,' Danny ordered, pointing to a large wooden box at the back of the space. 'And don't move or make a sound.'

She sat, and watched wide-eyed as a man she hadn't seen before – Will, they called him – pulled some packs of white powder from a briefcase and handed them over to Conn and the others who had now all joined him. She was shaking like a leaf. She couldn't stop it. She'd never felt so scared in her life – or so ashamed. She'd betrayed Goldie and Finn, saying she'd be part of Conn's team. They'd never have caved as quickly as she had. She was a coward. She stifled a sob. She couldn't bear to think about what might happen afterwards – if they killed Finn and Goldie. It was like a knife physically piercing her heart. She clasped her hands around her knees and started a slow, rhythmic rock, backwards and forwards. She wouldn't think about it – or the fact that the only person left then to look after her, would be Conn.

'The money?' the man, Will, asked, and Sam, Greg and the third man hauled their own briefcases onto the table.

'There's fifty grand in each bag,' Conn told him, adding his own bag to the pile. 'Two hundred grand in all. You count it while we check the stuff.'

Silence followed. Alyssa had never seen so much money passing hands and she stared, open mouthed.

'*Armed police. You are surrounded. Come out with your hands up.*'

Heads jerked up, horror reflected on every face.

'Fuck!'

'What the–'

'*Conn*! What's going on?'

Conn looked stunned. 'I don't know. I don't know.'

'I repeat. This is the police. Come out with your hands up or we'll storm the building.'

'*You bastard. You betrayed us.*'

'No! Don't be ridiculous. I don't know any more than you do, why they're here.'

'Is there another way out?'

'No.'

Conn swung round, casting about him wildly. His eyes settled on Alyssa. In an instant, he'd leapt from his chair and run to the back of the unit, yanking her viciously to her feet and hauling her over to the side door. He threw open the small window next to it and thrust her forward so they could see her.

'We got a hostage,' he shouted. 'Stay away or I swear I'll kill her. Back off now.'

His body was shaking uncontrollably behind hers as he held her. She didn't know if it was from the drugs he'd taken, or from fear, and she jerked as she felt the sharp blade of a knife press into her throat. 'Don't move,' he spat. 'Or you're dead.'

She whimpered, her legs buckling, but his grip kept her upright. Through the small window, she could see that the yard outside was transformed. There were bright lights and cars everywhere and she could see a policeman standing behind one of the cars, a large tannoy in his hand. 'Connor Stephens. This is the police, and we are armed. Put the knife down and come out. Don't make things worse for yourself.'

'Back off,' Conn yelled. 'Do you hear me? I mean it, I'll do it. Watch me – you see if I don't.' Alyssa felt him move as he manoeuvred an arm to get a better grip on her, and next thing she knew a loud bang rent the air. She screamed, expecting to feel the knife slash her neck at any moment, but then, unbelievably, Connors' grip went slack as he slid to the floor. She looked down in horror at the hole in his head and screamed again.

Everyone in the lock-up froze as they stared at Connors' inert form in disbelief, and Alyssa was no exception. She knew the door was there, inches from her shaking body, but she was in shock, unable to make the move that would lead her to freedom and safety.

'Grab her! Quick!' It was Sam's voice as he lunged towards her, and it was all the impetus she needed to jerk her out of her shock back into the danger of her own situation. She made a dive for the door, fumbling with the knob as she yanked it open. She was aware of a second person launching himself in her direction, colliding with Sam as he did so. It was Greg and, in the split second that their eyes met, she knew he'd done it deliberately to give her a chance of escape.

'Shit,' she heard his exclamation. 'Quick, she's getting away.'

She felt a hand grab her dress. *She wasn't going to make it.*

But the scent of freedom spurred her on. With a frantic tug, she tore the material free of that grasp and raced, sobbing, out into the cold, night air.

'Don't shoot, don't kill me,' she screamed, running towards the lights. She ran as fast as she could, expecting a bullet to drop her dead to the ground at any moment, like Conn. But it didn't happen. And then she was crashing into the strong, solid bulk of another human being. Someone who wrapped his arms around her and told her it was alright, she was safe. And what a brave girl she'd been.

And as she clung to him tightly, sobbing into his jacket, she was glad he didn't know the truth. That she wasn't brave at all. She was a coward who would have done anything to save her own skin.

CHAPTER FORTY-TWO

Harry poured himself another coffee, knowing he should be drinking decaf if he wanted to get any sleep at all, yet needing the caffeine to keep him awake. It was gone two in the morning, and he'd spent the last hour and a half flicking listlessly through the files on Barbara Harding and Elena Mancini, fruitlessly noting all the links they had in common. His mind just hadn't been on it because he was on tenterhooks waiting for an update from DI Chambers – and the longer he waited the more intense the sick feeling in the pit of his stomach became. He should have heard something by now.

His phone rang and he pounced on it. It was Chambers.

'Successful result, except that we were forced to take Connors out. He had a knife to the girl's throat and made a move which was considered to be a danger to her life. But we rounded the rest of them up – together with a big haul that they were in the process of divvying up – and your girl's safe. They're taking her to the hospital now for a check over – looks like they plied her with those cannabis-laced sweets that are flooding the country. There were thousands of those in the stash we picked up, disguised as Haribos, Kinder eggs, Mars bars, you name it – it's a frightening development. Anyway, the foster mother and brother have been driven to the hospital to see her. The paramedic thinks she'll be fine.'

'Thank Christ for that, and thanks for letting me know. I've been on tenterhooks waiting for this call. Good to know I can head home now.'

'Huh, more than I can do. But once we've tidied things up and I hit the sack, I'll be staying there for at least ten hours, I'm telling you that.'

Which was more than he'd be doing, Harry thought ruefully, as they ended the call. It was Saturday, and wouldn't he just love a lie-in. But he'd need to be back in the office first thing and get his mind back on the Barbara Harding case before anyone else ended up dying.

He sighed as he got up from his desk and picked up his jacket. There was someone else who'd be expecting him to have some time off today, as well – his mother – who was still waiting to have a heart to heart with him. He was tempted to stay the night at Claire's to delay that conversation; he hadn't had time to sort his own head out, let alone get it around hers. But he had to face her at some point, so he'd go home and set the alarm, to give them some time to talk in the morning before he headed back in.

It seemed no time at all before his alarm went off at six-thirty, and Harry groaned, burying his head under the pillow in a fruitless attempt to escape it. He dragged himself from the comfort of his bed into the shower and took a deep breath before giving himself a burst of cold water at the end. Brutal, but it did the trick waking him up.

Downstairs, he could hear the radio on in the kitchen which meant his mum was up, and he took a breath before going downstairs to join her.

'Hey, Mum.'

'Morning. You were late last night. I gave up waiting for you.'

'Yes, it was gone three before I got to bed. I told you I'm in the middle of a complicated case, and it's not getting any simpler. I need to get back in as soon as I've had some breakfast.'

'Oh, Harry, you need some sleep. And we need to talk.'

'You're right on both counts, but I'm sorry, it's just not the sort of job I can pick and choose when I go in. Without sounding too dramatic, people's lives are at stake.'

He moved over to the cupboard and pulled out some cereals. 'How did it go with Dad last night?'

'Not good. He just doesn't seem to get how huge all this is. How it's completely shattered my trust in him. He said that he'd been an idiot but that he'd loved me and hadn't wanted to lose me, or ruin what we had. He couldn't see that he'd already done that by having the affair. But he's right. I don't know if I could have accepted him fathering another child on top of being unfaithful, especially when I always quite wanted a second one myself, but at least it would have been out in the open and we'd have dealt with it at the time. To find out now, and know that he's been deceiving me for the last thirty years ... you get what I'm saying, don't you?

'Of course, I do.'

'I'm too old for it all. But I also feel I'm too old to start over again with a new life on my own.'

Her eyes welled up and Harry got up from his seat and put his arm around her. 'Come on, fifty-nine isn't old, but does that mean you and Dad are going to try and work things out?'

'I don't know. I've told him I need time to think things through. But if he thinks we can sit down and play happy families, he's got another think coming.'

It would take time Harry thought as he took his leave of her, and whatever the outcome, it was a bumpy road ahead. Maybe she'd never come round to accepting Angela's presence in their family.

In the car, he called his father.

'Harry? Bloody hell, what time do you call this?'

'Sorry, Dad, I'm on my way into work and just wanted to check you're okay.'

There was a silence, then: 'Things aren't good. I take it you've spoken to your mother. She wants nothing to do with me.'

'She's hurting. Give her time.'

'Well, I'm rattling around in this bloody hotel, not knowing what to do with myself. I know I screwed up and now I'm paying the price. God knows what we'll be doing about Christmas.'

'No point even thinking about that at the moment, you just need to give Mum the space she needs and hope you can come back from this.'

'I know.' He hesitated. 'Thanks for sending me Angie's number, I'm meeting up with her for dinner tonight if you want to join us?' There was another pause before he added. 'You don't know how I've longed to be able to say those words to you. It's been hard keeping that compartment of my life secret. I'm glad it's out in the open to be honest.' His voice was tired and emotional, and Harry's own emotions welled up in response.

'I'm not ready for that yet, Dad. I will see Angela again but on a one to one, when I've had time to digest stuff. Tell her that from me, will you? That I'll be in touch?'

He switched off the call and his feelings with it. By the time he walked into the incident room, he was back on track, focused on the case in hand.

"Morning,' Beth said.

He looked at her in surprise. 'Good on you for getting in so early. How was it at the hospital?'

'Both the girls are still there and somewhat the worse for wear from cannabis and alcohol consumption, although Hayley was the one they were most concerned about. I couldn't get a coherent statement out of her last night, but I told her parents someone would be back today to get one. That DI Chambers came to the hospital to check on them and he said he'll organise their statements as it's part of their investigation. He seemed a decent sort.'

'Yeah. Well, that's good. One thing less to worry about. We can concentrate on our own investigation now. And first things first, we need to get Abara back in, and get a statement off him about who was or wasn't driving Connor Stephens' car the day Barbara Harding was killed.'

'He was still at the hospital when I left. He said as soon as Alyssa was back home with Goldie, he'd come in. He's worried about their safety. He said Conn's net spreads wide. I told him we might need to put them up in a safe house. It didn't go down well.'

'It never does but I expect they'll come round to it.'

'DI Chambers said they'd be doing forensic sweeps of the hotel room, lock up and all the cars and they'd let us have anything relevant to our investigation.'

'It'll be good to see if they find anything useful in Connors' car. I'll also get Dave to check the Holmes data for a list of items stolen from those burglaries and Barbara Harding, and hand that over to them. See if any of it's stashed at Connors' home or in the lock-up.'

Beth looked at her watch and got up. 'I spoke to Paul Cunningham just before you came in – Mia's boyfriend?' she added, when he frowned.

'Oh, yeah.'

'I told him we had a few questions to ask him. He's got a hospital appointment this morning and didn't have time to come in first, so I said I'd go over to him early. I know you wanted to get that interview in the bag.'

'Hospital appointment on a Saturday?'

'Probably private.'

'Make sure you take someone with you. We don't know who is, or who isn't, dangerous. But whoever did those killings is ruthless.'

'Think I can't handle myself, Harry?'

'Not at all, just being sensible.

Beth grinned. 'Okay. I'll sort it.'

It was Mia who answered the door, and she looked at Beth curiously. 'Why do you want to see Paul?'

'I'll talk to him about that. This is PC Hammond. Can we come in?'

The girl shrugged and opened the door wider. 'Paul, the police are here,' she called down the hallway.

'Just coming.'

She showed them into the lounge. 'Have you got any news yet on Aunt Barbara?'

'We're getting there, but it takes time. That's why we keep asking questions of people. Ah, Mr Cunningham.'

He was impeccably dressed in designer clothes, his hair still sleeked from his shower. A waft of expensive aftershave teased Beth's nostrils. Smooth bastard, she thought.

'How can I help you? I've got ten minutes before I need to leave.'

Beth hesitated. She would have loved to have said what she had to say in front of his girlfriend – see her reaction to that – but it seemed unnecessarily cruel to the poor girl.

'Could we have a word in private?' She looked at Mia enquiringly and the girl shrugged, leaving the room and pulling the door to behind her.

'Something's come to our attention that we want to follow up on. I understand you were involved with a young woman a few years back, who accused you of defrauding her of twenty-five thousand pounds, claiming it was for an investment that would return her money five-fold. I'm sure you can see why that might be of interest to us with regard to Barbara Harding's investigation?'

'I don't see why at all. That was over four years ago and a complete misunderstanding,' Paul said. 'Louise was perfectly aware of the risks involved. It was an investment that went belly up. It happens.'

'But she was your girlfriend at the time, right? Not just a client.'

'Yes she was. All very sad because it broke us up. If you've looked into it, you'll see that no charges were ever brought. I think that speaks for itself.'

'All it says is that it was a high-profile family who didn't want embarrassing publicity, and they were wealthy enough to take the loss. Otherwise, it might have been a very different story for you.'

'Well, there you go. Funny old life, isn't it? They were financiers themselves. They understood that things can go wrong. All that's a very different story to the situation between Mia and me, now.'

'How long have you been seeing each other?'

He shrugged. 'About nine months or so.'

'And you met her before or after she moved in with Barbara?'

'I don't see what that's got to do with anything.'

'Just answer the question please. How did you meet?'

'I happened to be walking past the house when she pulled into Barbara's drive one evening. We got talking and the rest, as they say...'

'And you were walking past the house because, what ... you have friends in the road?'

He stared her out. 'No, I was simply out walking early one evening, admiring the houses.'

'Even though it's nowhere near where you live.'

'I'd played golf that day with a friend at Hadley and thought I'd have a wander around the area. I'm always looking for potential places to move to.'

'Or possibly for potential rich girlfriends?'

'I take exception to that. It's untrue and offensive.'

'Just doing my job.' Beth closed her notebook. 'That's it for now. I'd like a few words with Mia but no need for you to delay your appointment any longer.'

'I'd rather be here when you speak to Mia, and this is my flat. Are you going to tell her about Louise?'

'If I feel it's appropriate. I need to interview her alone, like I did you. I can either do it here or, if that's a problem for you, I can ask her to come down to the station.'

He scowled at her. 'Fine.'

He walked over to the door and called out to where Mia was in the kitchen. 'Your turn, Mia. Give me a shout when you've finished.'

Mia looked nervous as she sat down on the sofa and faced Beth. 'What's going on? Why are you interviewing us? Mum said I should get a solicitor if you singled me out for questioning.'

'That's up to you, pet.' Beth smiled, softening her voice to try and put the girl at ease. 'I just have a couple of questions and if you don't want to answer them without a solicitor, that's fine. We're just trying to get our facts straight.'

The girl hesitated, then shrugged. 'Okay.'

'Your boyfriend. You've been going out about nine months. Is that right?'

The girl nodded.

'I'm curious to know ... has he ever suggested you invest money in anything?'

The girl's eyes flew open. She had the look about her of someone who's just been blindsided.

'Why are you asking that?'

'Has he ever mentioned an ex-girlfriend of his called Louise?'

Mia shook her head.

'You might want to ask him about her,' Beth said. 'Then if you want any more info, give me a call.'

'You're frightening me. What's he done? Last night–'

Beth looked at her keenly. 'Last night?'

Mia plucked at the material of her dress where it covered her knees. 'I don't know. I don't know what you're talking about, but ... last night he mentioned a new app that he was going to invest in, but he didn't have all the money he needed. He thought we should invest together when my money from Barbara comes through, and said it had the potential to make ten times what we put into it when the company got sold.'

The door opened, and Paul burst in. 'Don't say any more, Mia, and don't listen to her. She's trying to turn you against me. The stupid cow doesn't know what she's talking about.'

'Your boyfriend was accused of swindling a previous girlfriend out of twenty-five thousand pounds,' Beth said, ignoring him. 'He persuaded her to lend him some money to invest in a start-up company that apparently then went bust. Only it turns out it was a company he'd set up with another man and they misappropriated the funds.'

Mia turned to Paul in bemusement. 'Paul?'

'All lies,' he snapped.

She shook her head. 'But you were only saying last night about me investing Barbara's money with you in that start-up company.'

'Yeah, but that's a much safer bet. I told you I'd show you all the info on it before we decided. You don't have to do it if you don't want to.'

'But you were banging on at me last night when I said I wasn't sure, saying we should do it as soon as the money came through ... that it was too good an opportunity to miss.'

She switched her gaze back to Beth. 'Did he really do that? Swindle that girl out of money?'

'It never went to court,' Beth said, 'but we've looked into the investigation that was carried out and I'm afraid it very much looks like your boyfriend made off with the money.'

'Don't listen to her, Mia. They've got no proof to back up their claims. She's trying to spook you and turn you against me.'

'And why would I do that?' Beth countered. 'I'm simply stating the facts as they've been presented.'

'Well, your facts are wrong, and you know where you can stuff them.'

'Charming,' Beth said. She turned back to Mia. 'I see from your statements you claimed to be together last Saturday from about five o'clock onwards?'

'Yes. I finished work at four and went straight over to Paul's. We went out for dinner that night and came back and watched television.'

'And you, Mr Cunningham, said you were playing golf with a mate at Hadley Golf Club that morning. We spoke to your friend, and he confirms you had a drink afterwards and separated at about one. Where did you go after that, between, say, one and three?'

'I went to Waitrose in Barnet and did some shopping for the week-end and then went home. And before you ask, no, no-one saw me but I did pay by credit card so I assume you can check it out?'

'Okay, we'll be doing that, but it does leave a gap just around the time Barbara was killed. Did you know about the key she kept in her back garden?'

'No.'

Mia's look was sharp. 'You did, Paul. Don't you remember back in the Spring, when Barbara was out with friends, and you realised you'd left your wallet there? I told you where the key was then.'

He scowled. 'Well, perhaps you did but I forgot, okay? If you remember, we ended up going round that evening to pick the wallet up and stayed for supper, so I didn't use it. And I've had no reason to use it since then. Christ, Mia, you're not accusing me of murdering your aunt now?'

Beth studied the two of them. There was a window of opportunity; it was a small one, but it was there. He'd have to be one cool customer though, to murder someone and go straight from the scene to do his weekend shopping.

'And last Wednesday, the day Elena was killed?'

'I already told you. I dropped Elena off at the station, went home and then went back to Barbara's house for supper before coming back here with Mia.'

Again, enough of a window of opportunity to stash Elena's body in the boot of his car to dump later that night if he was worried about her contesting the will.

Beth stood up. 'Okay, we've got a few more things to check out – including your Waitrose receipt, Mr Cunningham. We'll get back to you if we need anything more, but please make sure we can easily contact you.'

'I want to come with you.' Mia's voice was distraught, and she wouldn't look at Paul. 'I don't want to stay here.'

'Mia!'

She ignored him, staring at Beth with misty eyes. 'I'll just grab some bits. Will you wait for me? I only need a lift to the station.'

'That's fine, pet. No worries.'

CHAPTER FORTY-THREE

'Bingo!' Dave Freeman's excitement was palpable as the analyst highlighted an email and hit print. 'Sir, I think I've got something here that you're going to be well pleased with.'

He jumped up from his seat and moved over to the printer to retrieve the document, handing it to Harry with a flourish.

Harry scanned the contents and felt the same sort of adrenalin rush that he got when he drank a strong cup of coffee. 'Good work, Dave. Let's get him in, and while we're at it, request Matteo Mancini to come in too. I think it's time to turn up the pressure.'

Matteo Mancini's stare was hostile when Harry walked into the interview room. 'What's going on? Why do you need to see me again? This is beginning to feel like harassment and my wife needs me at the moment. She's pregnant and not well.'

Harry sat down at the table and opened his file. 'Thanks for coming in, Mr. Mancini. We requested this interview because some new information has come to light today regarding your father, and I wanted to speak to you about it before we speak to him.'

'What information? What are you talking about?'

Harry's phone buzzed and he looked at it impatiently, but when he saw who it was, he got up from his chair and went to the corner of the room.

'Geoff, is it urgent? I'm just starting my interview with Matteo Mancini.'

He frowned as the other man quickly relayed the reason for his call.

'Right. He's probably trying to leave the country. Have you got ports and airports covered? And Euro-tunnel? Okay, sounds like you're on it. Let me know as soon as you hear anything.'

He ended the call and returned to take his seat opposite Matteo.

He watched the other man closely as he framed his question. 'We've had some intelligence come through this morning. Were you aware that Lorenzo Mancini is not your father's real name?'

Matteo looked shocked. 'What? What are you talking about? Of course it is.'

Harry shook his head. 'His fingerprints have come back as a match to someone wanted in Italy in connection with organised crime out there, back in the eighties. We believe he moved to the UK with a new identity to escape arrest.'

'That's rubbish. He came over when I was a baby because he and my mother felt there were more opportunities over here.'

'He came over because he was wanted for murder, amongst other things.'

'No! You're lying.'

'Has he ever gone back to Italy? Taken you there on holiday perhaps, to meet other members of your family?'

'He doesn't have any family. He was an only child, and his parents are dead.'

'None of that is true. His real name is Alessandro Bertolami and his mother, and two sisters are very much alive. We're bringing him in for questioning over the deaths of both Barbara Harding and your mother – only that was one of my colleagues on the phone, telling me that he's done a runner. Probably because he knew we'd come up with a match for him from the fingerprints we took.'

Matteo looked from one to the other in complete and utter shock. 'No, this can't be right. You've got it wrong. He's not a murderer.' He turned to Beth. 'You saw how cut up he was when you told him my mother was dead.'

'We don't know what happened yet,' Beth said. 'Maybe it was an accident, and he was genuinely upset.'

Matteo jumped up from the table. 'I want to speak to him before I speak to you. You can't stop me.'

'Please calm down, Mr Mancini.' Harry said. 'You won't be seeing him for a while once we've brought him in. Even if he's innocent of Barbara's and your mother's murders, we'll be advising Interpol that we're holding him, and no doubt they'll want to extradite him to Italy in connection with the serious charges he faces there.'

Matteo stared at him in disbelief, then slumped back into his chair and buried his head in his hands. When he raised it, his face was a mixture of emotions. 'I don't know what to think. If he killed my mother I can never forgive him. She...' He broke off.

'Yes?' Harry prompted.

The other man shook his head, his expression tortured.

'We just want to get at the truth,' Harry said. 'As I believe you do. If there's anything more you want to tell us?'

For a long moment Matteo said nothing and Harry shot Beth a quick warning look to stop her from breaking the silence. If the man needed time, they'd give it to him.

Finally, he seemed to come to a decision, his voice heavy as he said. 'I told you that in our phone conversation on Wednesday, Mama said she was going to leave my father and divorce him. I don't know why she didn't do it years ago. He didn't treat her well. She said it was because they lived apart during the week anyway, and they had a good social life at weekends with the Italian Club and other friends – and financially it would have been tough. But what I didn't tell you, was ... the reason she was going to leave him now, was because she suspected him of killing Barbara. She said she knew the solicitor was going to Barbara's on Saturday and she'd told my father that. He was the only other person who knew, and it felt like too much of a coincidence that Barbara should be murdered that same day. I couldn't believe it. I said that Papa has his faults, but I couldn't believe he'd do anything like that. I told her she was crazy ... that if she divorced him he'd probably be entitled to half the money anyway, but she said no, she was leaving, and he wouldn't dare stop her because she knew things about him that he wouldn't want publicised.'

'What sort of things?'

'She didn't say. Maybe it was the stuff you're talking about, but ... their marriage wasn't the best. My dad can be ... aggressive sometimes. I assumed it was something to do with that.'

Harry leant forward. 'Are we talking domestic violence here?'

Matteo nodded.

'Against just your mother, or you as well? Was he physically violent towards you as a child? Did he hit your mum?'

Matteo shifted uncomfortably in his seat. 'Sometimes,' he mumbled. 'But whenever he lashed out at us it was always in the heat of the moment, and he was always sorry afterwards. He hasn't done anything like that recently, I'm sure. She'd have told me.'

'A lot of women don't speak out,' Harry said, 'especially if they think it will cause more problems than it solves.'

Matteo looked at him and took a deep breath, before saying. 'I went through a difficult period when I was a teenager; I had anger issues because I felt so frustrated that I couldn't help my mum. I saw a counsellor who told me that my issues were more than likely brought on by Dad's aggression; that it wasn't my fault. It helped. But maybe … maybe that was why Mama chose not to say anything if my father was treating her badly. Maybe she worried that now I'm an adult I might not take things sitting down, and, as you said, it might cause more problems than it solved.'

He turned back to Beth. 'I didn't tell you about my conversation with my mother because at the time, I didn't believe it and I thought Dad was going through enough, but … now I don't know what to think.'

His voice broke and he started to sob.

Harry closed his file. 'Okay, I think that's answered enough of our questions for now. You may as well head off home. In view of the Interpol connection, it's unlikely we'll be releasing your father, and he won't be allowed visitors for a while, but we'll keep you in the picture.'

'So, what did you think of all that?' Beth said, as they made their way back to the office.

'I'm thinking that things aren't looking good for Lorenzo Mancini if we find him, and that with a bit of luck, we'll get some dregs of the weekend after all.'

CHAPTER FORTY-FOUR

I t was a tense two hours, but the call when it came through brought a smile to Harry's face. He hung up the phone and looked round at the others in the office.

'They've got him. Picked him up at Luton airport, booked on a flight to Catania. They're bringing him in now. Thank God the system does sometimes work.'

'What's this about?' Lorenzo Mancini demanded belligerently two and a half hours later, when Harry finally joined him and his solicitor in the interview room. 'Why have you arrested me? I was on my way to visit relatives. A man needs to be with his family at a sad time like this.'

'I thought Matteo was the only family you have,' Harry responded coolly. 'At least, that's what he told us. But before we go any further I need to advise you that we're interviewing you under caution, so we just need to get the formalities out of the way.'

Once that had been done, Harry faced him squarely across the table.

'Why were you leaving the country in such a hurry, Mr Mancini?'

He looked agitated. 'I told you, I wanted to go home to share my grief over my wife's tragic death with our families. But then your people come, and they arrest me. I don't understand why. I have just been bereaved; can you not respect that?' He mopped at his eyes with a handkerchief. 'To do it like this makes me feel like a criminal.'

'Perhaps that's because you are a criminal,' Harry said coolly.

The man stared at him. Harry had his full attention now.

'We've had some information come through this morning that shows you've been leading a double life, Mr Mancini. For a start, Mancini isn't your real family name, is it?'

The man darted a quick look at his solicitor, before replying. 'Of course it is. I do not know why you would say this.'

'I think you do. You see, we've had your fingerprints come back now and they match those of a man called Alessandro Bertolami – wanted by Interpol in connection with a number of serious offences in Italy back in the eighties, including murder. Would you like to talk to me about that?'

The change in Lorenzo's expression was impressive, as it hardened. 'No, I would not. I repeat, I do not know what you are talking about.'

'I thought you might say that, so let's stick to our current investigation for the time being, shall we? The murders of Barbara Harding and your wife.'

'You cannot think for one minute that I killed them?'

'That's exactly what I am thinking unless you can convince me otherwise. Let me put some facts together for you, so that you can understand why.'

Harry leaned forward on the desk. 'One: you have a history of violence, both in Italy and here in the UK, where, according to your son, you hit him as a child, and also your wife.'

'He's lying.'

'Your family's GP records note concern that your wife may have been a victim of domestic abuse, and that Matteo also had a couple of unexplained injuries. However, as is often the case, your wife didn't speak up and they could get no proof of any of it. Matteo also had significant anxiety and anger issues as he got older, which it was concluded were more than likely brought on by an overly domineering father figure.

'Two: you knew your wife was due to inherit a considerable amount of money from Barbara, and you also knew that Barbara was about to change her will. We understand that she had, on occasion, threatened to cut everyone out and while there was no real reason to suspect she would disinherit Elena completely, she had stated quite clearly that she wanted to leave more money to charity, and perhaps you were concerned that she might reduce your wife's legacy? That could have been a significant amount of money to miss out on.

'Three: Elena knew about the meeting with the solicitors on Saturday and according to your son, she'd told you about that meeting. It was originally planned for four pm but unbeknown to anyone, it was brought forward to the morning due to personal reasons on the part of the solicitor involved. Barbara was murdered at around one thirty pm, which should have given you plenty of time to kill her and exit the house before the original planned meeting you still believed was happening at four.'

'You cannot have proof of any of this. My wife told me about no such meeting, I had not seen her since the Monday before that.'

'The meeting was arranged more than three weeks ago.'

'So why did no one see my car if I was there?'

'We're checking CCTV now for any images of it along the roads either end of Beechwood Way, from where it's possible to access the footpath at the back of Barbara's garden.'

'I told you; I was at the pub with friends that day. Ask them.'

'We have, and according to them, you left early, around twelve thirty. To go to the betting shop, you said. Yet you told us you had been at the pub for most of the afternoon.'

Lorenzo shrugged. 'I gamble a little, and Matteo and Elena, they disapprove. That is why I did not say this at the time.'

'You can see how it doesn't look good for you that you lied.'

Harry glanced at his notes and then back to Lorenzo. 'We have one final reason why we suspect you of these crimes, and that is because your wife suspected you. Were you aware of that?'

He gave a scornful laugh. 'Pah, that is ridiculous. Who told you that?'

'Your son. He was quite distressed when we told him about your history, and finally he admitted that his mother had told him on the day she was killed, that she suspected you of killing Barbara because you were worried she might cut Elena out of her will, or significantly reduce the legacy. She also told him that she was going to keep the money for herself and divorce you. Did she tell you that when she got home? Is that why you killed her? Perhaps you didn't mean to, but you argued, and things got out of hand?'

'No!'

'Are you saying your son is lying, then?'

'He is misguided.' He shrugged. 'We do not have an easy relationship. It is his way of getting his own back.'

'On the contrary, he tried to cover for you to start with, but the realisation that you may not only have killed Barbara, but also his mother...'

'You have no proof of any of it and to suggest that I would cold-bloodedly murder my own wife is ridiculous. Prove it if you can, but I think you will have a problem. My son has always had a temper, just like his father you might say, and much as I do not like to say this, he has not always been successful in controlling it. There were times he got into trouble when he was younger. Maybe it is him you should be looking into. It grieves me to say this, but yes, he has a vicious streak in him, and I can see him losing control and lashing out at his mother. I deny everything you have accused me of, and I demand you let me go home immediately.'

'I'm afraid we can't do that, Mr Mancini. You're under arrest and we'll be holding you here at the station pending further questioning. We're checking some final details and my officers are searching your premises as we speak. We'll also be bringing your car in for forensic examination. On top of all that, someone from Interpol will be coming in to interview you in relation to the historical charges against you. In my opinion ... it's unlikely you'll be going anywhere other than a prison cell.'

CHAPTER FORTY-FIVE

H arry grabbed a quick snack from the canteen before heading back to the office.

'Okay, everyone, make your way to the incident room. We need to piece together everything we've got and see what's still missing, to try and put this case to bed. Grab a drink if you need one and we'll meet up in five minutes.'

'Finn Abara came in about the car and burglaries,' Beth said. 'Geoff's interviewing him now and said he'll join us, but I listened in for a while and heard him saying that it wasn't him driving the car last Saturday afternoon, and that he only said that because Conn threatened to harm Alyssa. He's very anxious though about their safety. Says he knows Conn's gang will try to get to them before any trial.'

'Then maybe he needs to have a re-think about the safe house,' Harry said. 'That would be the best plan all round.'

He grabbed two coffees from the machine and did a quick detour via DCI Murray's office.

'Ah, thanks,' Murray said, taking one of the cups. 'How did the interview go?'

'Good. I reckon we're nearly there and I'm holding Lorenzo Mancini. We just need to narrow our searches down to him now and firm up the evidence. The only disappointing thing is that his fingerprints don't match the unknown ones on the settee where the cushion was taken to smother Barbara Harding.'

'He could have worn gloves, or those other prints could be anyone's, even the cleaning company she got in.'

'I know. It would just have made things tidier. Interpol are sending over everything they've got on him. By the sound of it, he'll be going away for a long time even if he isn't guilty of murdering our two victims.'

'By the way, I've just had a call from DI Chambers. He seemed very pleased with himself. Apparently, they found all manner of stuff in Connor Stephens' lock up. Plenty of stolen goods – some of which link to the burglary last Saturday in Barbara Harding's road – not to mention the huge drugs haul they grabbed. What with that and force-feeding the girls drugs and alcohol, that particular gang isn't going to get off lightly. Still nothing linking Stephens with the Barbara Harding investigation though.'

'He was a nasty bit of work. There were a couple of older girls with them at the hotel last night. I reckon they'll have a story to tell if they're handled right. Finn Abara's given a statement retracting the one he made saying he was driving Connors' car the night of the burglary. He said he was being blackmailed into doing that to protect his sister.'

'You think he's out of the frame then?'

'Yes, sir, I do. I'm as sure as I can be that he's been trying to steer clear of Connor and his gang since his release from prison.'

'Okay. Keep me posted. I've got a couple of calls to make now. See if you can have it tied up by the time I've finished.'

Harry laughed. 'In your dreams.'

The atmosphere in the incident room was tense, as people pored over computer printouts and scribbled notes, pooling their information.

'Anything new?' Harry asked, looking around the room.

Beth pulled out her notes. 'It seems Elena never got on a tube at Barnet on Wednesday. She took a cab instead. We've found CCTV footage of her getting into one at Barnet station at five o'clock, which explains why we couldn't find any images of her after that at Cockfosters or Finchley stations. We're checking with the drivers now to see if we can find out who picked her up and if they remember where they dropped her. I'll let you know as soon as I do, but it makes it less likely that Paul Cunningham was involved in her death. Dave also checked out his Waitrose receipt on the day Barbara was killed, and his credit card shows that he was paying for his shopping at 13.50hrs, which would make it tight for him to have fitted a murder in.'

'I'm going through the CCTV footage again checking for Lorenzo Mancini's car now,' Dave said. 'To see if we can find it anywhere en route to Barbara Harding's house, for the Saturday or early hours of Thursday morning. If we can find proof of that, I reckon we'll have him.'

The phone rang on Beth's desk, and she answered it.

'Okay, thanks, I'll tell DI Briscombe.' She hung up and turned to Harry. 'That was uniform. They've had a call come in from Matteo Mancini's neighbour complaining about a disturbance at the flat. They said that as he's involved in the case we're investigating, they thought we might want to deal with it.'

'And they're right. Anyone else got anything to say before we go? No? Well, keep on it.'

CHAPTER FORTY-SIX

A woman in her sixties answered the door. She looked strained and upset, and from upstairs, they could hear a lot of shouting.

Harry showed her his card. 'There's been a report of a disturbance at this address. Is Mr Mancini in?'

'Yes, but … it's not a good time.' Her glance flicked edgily to the upstairs rooms.

'Is everything alright?' Harry asked, following her gaze.

'Yes, yes.'

'And you are?'

'Marina Russo. My daughter Sophia is married to Matteo.'

'Ah, I see. Well, we've had a complaint about the noise, perhaps I could have a quick word with Matteo.'

'No. No, it is alright. I will tell them to be quieter.' She offered a nervous smile. 'We are sorry to have been a nuisance.'

The sound of a woman's voice screaming in anger in Italian, gave Harry the excuse he needed. 'I think, if you don't mind, I'd better go up and tell them myself. It'll only take a minute.'

For a moment, he thought she was going to refuse to let him in, but then, with a resigned shrug she stepped aside. The arguing in the room stopped the minute they walked in, and Matteo looked angry at the interruption.

'What now?' he demanded. 'Are you never going to leave me in peace?'

'Well, if you conducted yourself a little more peacefully, then perhaps your neighbours wouldn't feel the need to call us out. According to them, there's been a lot of shouting and arguing going on for the last hour or so.'

He turned to the third occupant of the room, an older man.

'My father-in-law,' Matteo said before Harry even asked the question. 'And it's a private, family matter that we're discussing. I apologise if we've been a bit noisy, it's the continental temperament. We'll tone things down a bit.'

'Okay,' Harry's eyes did a sweep of the room, settled on an item on the floor by the fireplace, and did a double take. He stared at it, a frown creasing his brow.

'If there's nothing else?' Matteo said pointedly. 'Can I ask you to leave now?'

Harry hesitated, but there was nothing he could do at this point without a warrant, so he nodded at Beth and turned to leave the room. As they exited, his phone pinged, and he took it out of his pocket. The title on the message had him opening it straight away. He read it and stopped in his tracks, turning to look back at Matteo. 'By the way, just one more thing … you mentioned when questioned, that you hadn't visited Barbara Harding's house in a year or more?'

'That's right.'

'So, I'm wondering how you can explain the fact that your fingerprints have been found on the arm of the same settee where a cushion was used to smother Mrs Harding to death, last Saturday?'

There was a strangled gasp from Sophia, as she looked at her husband in horror.

'Matteo?' she said, when no one spoke.

He had the look of a trapped animal. 'Well ... I can't explain that. I mean ... maybe I did go round more recently, to pick my mother up or something. I don't know ... I could easily have done that and forgotten.'

'Yet you were quite adamant when you said that you hadn't been near the house.'

'Not in a while, I haven't, but if my fingerprints are on there, it could be from the last time I visited. I'm sure I read somewhere that DNA can last a long time.'

'That's true, but according to your mother, the carpets and sofas were professionally cleaned a couple of weeks ago, and she was adamant that she carried out a thorough clean of the whole house regularly, including polishing the wooden frames of the chairs and sofa. I'm afraid you're going to have to come back down to the station with me and answer a few more questions. And you too, Mrs Mancini, if you could. I'd also like to do a search of these premises and your cars, if you have no objection?'

'I do object,' Matteo glared at him. 'On what grounds? You already told me you knew it was my father who killed Barbara and my mum, so why are you trying to pin the blame on me, now?'

'*Matteo*!' Sophia's expression was horrified. 'How can you say that? It was you who killed Elena, you know it was.'

A stunned silence followed her words, and her hand flew to her mouth as she realised what she'd said.

'Sophia! What are you saying?' her mother demanded.

Her daughter shook her head, the tears spilling down her cheek. 'Oh, Mama, I'm sorry but it's true and it's why I've been saying that

I want to leave Matteo. You kept asking me what was wrong this last couple of days, why I was so upset – and that is why. It was so horrible, but Matteo killed Elena and I saw it.'

'Shut up.' Matteo shouted. 'Can't you see, this is what they want? To divide us? But how will our child fare without a father to bring him up? Have you thought about that? Don't say another word until we have a solicitor.'

But quick as a flash, Sophia rounded on him. 'No. It was hard enough going along with it, knowing it was an accident. But to hear you trying to blame your father like that...' She shook her head and said brokenly. 'How could you do that? Do you think I want such a man bringing up my child?'

She turned back to Harry. 'Elena rang Matteo when she was on her way home after being fired by that witch, Sylvia. They argued and Elena changed her mind about going home and got a taxi here. She and Matty had the most terrible argument. I heard her accuse him of killing Barbara because she said he was the only one she'd told about the solicitor coming that day. They were screaming at each other. I ran in to try and calm things down, just in time to see ... to see my husband strike his mother on the side of the face. She lost her balance and fell, cracking her head on the fireplace, there. The blood. It was awful, and so much of it. We could tell she was dead ... her eyes were just staring, and when Matteo felt for a pulse there was none. I said we should call an ambulance, but he said there was no point, we could see she was dead, and if the ambulance and police came he'd be sent to prison for manslaughter. He didn't mean to kill her, I know that, but...' She broke off. 'I've seen him angry before but never like that. He was completely out of control.'

'Sophia, stop. Please!'

She ignored him. 'I said I was going to call the police, but he got angry with me and told me if I did that, I'd be ruining not only his life but my own and our baby's too. He told me to go to my parents for a few days until things quietened down – think things through calmly. But I can't get it out of my head seeing him hitting her like that. Poor Elena. And now, to hear him trying to blame Lorenzo...' She collapsed down onto the sofa and buried her face in shaky hands as she sobbed. Straightaway, her mother sat down beside her and put her arm around her. 'Cara ... Cara ... you should have told us. But don't cry. It is not good for the baby. We will get through this, you, me, and papa. Together, we will get through it. You have done the right thing.'

Harry looked at Matteo. 'I think that's all we need for now. Beth, call it into the station that we want forensics down here and a search warrant. And when they get here, get them to take samples of that rug by the fireplace. I've a feeling it'll match with the fibres forensics found in Elena Mancini's hair.'

'I didn't mean to kill my mother. I loved her. It was an accident. At least back me up on that, Sophia,' he added desperately.

Harry shot a quick look over Beth's shoulder, pleased to see that she was already making a note of his confession in her notebook. They'd get him to sign that back at the station.

Sophia shook her head as she looked up, her cheeks wet with tears. 'I can't believe you've done this to us, Matteo.' Her tone had hardened, her eyes glittering with anger as she hurled the words at him. 'You've destroyed our life and everything we've worked so hard for. How could you be so stupid? You may not have meant to hurt Elena, but you lost your temper one too many times. And I know you were worried about the debt, but ... if it was you who also killed Barbara because you wanted the money...' Her eyes were locked on him in horror, as if seeing him for the first time. 'How can I have anything to do with a man who would do something like that?'

'*No!* Sophia. Don't say that. I love you; you know I do. And what about our child? I'm still its father.'

The fire seemed to go out of her as quickly as it had arisen, but there was a steely strength to her words as she said, 'Do you think I want our baby to have anything to do with the sordidness of all this? He or she deserves better than that ... a childhood as sweet and innocent as the one I had. As every child should have. There'll be no contact between you if I have my way. We're over. And so is our marriage.'

'*No!* You can't just finish it like that. I have rights–'

Sophia's parents were looking shocked at everything that was going on, but now her father stepped forward and said bitingly, 'You will have no rights over this child if we have anything to do with it. You need not worry about Sophia and the baby. We will help with the restaurant and support them for as long as we are needed. Until one day I hope she can find a man who is worthy of her. But that man will not be you.'

Matteo lunged forward as if to make a grab for him, but Harry and Beth were quicker and Beth pulled the restraining cuffs from her pocket and snapped them onto his wrists.

'Matteo Mancini,' Harry said. 'I'm arresting you on suspicion of the murders of Barbara Harding and Elena Mancini. You do not have to say anything, but it may harm your defence if you do not mention when questioned something which you later rely on in court.'

CHAPTER FORTY-SEVEN

'The evidence is coming in thick and fast now,' Geoff said, the minute Harry walked back into his office.

'Good. We've brought Matteo Mancini into custody over the murder of Elena Mancini, and with the fingerprints they found on the settee arm, there's a strong possibility that he also killed Barbara Harding. I'll question him formally tomorrow once we've put everything together. But it needs to be solid. We can't afford to mess it up. What have you got?'

'Well, to start with, like I said in my text, his fingerprints came back as a match for those found on the arm of the settee and forensics are rushing through his DNA to see if it matches with skin samples found beneath her fingernails. As well as that, Beth just rang in. They've found Barbara Harding's missing money and jewellery in an empty rat poison box in Mancini's garden shed, as well as four small antique handbags that match Barbara's collection, in a cupboard above his wardrobe. There's no plausible excuse for him having those items, other than that he took them when he attacked her. Dave has also come up trumps with the cab driver who picked Elena up from Barnet. He said he remembered her because she was visibly upset and when he asked her if she was okay, she said she was fine, just family problems. And guess where he dropped her off?'

'I'm hoping outside Matteo's restaurant?'

'Yup. Around six o'clock, he thought. And now, maybe best of all, we've got Matteo on CCTV, parking his car quite a way down on the main road, at 13.06 hrs on the Saturday Barbara was murdered. He gets out and walks back in the direction of the footpath that leads to Barbara's back garden. Then we lose him. But it's enough to put him in the vicinity at the time of her murder, with access to her garden via that path. We also have him returning to the car half an hour later.'

'Good work. What about early hours of Thursday morning? We've got his signed confession admitting he killed his mother, but every bit of evidence helps.'

'Yup, we've got that too. We've isolated images of his car approaching the bottom end of Barbara's road at 02.03hrs on Thursday morning. We don't see him further along the road, which means he could well have turned into Beechwood Way. Fifteen minutes later, we've got him back on the main road, heading home again. It puts him near the scene of the crime at the right time.'

Harry straightened up. 'Amazing what you can do once you've got the right information to input. Well done – it's a headache I know trawling through that lot. See if forensics can prioritise Matteo's flat and car, will you? Tell them we're on a ticking time clock. If we can find traces of Elena Mancini's DNA in the boot and the hair fibres from the rug are a match to her head wound, that, with his wife's testimony, means we've got that one pretty well sewn up. And another top priority – we need to get a detailed witness statement from Sophia Mancini as soon as possible and establish exactly how involved she was in all this.' He looked at his watch. 'We need to stay focused – keep our eye on the custody clock and make sure we've got everything water-tight for the interview tomorrow. It's going to be a long day and night for everyone, I'm afraid. Get Beth to run the file past the CPS for their initial thoughts, when she gets in, will you?'

***

At ten o'clock that night, Harry closed his file and looked around in quiet appreciation at the team around him. They'd been working solidly for the last six hours, confirming witness statements, checking and cross-checking evidence and pulling everything together; taking only the briefest of breaks before getting back to their individual tasks. His file was now crammed full of relevant facts and data, all of which would hopefully give them a solid case to present to the CPS.

'Well done, everyone. You've done a great job and I think we've got it as tight as we can get it. I'll hit him hard with all this in the interview tomorrow, and fingers crossed it'll stick, but in the meantime, I think we should all head home and get a bloody good night's sleep.'

CHAPTER FORTY-EIGHT

H arry bolted his breakfast down and rushed into his office an hour and a half before the planned interview with Matteo Mancini and his solicitor at ten o'clock. He was exhausted but felt he needed to go through the file one more time to make sure he hadn't missed anything or left any loopholes for Mancini's solicitor to jump on. He sat down at his desk with the coffee he'd just made and picked up the newspaper someone had put in his in-tray. The headlines caught his attention immediately and he started to read.

POLICE MARKSMAN KILLS ONE, AND SEVERAL OTH-ERS ARRESTED IN HATFIELD DRUGS BUST.

The Eastern Region Specialist Operation Unit (ERSOU) supported by officers from Herts & Cambridgeshire Constabulary, carried out warrants in Hatfield in the early hours of this morning.

Approximately 15 kilograms of cocaine and other illegal substances, were found in a lock-up on a Hatfield estate, with an estimated street value of over £1.2 million. One man was shot dead, and five other men arrested during the warrants, and it's expected that formal charges will be brought later today ahead of a court appearance at Cambridge Crown

Court. As is usual in these circumstances, the shooting has been referred to IOPC (Independent Office for Police Conduct).

Detective Inspector James Chambers from ERSOU said: 'We can't comment on the specifics of this case, but this is a significant seizure of Class A drugs, and we are pleased that we have prevented them from filtering onto the streets.

'We invite anyone with information relating to drugs dealings to come forward and share their information with us. That way we can gather intelligence into organised crime, and together we can build better and safer communities for our children to grow up in. All information received will be treated in the strictest confidence.'

'Good result,' Dave Freeman said from his side. 'And good results on our investigation too. I've been compiling stuff for the official report. It's a strong case.'

'Do you ever go home?'

The other man grinned. 'Occasionally, but home is a one-bed flat and boring as hell if I haven't got anything planned for the weekend. Might just as well be here.'

'Dangerous thinking,' Harry said. 'We all do it, but it's too easy to get sucked into forgetting there's a life outside of all this. That's what our esteemed boss says, anyway, and I know he's right, even if I do ignore his advice half the time. Still ... now you're here ... let's compare notes one more time to make sure I haven't missed anything.'

***

Matteo Mancini looked tense and on edge as he sat across the table from Harry and Beth with his solicitor. He watched as Beth went through the process of setting up the recorder and switching it on, then sat up straighter as she completed the introductions and other legal requirements. Once formalities had been completed, he looked at Harry, clearly waiting for him to speak first.

'Right,' Harry said, 'we all know why you're here and we've already established that you were responsible for your mother's death.'

'It was an accident; you heard my wife say that.'

'We have her signed statement to the effect it was an argument that got out of hand, but at the end of the day, you were still responsible for Elena's death and went to significant trouble to cover it up. Perhaps you'd like to tell us exactly what happened that day?'

Matteo and his solicitor exchanged brief glances and Harry crossed his fingers, hoping they hadn't agreed on a "no comment" approach. Then he returned his gaze to Harry and gave a little shrug.

'It was as I told you. Mama rang to tell me what Barbara's will had said. She was angry at having been fired but happy because she'd been left a hundred thousand pounds. She told me she was going to leave my father because she suspected him of having killed Barbara because he was the only one she'd told about the solicitor going round. We argued because at first I didn't believe it and I knew if she left Dad he'd expect to come and live with me and Sophia, and we don't have room for him. I told her she'd married him, and it was her duty as his wife to stand by him.'

'Even though you knew he knocked her around?'

Matteo shrugged. 'As far as I knew, that had stopped. She was only there two days a week. But she told me she'd had enough of being pushed around by the men in her family, she would give me ten thousand pounds towards my debt, and she'd use the rest of her money to make a clean break from Dad. I'm afraid I was so angry that I hung up on her. A little while later, she turned up at the door saying she didn't like arguing like that and we needed to clear the air. But we just ended up arguing more. She was so stubborn, saying how she'd put up with him all these years and now it was my turn to have him and see what it was like. We were shouting at each other. Sophia came in and tried to calm things down but when my mother accused me of being just like my dad, I lost it, and lashed out at her. I didn't mean to. I couldn't believe what I'd done. And when I saw her lying there and realised she was dead ...' He took a deep, shuddering breath, and for the first time, Harry felt he was seeing genuine remorse. 'It made me think she was right ... that maybe I am like my father.' He stared off, clearly lost in the memory of the moment, before returning his gaze to Harry. 'After that, I panicked. Sophia kept saying we should call an ambulance, but I knew it was too late for that. All I could think was that we had a baby on the way, and I couldn't abandon my family by being sent to prison for a crime I hadn't intended committing. It's all such a terrible mess.' He buried his head in his hands.

'It is,' Harry said, 'and I would add here that we do have forensic and other evidence, in the form of witness statements and CCTV, supporting the fact that your mother came to your flat after your conversation and was killed on your premises. However, whilst we can accept that it was an accident – an argument that got out of hand – what isn't excusable is the fact that you then went to great pains to dispose of her body so that it wouldn't be tracked back to you.'

'I know that was a terrible thing to do,' Matteo said, 'but I wasn't thinking straight, and people do stupid things when they panic.'

'Why the woods behind Barbara's house?'

'I'm sorry?'

'Why did you leave Elena there? Plenty of nearer places for you to dispose of a body.'

Matteo flinched at his choice of words, but his gaze was straight as it met Harry's. 'I felt terrible about what I'd done, and I knew the place was empty and I was unlikely to be seen, and that she'd be found quickly. I wanted that.'

'Nothing to do with the fact you hoped it might be pinned on one of the occupants of the house she argued with that day?'

His mouth tightened. 'No. I'll never forgive myself for what I did to Mamma, and I hold my hands up to that. But not Barbara. I won't take the blame for her murder – and for what it's worth, though I hate to say it, I think my mother was right ... I think it was my father who did that.'

'Oh? And what makes you say that?'

'Because I'm not a murderer. You told me yourself that he's wanted in Italy, and I've given it a lot of thought. He's a violent man – as a child I was a victim of his violence, as was my mother. He could just as easily have got into Barbara's house that afternoon, as me, and he had just as big a motive. My parents were relying on that inheritance for their retirement, and Dad didn't know that Mum was planning on leaving him. She'd mentioned a couple of times how Barbara had recently talked about giving smaller legacies to people because she wanted to donate more to charities for the blind. Dad's ruthless when he wants something and the more I think about it, the more I believe now that he could have done it if he knew the solicitor was going round to change Barbara's will.'

'Let me stop you right there because, if you recall, your wife claimed that the reason you argued with Elena was because your mother suspected *you* of killing Barbara, not your father. We now have Sophia's signed witness statement to the effect that she overheard Elena saying that *you* were the only person she'd told about the solicitor's visit.'

'She's lying.'

'And why would she do that?'

'You heard her. Because she wants nothing more to do with me. My mother's death was an accident. My solicitor advises me that will probably be a manslaughter charge. But I'll go down for a lot longer if I get convicted of Barbara's murder and that would suit my wife and her family.'

Amazing how quickly people's loyalties and priorities changed, Harry mused. Matteo wasn't going to make things easy for his wife, going forward.

'Anyway,' Matteo added. 'What motive would I have to want Barbara dead? I hardly knew the woman.'

'Perhaps because you were in debt and with Barbara dead, you were banking on your mother giving you enough of her inheritance to significantly reduce that debt? Your wife claims the bank were going to foreclose unless you came up with at least thirty thousand pounds before Christmas and you were under a lot of stress because of that. It would be very convenient for you if Barbara were to die. Then suddenly, Barbara's making noises about changing her will and leaving most of it to charity. The same goes for you as your father. If she'd significantly reduced your mother's legacy that would seriously have impacted on what your mum gave you and what you in turn were able to give to the bank.'

'That's all supposition.'

'Maybe, but we'll get clarification on the debt issue from the bank tomorrow, and you seem to be forgetting that we have your fingerprints on the arm of the settee in Barbara Harding's lounge. That puts you in the house recently, whereas you claimed not to have been there in over a year.'

'No, I haven't forgotten but I remembered last night that I did go round to the house more recently to pick Mum up. It was a Saturday morning a few weeks back. No one else was there but I went in briefly and waited in the lounge, chatting to Barbara, until my mum was ready.'

'Convenient that. That there's no one still alive to contradict you. It's a good thing for us that we've come up with some more evidence.'

Matteo looked at him uneasily. 'What evidence?'

Harry pulled out another folder. 'As well as the fingerprints on the settee, we have skin samples retrieved from beneath Barbara's finger-nails that match your DNA. I've also been notified that traces of blood on the steering wheel of your car are a match to Barbara Harding's blood. We also searched your garden shed, and I'm sure you know what we discovered there, concealed in a tin of rat poison? Barbara's missing jewellery and over a thousand pounds in notes – the serial numbers of which match those withdrawn by her from the bank. We also found her handbag collection – a very valuable collection that your wife tells us Elena had made mention of on several occasions. All of that, together with CCTV that we're currently pulling together confirming that you were near her house the afternoon she was killed, give us enough evidence, I believe, to have you put away for a very long time. Oh, and by the way, your wife has now confirmed that you left the restaurant earlier on Saturday than stated in your interview, saying that you needed to get some urgent supplies for the evening's dinner menu.'

Harry stopped talking and looked at the other man across the table. 'If you can disprove any of that, or explain it away, I'd suggest now's your time to do it.'

Matteo's shoulders sagged and he looked almost lost as he looked to his solicitor for guidance. The man leant forward and whispered something in his ear and Matteo stiffened his spine. He took a deep breath, his face an emotionless mask as he met Harry's gaze.

'I have nothing further to say at this time,' he stated.

Harry stood up and gathered his files together. 'Then I think that's about it. We've been in discussions with the Crown Prosecution Service, and we believe, as do they, that we have enough evidence to charge you. Beth ... if you'd do the honours?'

Beth's soft Northumberland lilt as he exited the room, was music to his ears.

CHAPTER FORTY-NINE

B eth stared out of the window later that day as various members of the team climbed into their cars and headed for the pub. It had been a long week and all she really wanted to do was climb into bed and sleep. The funeral had been emotionally draining, forcing her, as it had, to acknowledge what a dysfunctional family she had. She might try to shrug it off, pretend that it didn't bother her, but it did. She couldn't help thinking back to the scene earlier in the day in the Mancinis' flat – Sophia's mother putting her arm around her daughter and hugging her, telling her she wasn't alone, they'd get through it together. And her father, standing up to Matteo and telling him that he'd be there for his daughter for as long as she needed him. What a far cry from her own situation, where she'd brought herself and Isi up and thankfully made a reasonable job of it, despite her parents rather than because of them. It should encourage her really to see a family bond like that, make her realise that there was another way … a better way. So why had it just left her feeling depressed?

'Hey.' Geoff came up behind her, making her jump. 'Penny for 'em. You look miles away. You coming to the pub?'

She sighed. 'I was just thinking how lucky Sophia is to have such a supportive family. It was nice to see.'

Geoff looked at her closely. 'I bet you'd be just as supportive to Isi, or your brother, Ryan, if they needed your help.'

'I guess.'

'We make our own lives, Beth. And you're doing bloody well with yours. No point getting bogged down in things you can't change.'

'What are you? Some sort of analyst now?'

'Could be if you pay me enough.'

She smiled. 'I think I might give the pub a miss tonight.'

'Come. It'll cheer you up. Have a couple of drinks if you need to, I can drop you home.'

'You're a good mate, Geoff.'

He grinned. 'We're good mates to each other – and I can be a stupid arse sometimes, I know. Enough to test the patience of a saint, my sister always says.'

'Who, you? Never! Okay, I'll come. First drink's on me. Where's Harry?'

'Just filling the boss in. He said he'll join us.'

***

'Well done, Harry. A good team effort,' Murray said, taking the report from him.

'Well, there's still lots to do to make it water-tight for the CPS, and we're still working hard on that, but we're lucky with the team we've got, for sure. And once we got the breakthrough of Mancini's prints on the settee, it was pretty straightforward detection work after that. So much easier once you have a concrete suspect to pin things on.'

'Tell me about it.' Murray chuckled. 'But I suppose if we had the luxury of knowing in advance who did it, we'd be out of a job.'

He got up from his chair and reached for his jacket. 'Is everyone going to the pub?'

'Yup. You joining us?'

'Just a quick one to show my face.'

'I don't think anyone's staying late. We're all knackered, and the days of celebrating successes in style are long gone.'

'Not like it used to be that's for sure. And probably a good thing too.'

Harry ordered a drink for himself and Murray and made his way to where the rest of the team were sitting.

'Cheers, everyone, and well done. With a bit of luck, we'll get an early night tonight. And I'm sure you're all ready for that.'

He thought of his own home and the situation awaiting him back there and was tempted to volunteer for overtime.

He took the seat next to Beth. 'You okay? We haven't really talked about your dad at all. I know you said it hadn't been easy, but I hope you're not feeling too low?'

'Nah, I'm fine,' she grinned, 'and this is helpin' right enough. Geoff's just gone to get me another.' She held up a large glass of wine that had already been almost fully consumed. 'An' don't worry,' she added. 'I can tell you're about to give me some preachy advice, but he's seeing me home, so no chance of me getting into too much trouble, okay?' Her Northumberland accent was more pronounced with the booze and Harry smiled. 'Glad to hear it,' was all he said. 'Let your hair down and have a bit of fun. You deserve it. I'll be back in a minute.'

He stood up and exited the pub, pulling his phone out of his pocket.

'Hi,' Claire answered.

'Hi. I know we talked about me coming over to yours later, but I think I need to go home and spend some time with my mum. She's struggling.'

'No worries. I've been reading up about the Christmas market in Strasbourg. It looks amazing. I'm so excited.'

Harry grinned, his own spirits lifting. 'Me too. I think I'll be more than ready for that to help prepare me for the Christmas I'm going to have.'

'It might not be as bad as you think.'

'It'll be worse, believe me. And I'm telling you now, we're only going on that holiday on one condition. We make a pact not to mention my family's trials and tribulations while we're out there. I want to forget everything and have a great time. Selfish of me I know, but...'

'I don't blame you and I couldn't agree more. That job on its own is enough to knock the stuffing out of you. We're going to have a fab time and you're going to think about nothing else other than that – and me! How's the investigation coming on?'

'It's done. I'll fill you in when I see you. I'll call you tomorrow when I know what's going on at home.'

'Okay, good luck. I'm having a TV night watching one of my favourite slushy films. It's an oldie, but a goodie.'

Harry chuckled. Claire loved her feel-good romances. 'Which one is it this time?'

'You've Got Mail, Meg Ryan and Tom Hanks. Count yourself lucky you've not been forced to watch it yet. Your time will come if you plan on sticking around. And that's official!'

In the past, that kind of statement would have instantly triggered Harry's fight or flight response. But with Claire, he simply resigned himself to an hour and a half of purgatory, and it felt good. 'We'll see about that. I'll expect to earn a lot of brownie points.'

'And you'll get them. Pity you're not here tonight for me to show my appreciation!'

'I'd better go before I change my mind about that. Catch you tomorrow.'

An hour later and the pub gathering was breaking up. 'Anyone need a lift?' Harry called out, refusing to acknowledge that it was yet another way of delaying what lay waiting for him at home. No one raised a hand and twenty-five minutes later he was letting himself into his house and hanging up his jacket.

Both his parents were in the lounge, and it was obvious straight away that his mother had been crying again. He hated seeing her so upset. He waited for one of them to speak.

'Hi, Harry.' It was his father who filled the silence. 'How's your day been?'

'Don't expect much from him,' his mother said bitterly. 'He'll be heading out again in five minutes.'

'Actually, I won't, Mum. We've had major breakthroughs in the case today and we're all taking some well-earned rest. I'll need to go in tomorrow morning to finalise the interviews, but tonight I'm free – though I won't be late to bed. What's happening about supper?'

His mother shrugged. 'Haven't even thought about it.'

Harry looked at his watch. 'Well, it's seven o'clock and we need to eat. How about I get us a takeaway? Your choice.'

'You choose it, Harry. I'm not that hungry anyway.'

About to settle on an Indian because they all knew how much his dad liked curries, he changed his mind. Maybe better not to be seen pandering to his father at the moment. Christ, was it always going to be like this?

'I'll get us a pizza and I've got salad stuff in the fridge to go with it. I'll just get the menu so you can choose. Then we can sit down and talk...'

CHAPTER FIFTY

B eth opened her eyes and stared sleepily up at the ceiling. She had a hangover. No doubt about that. They'd come back here and cracked open another bottle of wine, and now she had a splitting headache and her mouth felt dry as a bone. She reached for the water glass by her bed and drank from it thirstily. She was aware that something felt out of kilter, and she frowned, trying to pinpoint what it was. Then a movement beside her brought it strikingly home. She whipped her head round and it all came flooding back. Geoff was lying there, sleeping deeply, his chest bare, apart from the layer of downy golden-brown hair covering it. She resisted an unexpected urge to run her fingers through it.

Oh, my God. So, she hadn't been dreaming when she'd had visions of herself being cradled in his arms in the night. More images flitted through her mind now, more intimate ones, and she felt the heat warm her cheeks. She needed to be on her own.

She inched herself sideways, as unobtrusively as she could, until she could slip out of the bed. Grabbing her dressing gown, she crept into the living-room and curled up in the corner of the settee. She sat there, shell-shocked. What had she been thinking? Geoff of all people. He was her best mate and she'd adamantly rejected any ideas of him being anything other than that.

Idiot, idiot, idiot!

She wasn't stupid. She'd recognised as they got closer that he gave her the same sort of anchor to her life that she'd had with Andy, and sometimes that unsettled her. She also recognised that he was an attractive man with one hell of a sex appeal to the ladies. Including her. But she'd always kept things strictly platonic. They both had, recognising that their friendship was special and not wanting to derail it. But now...

She looked up as the door opened and Geoff walked in. He was wearing her spare pink dressing-gown and in any other circumstances she'd have laughed out loud at the sight of him. It was one of the things she liked about him; that he was so comfortable in his own skin that he didn't give a toss about what people might think. And the truth of the matter was, despite the pink dressing-gown, he looked terrific and all male – something she was suddenly very conscious of.

She cleared her throat, her gaze settling somewhere in the region of the golden hairs just peeping through the vee of the dressing-gown neckline.

'Hey,' she said.

She could hear the amusement in his voice as he responded and could picture the twinkle in the deep brown of his eyes, even if she wasn't looking at him.

'You're going to want to talk, I know. But you want to do it over breakfast, or before? Or perhaps you're thinking we might not even make breakfast?'

She sighed. He knew her so well. But at least now she found she could look at him.

'I was drunk.'

His voice became serious. 'I wasn't exactly sober. But we talked about that if you remember?' He hesitated, then added, 'How we didn't want to do anything we'd both regret.'

'And now we have. I'm sorry, but that's how I feel. Our friendship means a lot to me – too much to risk losing it when things don't work out.'

'And what makes you so sure they wouldn't work out?'

'Come on. This is me we're talking about. I make a mess of everything I touch.'

'And how many times have I told you that's bullshit? So, you've got a bit of a crackpot family – do you think you're the only one? Don't let them affect you for the rest of your life, Beth. They don't define who you are. Move on and do better.'

He made it sound so easy. Out loud, she said. 'Last night was a mistake. We've got a good relationship as friends, one we've both said we'd hate to lose.'

'Lovers can be friends.'

Something in the rich timbre of his voice when he said the word lovers, made her heart do a little flip. It was unnerving, and she hoped not obvious to him, as she said flatly, 'Lovers come and go. Good friends are for life. Let's not ruin that.'

He studied her for a long moment, and she looked anywhere but into the rich warmth of that regard. His astute eyes wouldn't miss the agitated way she was plucking at her fingers, and she forced her hands to lie still in her lap. Then he gave a little shrug and smiled his easy-going smile. 'Okay, I know when I'm beaten, and if that's how you feel then you're probably right.'

She stared at him. 'You mean you agree with what I'm saying?'

'Not that it was a mistake, I can't agree with that. If you want the truth, it was great. But you're right when you say that what we have is special. I don't want to jeopardise that.'

'Yeah ... well ... we can forget it ever happened then, right?'

'Yep. Now, what do you fancy for breakfast? Got any eggs and bacon?'

Just the thought of that made her want to heave. She jumped up from the sofa, still feeling edgy, despite his easy capitulation.

'You help yourself to what you want while I grab a shower. Then it's back to the grindstone. You'll need to drive.'

CHAPTER FIFTY-ONE

Finn wandered into the kitchen, the previous day's post in his hands. 'Alyssa not up yet?' he asked Goldie, as he sat down at the breakfast table.

'No. She's exhausted after the last couple of days. We'll need to be gentle with her, Finn. It will have been traumatic her seeing Conn shot like that. She might need some counselling or something.'

'Yeah, I know. I worry about her, Goldie, and how she'll turn out.'

'She'll be fine – this has been a big wake-up call to her. But what she needs now is support. Not angry rantings from her older brother.'

'I know.'

'You worry about her, I get that, but she needs love in her life, not anger and blame. She looks up to you, and that's how we can turn her around from all this.'

'Yeah, but you and I both know, even with Conn gone, there's still plenty out there ready to take advantage of her and kids like her. It ain't easy breaking away from it once you've got sucked in. I came out of prison swearing never again ... that I'd turn my life around and do better for her. But what a joke. All I done was make things worse.'

'Don't think like that. None of this was your fault.'

'*Shit*!'

Goldie blinked as he uttered the expletive. He was staring at a letter in his hand, his eyes wide open in shock.

'What's up?'

He shook his head. 'This has to be some sort of fit-up, man.'

'What?'

'This letter. It says it'll be a while before everything's settled and I get the money, but Barbara left me twenty grand in her will to help me with my music – she can't have.'

'Let me see.' Goldie took the letter from him and scanned its contents. She gave him a broad smile. 'It looks genuine enough to me. You'll have to call them like they say, but ... bloody hell, boy. She must have thought you were good to do that. And all the music equipment as well – that'll save you a bob or two.'

He looked dazed. 'I can't believe it. She always said she believed in me more than I did myself.' His eyes watered up. 'With that money I can afford to pay someone to produce my best songs professionally and start sending them out.'

He jumped up from his chair, his face alight with excitement. 'She gave me a couple of names – I wrote'em down somewhere. People I could send them to and say she recommended me. Where did I put them? They must be somewhere in my room.'

'Morning.'

They both spun round as Alyssa walked into the room. Her eyes were sheepish as she looked from one to the other.

'How are you feeling?' Goldie asked.

'Alright.'

'Come here.'

The older woman opened her arms and Alyssa ran straight into them. 'I'm sorry,' she mumbled, her voice muffled.

'Don't you worry about it, girl. It weren't your fault.'

'I was stupid – I just didn't know how to stop once I started. I wanted to tell you, but Conn said we mustn't tell anyone what we was doing because he didn't want people knowing his business.'

'I warned you about all of that before I went into prison,' Finn said.

'I know you did.' Alyssa drew back from Goldie to look at him. 'But Conn was so nice to start with. Said things must be difficult at home with you inside and that you were his mate and he looked after his mates. That was when he started paying us for running errands for him after school, a way of earning a bit of pocket money.'

'That's what he did. Sucked you in until it was impossible to break away. It weren't your fault, he done it to me exactly the same way. Had me lie about the bloody car and go to prison for him – even made me feel a hero for doing it.'

He looked at Alyssa closely. 'You sure you're alright? You know me and Goldie's here for you?'

She nodded, but her face took on a haunted expression. 'It frightened me. Those men ... they were horrible. Apart from one. Greg his name was. He was nice to me and told me he didn't think I was cut out for what they was doing and to think about things when I got home.'

'Well, he was bloody right for sure. They didn't ... hurt you in any way?'

She shook her head. 'But I don't want to talk about it. I already told the police at the hospital, and they said they'll be going away for a long time.'

'But what happened with Conn, after you left us?'

'Only tell us if you want to,' Goldie said, ignoring Finn's irritated frown.

Alyssa hesitated. 'It was horrible,' she said finally. 'I was so scared.'

When she'd finished filling them in, she looked at her brother, the tears swimming in her eyes.

'Connor told me there was nothing he could do for you and Goldie, but if I behaved myself then I'd be alright; he could stop them from killing me. I didn't know what was happening to you. I thought maybe you was dead already. I was such a coward because I said all right, I'd do whatever he wanted.' The tears were running down her cheeks freely now. 'I hate myself for that.'

'Well, don't,' Finn said. 'I'd have done the same, anyone would.'

'Really?'

'You'd have been an idiot to say anything else.'

'It was so scary when he grabbed me and put the knife against my throat. He sort of jerked and I thought he was going to kill me, but then I heard a bang and he just fell to the ground.'

She shuddered, her eyes reflecting her horror.

'Don't say any more, lovey, you need to try and forget that.'

'I can't, Goldie ...'

Goldie drew her back into her arms and kissed the top of her head, hugging her tight. 'It'll take a bit of time, but you will. Don't think about it no more now.'

Alyssa looked up at her anxiously. 'I just want to go back to life like it was. But what if Conn's mates blame me for his death and come after me?'

'They won't, but we ain't hanging around to find out,' Finn broke in decisively. 'You remember that lady I worked for? The one who died?'

Alyssa nodded.

'Well, she left me some money. It'll take a while to come through so we'll let the police rehouse us in this safe house they're talking about until after the court case and as soon as we can, after that, I'll use some of that money to get us right away from here to a new start.'

'No, Finn, that money's for your music.'

'I ain't arguing, Goldie. It's a done deal.'

'But what about my work at the youth centre? I can't just leave it.'

'You've been doing that nearly ten years. There's plenty of others can take over. Alyssa needs you – and so do I. I don't remember much about my mum and dad, but I do remember they had high hopes for me and Alyssa and now I've got a bit of money behind me, maybe we can live up to 'em.'

Goldie looked at Alyssa. 'How would you feel about that? Moving?'

The girl hesitated, then nodded. 'I'd miss my friends, but I'm scared living here now, and it won't feel the same. But I know how much your work at the centre means to you...'

'You mean more,' Goldie said. 'And Finn's right, I done my time there – and I won't miss my cleaning job, that's for sure. New home, fresh start. Finn can get a gardening job and write his music. You can go to a new school and get straight A grades and I'll get myself another little job and take up knitting.' She chuckled. 'What's not to love about that?'

CHAPTER FIFTY-TWO

'I'm heading off now,' Harry said, as the clock approached midday, 'and I suggest you guys all do the same. I know the work doesn't end here but we've broken the back of it, and I think we all deserve something of a weekend. See you back here first thing tomorrow morning, and keep your fingers crossed, nothing comes in in the meantime.'

There was a spring to his step as he headed for his car. It always felt satisfying bringing an investigation to its rightful conclusion and this case was no exception. He looked at his watch. He was meeting Claire for a pub lunch at one, that just about gave him time for a quick detour.

It was Goldie who answered the door.

'I just wanted to check that Alyssa was okay. I heard she was out of hospital.'

'She's doing alright,' Goldie said in a low voice, 'but it shook her up good and proper. Come through.'

She ushered him into the lounge, where Alyssa and Finn were sitting, playing a board game.

'Hi,' he said, 'don't let me interrupt, I just dropped by to see how you're all doing and to let you know that we've charged a man in connection with the Barbara Harding investigation.' He picked his words with care, so as not to traumatise the girl any further.

'Who was it?' Finn asked.

'Elena's son, Matteo. I can't say anything at this stage that might compromise the court case, but I thought you'd like to know.'

Finn shook his head. 'Who'd have thought that? But thanks.' He glanced at Goldie then shifted his gaze back to Harry.

'I was going to call you tomorrow ... we changed our minds about the safe house. We'd like to take that offer up. I want to get us as far away from here as possible, start over.'

'Conn's gang will be going away for a long time but I'm glad you've come to that decision. It was another reason why I dropped round. You'll need to pack up the stuff you want to take and be ready to leave first thing in the morning. I'll make the call today to get the house sorted and I'll get someone over here to keep guard overnight.' He looked at Alyssa. 'I hear you had a bit of a hairy time. You okay now?'

She hung her head. 'Yeah.'

'Sounds like you were crucial to the police being able to move in and arrest them as quickly as they did. If you hadn't been so brave and run out like that, the stand-off would have been much longer with you in there as a hostage. Everyone was singing your praises.'

'Really?' Her eyes lit up. 'I guess. I hadn't thought about it like that.'

'There you go, sis, you're a hero,' Finn said, ruffling her hair.

'Yeah, well remember that next time you're having a go at me,' she said, shaking his hand off.

Harry looked at his watch. 'Better be off, I just wanted to tell you myself about the arrest we made, and that you're off the hook. Good luck with everything.'

Harry got to the pub before Claire. He started a tab, ordered a beer for himself and a glass of pinot grigio for her and made his way over to a free table. Acting on impulse, he pulled his phone from his pocket and dialled a number.

'Hi,' the voicemail said. 'This is Angie. Can't take your call right now but leave a message and I'll get back to you.'

He cleared his throat. 'It's Harry ... Briscombe. I was wondering if you're free any night this week to meet up for dinner?' He paused. He could add stuff about how it would be good to talk, sort out where they were going in the future, but she wasn't stupid. She'd know why he was calling. 'Hope you can make it. Give me a call.'

'So ... arranging illicit dinner dates behind my back,' Claire said, plonking her bag down on the floor.

'I was calling Angela.'

'I guessed that. I'm glad you're meeting up. It can't be an easy time for her.'

'Let's hope I don't make things worse.'

She sat down on the chair next to him. 'I think the only way you'd do that would be if you said you didn't want to see her again – and I don't somehow think you're going to do that.'

'No. In fact, the more I'm getting used to the idea, the more I'm quite excited about having a sister. It's one of the things I envy about you ... your family.'

'Yeah, well they can be a pain in the arse sometimes, be warned, but I wouldn't be without them.' She took a sip from her glass. 'Thanks for this. I was ready for it. How are things back at the ranch?'

Harry shook his head, a rueful smile playing around his mouth. 'It doesn't get any better, but at least they're talking. Dad insists that he loves mum and that was why he didn't tell her because he was frightened she'd leave him, and I think she sees that, and acknowledges that she probably would have done. I could be wrong, but I get the impression that maybe she's softening off a bit now she's got over the initial shock. But she's still adamant that she doesn't want to meet Angela.'

'Small steps. It's been a huge thing for her to come to terms with – she needs time to process it. Hopefully, she'll come round to seeing that it's not Angela's fault.'

'I hope so.'

Claire took a sip from her glass. 'So, the case is all solved?'

'Yup.' It felt good to be able to say that, but an unexpected sadness washed over him at the thought of two lives wasted because of one man's greed. Life could be ugly, and the more he came up against the darker side of it, the more it seemed to affect him.

As if tuning into his thoughts, Claire's hand reached out across the table towards his. 'You did well, Harry. You got justice for them.'

'Not much good to them though, is it?'

'Perhaps not but give yourself some credit. It's not just about catching murderers. It's also about getting closure for families and friends. If there weren't people like you out there, doing the job you do, they wouldn't get that. You help them find peace of mind, and when they've lost someone close, that becomes incredibly important.'

He took her outstretched hand in his and gripped it. She was right. There would always be people killing for no good reason, and it would always be an uphill battle trying to take them out – but each successful prosecution meant one less dangerous person on the street and justice for their victims.

It sounded corny, but it was why he did the job. He just needed to remind himself of that sometimes.

THE END

YOU'VE FINISHED, BEFORE YOU GO...

Thank you for reading *None So Blind*. I do hope you enjoyed it and if you did, I'd love it if you could take the time to leave a review on Amazon or Good Reads. Reviews are so helpful to both readers and authors in spreading the word. Just go to the book page on Amazon, scroll down to where it says Review This Product and write a few lines. Job done! If you'd like to take a look at any of my other books, just visit my Amazon Author page: https://www.amazon.co.uk/Carolyn-Mahony/e/B00GF7WDVQ

It's so random what forms the basis of a new story. In this case it was the simple thought popping into my head of how hard it must be for people who are blind, having to count every step as they walk around their house. I even found myself walking around my own home with my eyes closed, thus confirming to my husband what he'd always suspected ... that I really am mad! From that initial daydream, a story was born, as well as the decision to donate ten percent of my earnings on this book to charities for the blind. Now I need to close my eyes and conjure up another vision to give Harry his next case. Wish me luck.

With very best wishes,

Carolyn

PS If you haven't read my Prequel novella to the Harry Briscombe series, *Behind Closed Doors,* you can get it for free from my website here: https://carolynmahony.comThat will also sign you up for my infrequent newsletter where you will receive details of new releases and any special offers I may be running. Hope to see you there!

Printed in Great Britain
by Amazon